AUTHORS NOTE

After reflecting on pre-publication comments I had these thoughts.

When Johannes Kepler wrote his first major astronomical work, Mysterium Cosmographicum, about planetary orbits within our solar system, he included mathematical calculations as proof for his hypothesis. His ideas challenged the accepted belief in the law of circles, championed by Greek philosophers, as well as the religious belief that the earth did not move and all other celestial bodies revolved around it. These beliefs were well established and taken as fact by the scholars of his day. Had he not included the proofs for his ideas they would have stayed just that, unsubstantiated ideas.

Some people who read my book, The Eden Conspiracy, disagree with its foundational concept that comes from a biblical approach different than traditionally taught. This Bible based approach provides the hope of salvation to all those who were once thought of as lost. In my novel, I have included multiple Bible verses as verification for my ideas. As a Biblist, someone who believes the Bible to be the word of God, beliefs need to be supported by Bible scripture, if they aren't, that belief is merely an unsubstantiated idea.

Other readers were confused by the books classification category, as the content may not be what they were expecting. Exploring the validity of religious beliefs within a conversation between two people, can be difficult to categorize into a literary genre. Is it a novel, or is it a theological thesis? Either way, I hope you find the ideas presented to be thought provoking, biblically supported and well researched, but above all, entertaining. Here's what a couple reviewers thought of my book.

"Clayton Carlson's characters put their thoughts on the line and say what's on their minds as he takes the reader on an informative and entertaining journey."
Dani Martin

"This book seems to be confused as to what it is - Novel or theological treatise? The story line had definite possibilities and it would be great to expand on this but I don't think you could really consider this a novel when it is filled with pages and pages of scripture quotes. As to the theology I couldn't and wouldn't want to argue over it. I'm no theologian. I did read it over carefully and found myself thinking; So what? None of the ideas expressed by Adam affect my daily walk with God and that is where I want to direct my thoughts. Whatever life after death looks like and how and when we get there is fine with me. Jesus will be there - what else matters? And if Adam would find that simplistic? - sometimes it really is!"
Eva Wiebe

The Eden Conspiracy

Clayton B Carlson

Clayton B Carlson
Copyright 2017 Clayton B Carlson
ISBN-13: 978-1988226118
ISBN-10: 1988226112
Published by First Page Solutions (Kelowna BC, Canada)

TABLE OF CONTENT

CHAPTER 1
DIVINE APPOINTMENT

The brbrbrbrbrbr sound from the Jake brake could be barely heard over the classic rock blaring out of the speakers in the old blue relic of a truck's cab. The truck was vintage for sure and looked good for its age, but it was bordering on the Rat Rod side of respectable. Not as bad as the old truck in the movie Duel, with Dennis Weaver. This old Star still had some shine, although it did look menacing enough in your rear view mirror to make you move over. Adam didn't consider himself to be an aggressive driver, he did his best to be polite and efficient, but if you were needlessly in the way, his patience did have an end. He could be often heard quoting his favourite bumper sticker, 'Lead or Follow, But, GET OUT OF THE WAY'.

Dropping two gears and getting back into the Cummins's power band made the Jake bark to life like a pack of mad dogs. It didn't take long for the bobtail Western Star to lose its freeway speed as it made the slow right turn of the Sumas exit off ramp. As he rounded the corner Adam looked out his driver's side window at a disheveled hitch hiker trying to catch a ride by holding up a piece of cardboard box with Kelowna written in red crayon. "He's a newbie," Chuckled Adam, speaking to the empty cab, "Suitcase and all, who hitch hikes with a suitcase?"

Three minutes later Adam is backing under his reefer van at the grocery warehouse. A full length mural runs down both sides of the fifty three foot van displaying a well-endowed, naked woman, reclining back on one arm while eating a piece of fruit with a broad smile of complete satisfaction on her face. She is posed, relaxing under the shade of a large tree in the midst of a flower bed. Her most private body parts are barely hidden by the colourful flowers and leaves, just staying within the bounds of public modesty. EDEN'S DELIGHTS is boldly printed on a banner across the top of the mural proclaiming the company name.

After quickly cranking up the landing gear, then hooking up the light cord and air lines, Adam is back in the cab preparing to move his truck and trailer to the other side of the fenced yard where he parks clear of the loading bay dock. After spotting the rig out of the way he gets back out of the truck. With a single motion he swings out of the open cab door, his left hand gripping the top of the long grab handle attached to the truck's cab beside the door frame. Adam slowed his catapulting decent with his hand as it slips down the handle, his boots gingerly touch down onto the compact gravel parking lot.

Heading towards the back of the trailer he checks the fifth wheel connection, lights and kicks the tires of the truck, slowly making his way towards the back he checks for anything amiss. After more tire kicking at the trailer wheels, he quickly looks inside the empty trailer for any noticeable damage and then closes the large back doors latching them securely.

"This will be a quick trip back home," he thinks to himself. "I'll be just flying up those hills."

Repeating the same checks on the passenger side, he heads towards the front of the truck. Having circled the unit in a counter clockwise direction, checking as he went, Adam is satisfied with the equipment's condition. Opening the driver's door, he puts his work gloves together and sets them on the floor of the truck on top of the fire extinguisher between the driver's seat and door. Forcefully pushing the door shut he heads towards the warehouse, pausing to wipe dirt off of the quote painted on the side of the Western Star's front fender. The Quote is from the Bond movie Skyfall, 'Sometimes the old ways are best'. Chuckling he wipes his dusty hands off on his pants as he walks.

Once in the depot he makes a bee line for the bathroom, the door slams behind him and he bolts it closed. Five minutes later he emerges wiping soapy water off his now clean hands with paper towel.

Jack the warehouse manager waves to him from his office door. "Hey Adam," he bellows. "Have you got a minute?" Adam veers over towards the heavy set man in the stained white shirt.

"What's up?" inquires Adam. "I was just getting ready to leave."

"Are your log books all in order for this month?" demands Jack. "The damn CVSE has been riding my ass for the past month with audits. Even you owner-ops have to be accounted for. Are you sure you're not over on your time?"

Laughing Adam sings his response to Jack. "Ask me no questions, and I'll tell you no lies."

Jack's face lightens into his normal beaming smile. "You wouldn't have so much to sing about, if it was you having to pay the fines. Come to think of it, they only complain about small stuff with your paperwork, nothing worthy of a fine."

Adam smiles knowingly. "That's because I don't cheat."

Jack scoffs at the idea. "Ya right. I won't ask any questions, I don't want to make you a liar." Turning back into his office Jack mumbles to Adam. "Have a good trip, if that old thing makes it."

"Ya, ya, ya, it's not my old truck that has to sit while DPF and computer parts are on back order like those new ones of yours," retorts Adam with a grin. While tossing the wet crumpled paper towel into the trash can he adds sweetly. "Have a good day, and good luck with the CVSE."

Reclining in the driver's seat of his truck, Adam is using his hands free phone, talking to his wife back home. His side of the conversation can be heard, while her side sounded more like Charlie Brown's teacher.

"No! I'm not going to sit around down here for two days while the log book catches up."

"It's Sunday, I've called and the scales are closed, so there will be no pictures of the truck plates with traceable date and time stamps."

"I fueled up last night and I won't make any purchases with a card. I have some cash if I do need anything."

"Ya, ya, of course."

"No, don't be silly."

"I will park out at the Sindou farm when I get back. They said they could be loading on Tuesday afternoon and I won't have to pick it up until Wednesday."

"I know, I will, it's only four or five more hours and I will be home with you. Then we can have two days off together."

"I know."

"I love you too."

"I love you four."

"No, I love you more."

"Hay I know what I'll do. I saw a lost lamb looking for a ride on the way over here to pick up the trailer, If he's still there I'll give him a lift, he can keep me company all the way home."

"No, I've never seen him before."

"OK. Sure. I'll send you his picture when he gets in, just in case he's an axe murderer."

"Bye love."

"I love you too Lil."

After pushing the call end button, Adam reaches over to his laptop set up in the dash glove box, opening an audio file of mixed favourites, tunes soon fill the cab as he herds his big rig back towards the freeway and the newbie suitcase toting hitchhiker.

Adam sees the lone figure standing forlornly near the end of the on ramp at the edge of the road. He pulls his truck slowly past the cardboard destination sign and onto the paved shoulder. There wasn't a lot of room for the large trailer and it protruded awkwardly into the roadway.

"Lucky thing there's no traffic," thought Adam, as he impatiently waited for the hitchhiker to get to his truck. Adam kept checking his mirrors for the lone man with the suitcase but had not seen him coming yet. After what felt like ten minutes to Adam, he pulled the tab out from under the turn signal lever activating the four way flashers and then set the park brakes.

Mumbling to himself he jumped, as before, out of his truck. "Some people need a personal invitation to do anything. I haven't got all day," he said a bit angrily. Striding to the back of the trailer he went three paces past the end, whistled loudly and waved at the oblivious pedestrian who was standing staring off into the clouds. A sudden downpour of rain from the darkening sky seemed to get the hitchhikers attention. Dropping his cardboard sign, he held his suitcase above his head, in a futile attempt to shield himself from the sudden deluge. Dripping wet from the rain he dashed towards the passenger side of the truck. Adam ran ahead of him opening the passenger door wide, helping him up the fuel tank steps and into the warm dry cab. Adam had no sooner ran around the front of the truck and climbed behind the steering wheel that the rain stopped as quickly as it had started.

Earlier that morning on the outskirts of town, in a remote forested area, a lonely figure surveys what had been his home for the latest chapter of his life. The dorm room sits vacant and dank. It is small for two people, the cramped space made worse by the smell of sweaty socks and mildew. Condensation drips down the inside of the old single pain window, creating small swamps of greeny brown water on the windowsill. Two small dressers sitting side by side is all that separates the old metal cots. A thread bare tattered rug, little bigger than a table place mat, is on the floor beside each of the small beds to help avoid the cold cracked linoleum when getting up out of them.

The room reflects the Spartan, conservative values, of the small denominational Bible college that built the dorms seven decades earlier. Not much has changed within the Bible college since it was dedicated to the Lords service on that long ago August. Both buildings and teachings had not been altered or changed from that past age of strong authoritarian leadership.

It's been within these walls of learning that Isaac has spent the past fourteen months as he had stayed through the summer to take extra courses. Isaac was raised in the fundamentalist teachings of his loving, devout parents chosen denomination. He had been home schooled, repeatedly studying the bible scriptures validating the doctrines of their beliefs, which reinforced the Godly correctness of those beliefs in Isaac's mind.

Isaac didn't know how the adventures of his life would play out, but he knew who he trusted to get him to his final destination. He had always felt like he had a mission to accomplish in his life, although the mission statement was undefined, Isaac knew that he was on a mission from God. He was just waiting for God to open a door and he would gladly walk through it.

Speaking of doors, Isaac was about to walk through a big one. Earlier that week he had informed his parents on his decision to leave Bible college and go back home to help them with their small family painting business. His dad had fallen off a ladder, leaving him with a concussion and a broken leg. Isaac's parents tried to dissuade him from leaving college, siting the need to continue his schooling, but he would have none of it. Silently they were glad for his stubborn side, as they did need the help, and the mounting bills had to be paid.

Isaac's resolute decision to return home didn't sit well with the college dean though. The dean put a high value on his institutions instruction. He felt Isaac was throwing his education away for a small setback in his parents' life that they could get over by themselves. The dean urged Isaac to fast and pray for them while staying on at school, instead of abandoning his studies.

With Isaac's refusal and determination to go home to help his parents, the dean refused to refund Isaac's unused tuition fees, or his room and board which had been prepaid till the end of the school year. Furthermore the dean steadfastly refused to issue Isaac recognition for the school work that he had already completed. All of his college documentation would read 'INCOMPLETE'. If Isaac was to leave now, the dean made it clear there would be no coming back as long as he was in charge.

The ultimatums only served to strengthen Isaac's resolve to return home. He felt in his heart it was the right thing to do, and had faith that if it was a mistake God would work things out for the good regardless. After making his way out of the dorms, Isaac walked slowly down the college's windy, tree lined gravel driveway to the road.

Carrying all of his belongings in one old worn suitcase he prayed earnestly as he walked into his future.

"Father, I want to be doing your will in my life. Please guide me in the paths you want me to travel and teach me your wisdom. I want to learn about your mysteries. Let me not be shy in talking to others about my faith in you and the salvation only you provide."

Being a Sunday morning, the entire college was at chapel leaving Isaac alone to find his own way home. He was reluctant to spend any of the few dollars he had on a bus ticket home, so he planned to hitch whatever ride he could find. He felt bad about such an excursion on Sunday but had little choice but to start his trip as soon as he could. "An ox in the ditch," Isaac consoled himself, trying to remain positive about still having over three hundred miles to go before he could relax in his parents' home once again.

Approaching the road Isaac imagined being picked up by a family on their way to church. He rehearsed some witty ad lib lines just in case he might need them. The pickup that stopped for him not far from the college driveway had a lone occupant in it. The truck was old, run down, rusty, and had trouble idling as its brakes squealed to a stop. The driver filled the entire space allotted for the vehicle's operator. His tattooed arms bulged out of his chest straining the seams of his t-shirt.

"Want a ride? I'm going as far as the freeway."

"Yes please", Isaac replied excitedly. "That would be great. What takes you out this fine Sunday morning?" inquired Isaac, trying to make conversation to ease his nerves.

"I can't stay home on Sunday mornings", says the big man, wiping beads of sweat from his brow. "I live next to that dam college and every Sunday morning they raise such a ruckus I can't stand to be around here. I go into town for breakfast at Tim's by the freeway. I complained a few times about the noise, but it did no good. Those dam Bible thumpers got the law on their side. Where are you off to?" the big man asks, while carefully taking stock of Isaac.

"I'm going to hitch hike home to Kelowna," replied Isaac. "Getting to the freeway would be a great help."

"Huh," grunts the big man. "You better stay off the freeway if you're going to be hitch-hiking. The cops will fine you and drive you back to town. Your best bet is to make up a sign with where you want to go and stand on the on ramp before it enters the freeway. Technically on ramps aren't part of the freeway, but someone getting on might pick you up," he advises.

"Thanks," Isaac says. "I'll do that." The rest of the fifteen minute trip was silent except for the wheezing of the old pickup truck.

It was a four block walk for Isaac to get to the proper on ramp for the freeway after being dropped off by the big man. He found a stubby red wax crayon and a piece of cardboard in an open dumpster behind the Tim Horton's. Making the suggested destination sign, Isaac puts down his suitcase and plants himself near the freeway end of the on ramp just as an old semi-truck is taking the freeway exit. Isaac sees the truck driver's grizzled face as he passes by and wonders. "Why is that old guy working on the Lords day of rest? He should know better," he thought to himself, as his heart ached due to the loss of Godly wisdom that plagued modern society.

No other traffic was to be seen using Isaac's piece of the transportation system, just that one old truck, with the one old sinful driver. Isaac longed for the imagined family to show up and give him a ride on their way to church but he knew they would not be coming for him.

Forty minutes drag by before Isaac has his first glimpse of the huge rolling billboard of lustful sin heading his way. He could make out the naked woman on the side of the large semi-trailer as it came up Sumas Rd. before turning onto the on ramp heading for the freeway. The old truck's exhaust stacks smoked a dark grey as it pulled up the on ramps incline. Isaac watches in disapproving shock as the truck slows and comes to a stop just past where he stood.

"Is he stopping for me?" Isaac asks out loud. Pleading, he looks sky ward. "Oh God, please let someone else give me a ride, pleeeaaase."

"Maybe I can ignore him and he will leave," thinks Isaac. Not moving or acknowledging the parked semi a stone's throw away, Isaac stands motionless, face turned skyward. A whistle and a holler breaks into Isaac's thoughts, "Lord if this is from you please give me a sign." No sooner had that thought formulated in Isaac's brain that God responded with an attention grabbing blast of cold water pouring down on his head. Scrambling in obedience, Isaac dashes for the safety of the truck's cab, using his suitcase as a makeshift umbrella.

CHAPTER 2
CONDEMNATION

"What was taking you so long? I was almost ready to give up on you. We could have stayed dry if you had come when I stopped," scolded Adam, shaking off his rain soaked cap.

Isaac was silent, still trying to catch his breath and get his shivering under control. Water was coming off his hair in little streams running down his face and neck. Without waiting for a response, Adam had his phone in hand and was snapping a couple pics of his new passenger. Titling them, 'Wet lost lamb', he sent them off into cyberspace.

"There, all done," he said, putting his phone away. "I promised the wife I'd send pics of anyone I pick up. That way she knows who to look for if I don't come home."

Isaac stuttered with the chills, "I'm not too dangerous."

Adam had the brakes released and was going through the gears picking up speed quickly as he entered the east bound lanes of the freeway. Between shifts he cranked the heater fan to high and blistering heat began to rush out of the vent holes in the dash. Isaac could watch the colour of his wet denim jeans lighten as they dried out under the fiery blast. He reached out a white wrinkly finger to adjust the vent grills direction away from his scorching knee.

Cracking his side window open a bit to let the condensation escape the tight cab Adam brags. "It won't take long to warm up at 200 degrees. I put in an oversized heater core, and bigger fans. My name's Adam. Where abouts in Kelowna are you headed to?"

Feeling warmed and more comfortable, Isaac introduces himself and asks to be dropped off at the big mall where he would catch a city bus to his parents' house if they were unable to pick him up.

"Sure, I will be driving right past it," Adam replied. "What took you so long back there?" he questioned with some irritation.

"Well," Isaac states, sitting up a bit straighter in the surprisingly comfortable passenger seat. "I didn't want to get a ride from you!"

Without a hint of offence, Adam smiles and asks, "Oh, why not? You afraid of trucks or something. Beggars can't be choosers you know."

"No, it's nothing like that. I didn't want to ride with you because you seemed like a degenerate person driving a sinfully carnal truck and I was hoping for an uplifting, spirit building trip. In fact I was praying to God that you would go away, when he answered my cry of despair with that cloud burst, forcing me to get in with you."

The sincere nature of Isaac's statement had no negative affect on Adam's smile as he laughingly said, "Well things aren't always what they appear. That lady on the trailer is just a painting and she has less exposed than most of the fine classical European art people rave about. And even sinners are capable of doing good. I stopped to pick you up didn't I? And that rain thing, well we get those micro bursts from time to time. But we may be destined for a divine appointment, I guess we'll just have to wait and see what's in store for the trip."

Caught off guard by Adam's calm response and still hoping to get expelled from this rolling den of iniquity, Isaac pushes Adam for reasons why he was working on the Lords day, a special day set aside for rest and rejuvenation, not only for those who loved and followed God, but for all of mankind. Rounding off his comments for good measure, with statements about how the Old Testament Sabbath breakers were to be stoned for their transgressions.

Adam was quiet for a while formulating his response. Isaac took the pause as a quick moral victory. Finally Adam replied in a slow purposeful cadence.

"You are mixing up the Sabbath day and Sunday as if they weren't two completely separate things. The Sabbath God gave to Israel was to be kept on the seventh day, our Saturday. Not the first day of the week, which is our Sunday. The Sabbath rules don't apply to Sunday."

Having practiced in mock debates at school Isaac countered with some rehearsed retorts.

"The Apostles changed the Saturday Sabbath to Sunday when they started preaching to the Gentiles. Like when Paul brought that young man back to life after he fell out of a high window, they were meeting on the first day of the week, that's when they went to church, on Sunday."

Glancing quickly sideways, then back on the road, Adam saw Isaac furrow his brow and squint his eyes in aggression. Adam softly replies "Well I don't think that passage of the Bible says quite what you think it does."

Reaching over Adam opens the glove box, revealing a lap top. Closing the music program, he instructs Isaac, "Boot up the Bible study apps that it's loaded with".

Grinning, Adam winks at Isaac as he says. "Shouldn't judge a book by the cover. You should be able to find that passage somewhere in there, give it a try."

Growing uncertain of his first impression, Isaac quickly finds the scriptural passage in question. "Here it is," he says.

Reading triumphantly aloud for Adam to clearly hear, he brings to life Acts 20:7-14. In the New King James Version "Ministering at Troas," Isaac hollers, to be herd over the noisy old truck.

"7 Now on the first *day* of the week, when the disciples came together to break bread, Paul, ready to depart the next day, spoke to them and continued his message until midnight. 8 There were many lamps in the upper room where they were gathered together. 9 And in a window sat a certain young man named Eutychus, who was sinking into a deep sleep. He was overcome by sleep; and as Paul continued speaking, he fell down from the third story and was taken up dead. 10 But Paul went down, fell on him, and embracing *him* said, "Do not trouble yourselves, for his life is in him." 11 Now when he had come up, had broken bread and eaten, and talked a long while, even till daybreak, he departed. 12 And they brought the young man in alive, and they were not a little comforted."

"See," demanded Isaac. "They were having their communion church service on the first day of the week. The Bible proves it. There are many other scriptures that I can refer too, if you want?"

"No, not quite yet, let's deal with one section of scripture at a time," Adam advises. "At first read it does sound compellingly supportive of your position, but the timeline that it gives feels wrong somehow. Let's go over it again. They came together on the first day of the week and broke bread."

"Yes, they had a communion service!" Isaac broke in.

"Well it doesn't say that," said Adam. "To break bread was a common term used for eating a meal with friends. The Church usage of that term for communion, or the Lords supper, didn't come till much later. The first century church pooled their belongings and ate meals together so this would have been a common practice. To dogmatically say that they were having a church service using this text is a stretch. They simply came together for a meal, on the first day of the week."

The conversation pauses while Isaac verifies Adam's points. A quick Google search of, 'break bread', led to several sites supporting Adam's position.

Adam waits a long time for Isaac to stop typing and searching the web. "Can I take your silence as agreement?" Adam asks while giving Isaac a sideways glance. Isaac frowns and mutters illegibly.

"OK, so they came together for a meal on the first day of the week," Adam starts again. "Paul leaves for a trip the next morning at dawn. But rather than getting a good night's sleep he talks till midnight when the young guy falls to his death. After bringing him back to life they ate some more, then Paul talked until he departed at dawn. Read on to the end of the story Isaac," Adam instructs.

Isaac reads the rest of the account aloud to the end of verse 14.

"From Troas to Miletus"
"13 Then we went ahead to the ship and sailed to Assos, there intending to take Paul on board; for so he had given orders, intending himself to go on foot. 14 And when he met us at Assos, we took him on board and came to Mitylene."

"Thanks," said Adam. "That hike Paul left on was twenty one miles over mountainous terrain, between Troas and Assos. You can find some maps of his trips on line there. His companions sailed or rowed the boat around the tip of Asia Minor to Assos. Not a relaxing day either. Neither trip would have been classified as a Sabbaths day's journey by old testament law."

"That's why they left on their trip the next morning," interjected Isaac. "They met Sunday night and then left Monday morning."

Shaking his head Adam replies. "That only works if you keep track of days the way we do now in this modern age. We count days starting at midnight, but the Jewish day started and ended at sunset. Check Genesis chapter one, the days are counted from the evening to evening.

So the first day of the week when they got together to break bread, would have been to us, Saturday evening. Then, Paul talked until midnight of the first day of the week. To us, that would be the start of Sunday at midnight. Then the guy fell down dead. Paul revived him, ate some more, kept on talking till dawn and then did a twenty one mile hike over a mountain. Meanwhile his friends took the boat the long way around to Assos. That doesn't sound like a precedent setting way of modeling the new 'day of rest' to the church. Would you agree with that analysis?"

Isaac was silent in thought for a minute, "let me do some checking first," he said thoughtfully. "I had never thought of it like that before."

"Take your time," Adam said, as he adjusted the heater temperature. Then reaching into his cooler for an orange he started to peel it over the steering wheel while using his elbows to make slight course adjustments, keeping the truck speeding along in its proper lane.

After many different searches on the lap-top, Isaac finally broke the silence. "Yes, I suppose that this section of scripture wasn't the best one to prove my point about Sunday being the Lords day. There are others I should have used instead. What about…"

Adam loudly takes over the conversation. "Stop, stop, stop!" he says, holding his hand out, with the palm facing out towards Isaac's face. "We must decide about the last section of scripture before we move on. Does it support the Sabbath or Sunday? To me, it verifies keeping a Saturday Sabbath, not keeping Sunday as the Sabbath. It only supports Sunday if you count the days in an unbiblical way, from midnight to midnight. Do you agree or not?"

Isaac squirms in his seat, then begrudgingly agrees that it doesn't really support Sunday as the day of rest, but upholds Saturday.

"OK then, you can never use it in good conscience again to defend your belief for a Sunday day of rest, can you?"

Isaac hesitates for a moment, then looking straight at Adam says. "No, I don't suppose I can."

"Alright, what are the next scriptures we need to look at?" Adam asks as he slurps down the last piece of his orange.

"Just a second while I find them," Isaac says, fingers flying over the old lap top key board. He scrolls through sights until he finds the version he is happy with. "Here it is he blurts," and starts to read it out loud with renewed vigour.

"1 Corinthians 16:1-4 King James Version
Now concerning the collection for the saints, as I have given order to the churches of Galatia, even so do ye.
2 Upon the first day of the week let every one of you lay by him in store, as God hath prospered him, that there be no gatherings when I come.
3 And when I come, whomsoever ye shall approve by your letters, them will I send to bring your liberality unto Jerusalem.
4 And if it be meet that I go also, they shall go with me."

"There. You see? They were taking up an offering on the first day of the week to help the brethren in Jerusalem. They were to bring it with them to church. They held their service on the first day of the week, Sunday!" Isaac emphatically stated in exasperation.

"Well again it does appear to be saying that, if you already believe Sunday to be the day of worship, but there is nothing in there stating that Sunday should replace the Sabbath day. Paul was very blunt when he challenged and spearheaded the change to the practice of circumcision. Had he been changing the day of worship to Sunday, one would expect him to be much clearer with his assertion. Your proof is circumstantial at best and at worse misleading. There are other texts that will help clarify what is going on here. Look it up in the next book, 2 Corinthians. Use the New King James Version," Adam directs.

Scrolling through the book, Isaac scans the screen and quickly finds the passage, then reads it out loud.

"2 Corinthians 9: 1-5 New King James Version, Administering the Gift
Now concerning the ministering to the saints, it is superfluous for me to write to you; 2 for I know your willingness, about which I boast of you to the Macedonians, that Achaia was ready a year ago; and your zeal has stirred up the majority. 3 Yet I have sent the brethren, lest our boasting of you should be in vain in this respect, that, as I said, you may be ready; 4 lest if *some* Macedonians come with me and find you unprepared, we (not to mention you!) should be ashamed of this confident boasting. 5 Therefore I thought it necessary to exhort the brethren to go to you ahead of time, and prepare your generous gift beforehand, which *you had* previously promised, that it may be ready as *a matter of* generosity and not as a grudging obligation.

I don't see your point," Isaac complains.

Adam elaborates his position. "The point is, they were collecting a gift for the brethren in Jerusalem. Not taking up an offering to run the local church. They could have been setting aside their gifts individually every week for a long time. Then bringing them together before Paul came and their offerings were sent to Jerusalem. Paul just didn't want it to be gathered together when he was there, so it wouldn't look like they were doing it out of duty instead of love. Paul had been boasting to the Macedonian churches about the Corinthians and didn't want it to look bad to any Macedonian church members that might be accompanying him to Corinth. It was all about perceptions, not about the day of worship".

"Then why did he tell them to set aside their offerings on the first day of the week?" demanded Isaac.

"If you were to give an offering on how much God blessed you every week, wouldn't it make sense to wait until the week ended? Then you could make an accurate tally of the profits generated in the previous week. You could try to guess on Thursday but you would have no way of being sure until the week was over. Setting your offering aside on the first day of the week would make it easy to know how much you could give based upon the previous week. As well, it establishes a regular routine of giving a little at a time," explained Adam.

Taking the offensive Adam catches Isaac off guard by asking a couple questions. "If Paul was changing the day of worship to Sunday, why is it not recorded anywhere that he did? He kept going to the synagogues on the Sabbath as was his custom. He also kept track of the seasons by referring to the annual Sabbaths when recording Christian history for fellow Christians. If he was replacing these days of worship, why not use the updated days as reference points instead? Do a Google search for yourself and see."

Isaac is silent in his studies for a while, when he speaks again his voice has a softer tone to it. "I found the verse referring to the season, I think. Was it when he was on the boat trip, got caught in a storm and sunk?"

"Ya that's it," Replied Adam.

"Well it's not much of a reference. What annual Sabbath is it referring too? I'm not that familiar with the Jewish holy days. I would have never noticed it if you hadn't pointed it out," Isaac reads aloud Acts 27:9.

"Now when much time was spent, and when sailing was now dangerous, because the fast was now already past, Paul admonished them,"

"That's part of my point," Said Adam. "Why refer to a day that was to fall out of usage and the understanding of it to become lost to his future Christian audience? Why not say, late fall instead? Unless he didn't know those days would become forgotten through lack of use."

"Well maybe," Isaac paused to collect his thoughts. "That may be true, but it doesn't make having to keep a Saturday Sabbath binding on Christians today like you're trying to prove. The Sabbath was part of the law that Jesus did away with."

"Praise the Lord!" Adam exclaims loudly. "That's the first thing you've said that I can agree with. I wasn't trying to prove that Christians had to keep the Sabbath. You legalistically said that I was a sinner because I worked on Sunday. You went on to say that Sunday was the new Sabbath and should be kept in a legalistic way. I was pointing out the fact that Saturday was never replaced by Sunday in the Bible. I didn't say Christians had to keep the Sabbath day holy on Saturday, Sunday, or on any other day.

I wish Christians kept Wednesday as a day of worship. That would get them as far away as possible from the idea of having to keep Saturday, Sunday, or any day holy. Maybe then they would be less legalistic about everything else. I was pointing out that you were mixing up your days with no biblical support to back it up.

Jesus fulfilled the law's requirements for us on the cross. The torn temple veil demonstrates that to us, by making access directly to God possible. The last words Jesus spoke, told us, 'it is finished'. What was finished?" answering his own question Adam animatedly continues his rant. "The work Jesus came to earth to do, freeing all of humanity from the grip of sin, that, is what was finished. His sinless sacrificial life did that for us all. Christians are free from keeping outward laws that regulate our actions. Instead we are bound by the inward love of God that guides our thoughts and hearts. Our actions display our inward selves for all to see. Paul warned us about getting caught back into legalism in Galatians. 'Freedom is what we have—Christ has set us free! Stand, then, as free people, and do not allow yourselves to become slaves again'. Slaves to what? Slaves to laws and legalism. 'Have you not read? The sacrifice God wants is a willing spirit. God, you will not reject a heart that is broken and sorry for its sin'."

Nodding in agreement Isaac breaks in. "Yes, the Crucifixion and death of Jesus paid for our sins. His resurrection proof on, Sunday, is why we should keep his day special. The Lords Day, like when John was in the spirit on the Lords Day, when he wrote the book of Revelations. He wrote it on Sunday; we should worship the Lord on his day. Sunday!

Adam takes his eyes off the road for a moment and looks intently into the bright, young, wide eyes of Isaac. Turning his gaze back to the road he lets out a deep, heavy, sigh. "So tell me," Adam begins slowly. "What makes you so sure Jesus arose from the dead on Sunday?"

Giving Adam a puzzled look Isaac replies in bewilderment. "He arose on the third day. I thought you would have known that. Aren't you a follower of Jesus? Don't you believe in the resurrection of Jesus? That was the miracle Jesus gave to prove he was the son of God. I was starting to think you were a believer, but now I'm not so sure. Jesus was crucified on Friday and rose in victory over the grave on Sunday, just like the Bible says."

"I do believe in the resurrection of Jesus, and I do believe he rose just like he said he would." Adam tells Isaac reassuringly. "The problem is, I don't think you have looked at all of the scriptures to see how they fit together."

"Yes I have!" irritated, Isaac shoots back. "I have been to one of the best Bible colleges around, with well-trained scholarly professors and doctors of theology who have studied the scriptures for years. Yes, I do know the scriptures about the resurrection, thank you very much, probably better than some old trucker."

Ignoring Isaac, Adam guides the steering wheel with a slight amount of counter clockwise pressure, maneuvering his rig past, yet another truck in the slow lane. Quickly over taking and passing the slower lumbering semi, Adam checks his right hand mirror as he sings a line from a classic rock song. He provides his own back up instrumentals by making electric guitar and drum sounds with his mouth. "Life in the fast lane, surely you will lose your mind, life in the fast lane. Buna, nuna, nu, nu, nu, do, do do, do."

Giving Isaac a minute longer to cool down Adam changes the subject. "Those poor guys are stuck with speed limiters so they can't go faster than a hundred clicks. I prefer to at least go the speed limit. The boss tried to make me put one on, but it wouldn't work with my old mechanical engine. It had to be a, drive by wire, for the computer thingy to work." Laughing Adam adds. "And the boss wonders why I like my old truck. 'Sometimes the old ways are best'."

Sensing Isaac's tension starting to dissipate, he starts to talk again about the resurrection of Jesus. Getting no response, he glancing over to see Isaac slouched back in the passenger seat, his head resting against the side window, fast asleep. Time and the miles fly by, unobserved by Isaac.

CHAPTER 3
PROVE IT

Frost heaves in the road bounce the truck cab violently, banging Isaac's head hard against the cool side window, jarring him out of his slumber. Adam takes note of his waking, gives Isaac a moment to sort out his surroundings, then picks up the conversation where he had left off.

"You know, I never went to a fancy college like you. But that doesn't mean I haven't studied. I have lots of time to listen and think. I like to mull things over and look at a subject from every possible angle. I will do it for days. Now with the internet, research is so much easier than before. The company I contract to gets like a gazillion gigs of data per month with their satellite coverage contract. That's how they can keep in touch with all of the trucks. I can use it all I want. I just can't stream Netflix 24 hours a day is all. Anyway, between waiting to load produce and hours of service limits, I can get a lot of research done. There are audio posts I listen to and many topics to fact check. So, if you are ready to discuss the topic biblically, so am I."

"Sounds good to me," Isaac said with a growing clarity after his slumber. He was excited for the opportunity to exercise his biblical prowess and set this old trucker straight. "All points used have to be supported by the King James Version or the Strong's concordance using the words from the original texts. My profs say that other translations can misdirect a person if they are not careful. Only the sound word of God can be used and no source other than the Bible can be referenced to support an opinion." Isaac adds.

"That'll work for me," Adam replies nodding his head. "Good ground rules. Shall we start?"

"OK" Isaac begins hesitantly trying to remember where the conversation had ended. "I will admit that Paul doesn't specifically say to keep Sunday in place of Saturday, and the scriptures I used to show that he had were, well, circumstantial at best. And yes I agree that Jesus freed us from having to keep the old covenant law through his sacrifice." Isaac uses these retraction sentences to formulate where he wanted to start his rebuttal.

"But it is rock solidly clear, that the day Jesus was crucified was the preparation day for the Sabbath. Furthermore, it is also rock solid, that it was the first day of the week, while it was still dark before sunrise, that the women found the tomb empty. You can't disprove those facts using the Bible as source material."

"Absolutely, one hundred percent true. Congratulations, that's the second thing you've said that I can agree with," Adam says grinning.

"So now you agree that Jesus was crucified on Friday and rose on Sunday? Did the thought of having to prove, through bible scripture anything different, scare you?" Isaac sarcastically remarks.

"Nope, to all of those questions," replies Adam. "You're still wrong. Your first statement was true. The day Jesus was crucified was on the preparation day for the Sabbath and the women did find an empty tomb in the predawn darkness of the first day of the week. Those statements are, as you say, rock solid."

"So what's your problem?" Isaac was still sarcastic.

Checking his temper, Adam calmly replied. "It's not my problem. It's your lack of understanding of the bigger picture."

Still sarcastic Isaac sneers. "Ohh dooo tell, would you pleeaase enlighten me."

"Well since you've asked so nicely, it would be my pleasure," Adam says, saccharinly sweet, turning his face towards Isaac to display the biggest fake smile he could muster. "Let's start with verses talking about how long Jesus would be in the grave for. Your good with that keyboard, go find em!" he orders.

Isaac begins his search meticulously cutting and pasting each reference into a single document for future reference. "We'll use all of the accounts describing what Jesus, or others said, about how long Jesus would be in the grave," Isaac said looking for Adam's approval.

"Ya sure, that would be good," Adam says agreeably.

Before long Isaac proudly reveals his findings. "OK, these are the verses I could find about how long Jesus would be in the grave. I have put them into categories. First, is the sign Jesus gave to the Pharisees, then, in three days, on the third day and after three days," Isaac proceeds to read them aloud.

"Sign of Jonas.

Matthew 16:4 King James Version
A wicked and adulterous generation seeketh after a sign; and there shall no sign be given unto it, but the sign of the prophet Jonas. And he left them, and departed.
Luke 11:30
For as Jonas was a sign unto the Ninevites, so shall also the Son of man be to this generation.
Matthew 12: 40
For as Jonas was three days and three nights in the whale's belly; so shall the Son of man be three days and three nights in the heart of the earth.

In Three Days.

Matthew 27:40
and saying, "You who are going to destroy the temple and build it in three days, save yourself! Come down from the cross, if you are the Son of God!"

Mark 15:29

Those who passed by hurled insults at him, shaking their heads and saying, "So! You who are going to destroy the temple and build it in three days.

Matthew 26:61

And said, This fellow said, I am able to destroy the temple of God, and to build it in three days.

Mark 14:58

We heard him say, I will destroy this temple that is made with hands, and within three days I will build another made without hands.

John 2:19-21 KJV

Jesus answered and said unto them, Destroy this temple, and in three days I will raise it up. 20 Then said the Jews, Forty and six years was this temple in building, and wilt thou rear it up in three days? 21 But he spake of the temple of his body.

On The Third Day.

Luke 24:46

He told them, "This is what is written: The Messiah will suffer and rise from the dead on the third day,

Luke 24:21

but we had hoped that he was the one who was going to redeem Israel. And what is more, it is the third day since all this took place.

Luke 24:7

'The Son of Many must be delivered over to the hands of sinners, be crucified and on the third day be raised again.'

Luke 13:32

He replied, "Go tell that fox, 'I will keep on driving out demons and healing people today and tomorrow, and on the third day I will reach my goal.'

Luke 9:22

And he said, "The Son of Mane must suffer many things and be rejected by the elders, the chief priests and the teachers of the law, and he must be killed and on the third day be raised to life."

Matthew 20:19

and will hand him over to the Gentiles to be mocked and flogged and crucified. On the third day he will be raised to life!"

Matthew 17:22-23

And while they abode in Galilee, Jesus said unto them, The Son of man shall be betrayed into the hands of men: 23 And they shall kill him, and the third day he shall be raised again. And they were exceeding sorry.

Mark 9:31

For he taught his disciples, and said unto them, The Son of man is delivered into the hands of men, and they shall kill him; and after that he is killed, he shall rise the third day.

Mark 10:34

And they shall mock him, and shall scourge him, and shall spit upon him, and shall kill him: and the third day he shall rise again.

Luke 18:33

And they shall scourge him, and put him to death: and the third day he shall rise again.

1 Corinthians 15:4

And that he was buried, and that he rose again the third day according to the scriptures:

Acts 10:40

Him God raised up the third day, and shewed him openly; After three Days.

Matthew 27:63 KJV

Saying, Sir, we remember that that deceiver said, while he was yet alive, After three days I will rise again.

Mark 8:31

And he began to teach them, that the Son of man must suffer many things, and be rejected of the elders, and of the chief priests, and scribes, and be killed, and after three days rise again.

So you can see Jesus was in the grave for three days," Isaac said.

"OK. That would put Jesus in the tomb for 72 hours then wouldn't it? Three 24 hour days," Adam calculates.

"No. The term day was a figure of speech, any portion of the day would work," corrected Isaac patiently, momentarily losing his sarcastic tone. "There are other examples of that in the Bible."

"Yes, I have seen them, but Jesus used the story of Jonas as his test of divinity, breaking the three days into three days and three nights. So to fulfill that, you would need some part of each day and night. Friday sunset to predawn first day of the week would not have the needed time, there would need to be a daylight and night portion from each day. Or he may have completed the whole 72 hours so that the Pharisees would have no grounds on which to deny his divinity.

After all, he knew they would use the tiniest excuse to reject him; they had been doing that for the last three and a half years of his life. It doesn't make sense for him to give a sign to prove he was the son of God to the Pharisees and then give them an excuse to ignore it.

Had Jesus been talking to his friends then a figure of speech would have been alright. But not for the Pharisees, they were nit-picky lawyers all about the smallest jot and tittle. No, he would have wanted to be more precise than a figure of speech. Besides, look at his statements, in three days, on the third day, and after three days. The only way these three statements can all work is if it was exactly three days, 72 hours," Adan argued.

"I can see your point about the Pharisees; they did hate Jesus and used any excuse to reject him. However you are forgetting two important facts," Isaac declares. "The first is that Jesus was crucified on the preparation day and second is the two men walking on the road who met Jesus, they said it was the third day since Jesus had been killed. If he had been in the grave for 72 hours, for the full three days and nights, then they would have been talking to Jesus on the fourth day, not the third. It's not possible for him to be in the grave for a full 72 hours and then talk to people during the daylight portion of the third day."

"Your second point is a puzzler. I will have to do a bit more research on it. It does seem to put the full 72 hours into question," Adam admits. "But your first point is fairly easy to figure out. They were Crucifying Jesus on the preparation day for the annual Sabbath of Unleavened Bread. Jesus was literally being slaughtered as our Passover lamb.

I find the symbolism quite poignant. These annual Sabbaths could land on any day of the week, depending on the year. They were to be treated holy like a regular weekly Sabbath day. Like the fast day Paul used when referring to the autumn season, it was also one of the annual Sabbath days."

"I don't know much about these annual Sabbaths," Isaac admits.

"Well then you better look them up. I wouldn't want you to trust me about the Bible. You need to prove it for yourself," Adam says encouragingly.

Isaac begins another search on the lap top, this time to find scriptures on the mysterious annual Sabbaths and how they were to be kept. "There are several different texts describing the annual feast days, but this list in Leviticus 23 is fairly concise. The wording used, treats the weekly and annual Sabbaths the same, as holy convocations, to be the feasts of the Lord. I have never read about them before," Isaac said with a sheepish tone. He reads the entire chapter, pausing at times to reflect on the newly discovered biblical content.

"Leviticus 23 KJV
1 And the LORD spake unto Moses, saying,
2 Speak unto the children of Israel, and say unto them, Concerning the feasts of the LORD, which ye shall proclaim to be holy convocations, even these are my feasts.

3 Six days shall work be done: but the seventh day is the sabbath of rest, an holy convocation; ye shall do no work therein: it is the sabbath of the LORD in all your dwellings.

4 These are the feasts of the LORD, even holy convocations, which ye shall proclaim in their seasons.

5 In the fourteenth day of the first month at even is the LORD's passover.

6 And on the fifteenth day of the same month is the feast of unleavened bread unto the LORD: seven days ye must eat unleavened bread.

7 In the first day ye shall have an holy convocation: ye shall do no servile work therein.

8 But ye shall offer an offering made by fire unto the LORD seven days: in the seventh day is an holy convocation: ye shall do no servile work therein.

9 And the LORD spake unto Moses, saying,

10 Speak unto the children of Israel, and say unto them, When ye be come into the land which I give unto you, and shall reap the harvest thereof, then ye shall bring a sheaf of the firstfruits of your harvest unto the priest:

11 And he shall wave the sheaf before the LORD, to be accepted for you: on the morrow after the sabbath the priest shall wave it.

12 And ye shall offer that day when ye wave the sheaf an he lamb without blemish of the first year for a burnt offering unto the LORD.

13 And the meat offering thereof shall be two tenth deals of fine flour mingled with oil, an offering made by fire unto the LORD for a sweet savour: and the drink offering thereof shall be of wine, the fourth part of an hin.

14 And ye shall eat neither bread, nor parched corn, nor green ears, until the selfsame day that ye have brought an offering unto your God: it shall be a statute for ever throughout your generations in all your dwellings.

15 And ye shall count unto you from the morrow after the sabbath, from the day that ye brought the sheaf of the wave offering; seven sabbaths shall be complete:

16 Even unto the morrow after the seventh sabbath shall ye number fifty days; and ye shall offer a new meat offering unto the LORD.

17 Ye shall bring out of your habitations two wave loaves of two tenth deals; they shall be of fine flour; they shall be baken with leaven; they are the firstfruits unto the LORD.

18 And ye shall offer with the bread seven lambs without blemish of the first year, and one young bullock, and two rams: they shall be for a burnt offering unto the LORD, with their meat offering, and their drink offerings, even an offering made by fire, of sweet savour unto the LORD.

19 Then ye shall sacrifice one kid of the goats for a sin offering, and two lambs of the first year for a sacrifice of peace offerings.

20 And the priest shall wave them with the bread of the firstfruits for a wave offering before the LORD, with the two lambs: they shall be holy to the LORD for the priest.

21 And ye shall proclaim on the selfsame day, that it may be an holy convocation unto you: ye shall do no servile work therein: it shall be a statute for ever in all your dwellings throughout your generations.

22 And when ye reap the harvest of your land, thou shalt not make clean riddance of the corners of thy field when thou reapest, neither shalt thou gather any gleaning of

thy harvest: thou shalt leave them unto the poor, and to the stranger: I am the LORD your God.

23 And the LORD spake unto Moses, saying,

24 Speak unto the children of Israel, saying, In the seventh month, in the first day of the month, shall ye have a sabbath, a memorial of blowing of trumpets, an holy convocation.

25 Ye shall do no servile work therein: but ye shall offer an offering made by fire unto the LORD.

26 And the LORD spake unto Moses, saying,

27 Also on the tenth day of this seventh month there shall be a day of atonement: it shall be an holy convocation unto you; and ye shall afflict your souls, and offer an offering made by fire unto the LORD.

28 And ye shall do no work in that same day: for it is a day of atonement, to make an atonement for you before the LORD your God.

29 For whatsoever soul it be that shall not be afflicted in that same day, he shall be cut off from among his people.

30 And whatsoever soul it be that doeth any work in that same day, the same soul will I destroy from among his people.

31 Ye shall do no manner of work: it shall be a statute for ever throughout your generations in all your dwellings.

32 It shall be unto you a sabbath of rest, and ye shall afflict your souls: in the ninth day of the month at even, from even unto even, shall ye celebrate your sabbath.

33 And the LORD spake unto Moses, saying,

34 Speak unto the children of Israel, saying, The fifteenth day of this seventh month shall be the feast of tabernacles for seven days unto the LORD.

35 On the first day shall be an holy convocation: ye shall do no servile work therein.

36 Seven days ye shall offer an offering made by fire unto the LORD: on the eighth day shall be an holy convocation unto you; and ye shall offer an offering made by fire unto the LORD: it is a solemn assembly; and ye shall do no servile work therein.

37 These are the feasts of the LORD, which ye shall proclaim to be holy convocations, to offer an offering made by fire unto the LORD, a burnt offering, and a meat offering, a sacrifice, and drink offerings, every thing upon his day:

38 Beside the sabbaths of the LORD, and beside your gifts, and beside all your vows, and beside all your freewill offerings, which ye give unto the LORD.

39 Also in the fifteenth day of the seventh month, when ye have gathered in the fruit of the land, ye shall keep a feast unto the LORD seven days: on the first day shall be a sabbath, and on the eighth day shall be a sabbath.

40 And ye shall take you on the first day the boughs of goodly trees, branches of palm trees, and the boughs of thick trees, and willows of the brook; and ye shall rejoice before the LORD your God seven days.

41 And ye shall keep it a feast unto the LORD seven days in the year. It shall be a statute for ever in your generations: ye shall celebrate it in the seventh month.

42 Ye shall dwell in booths seven days; all that are Israelites born shall dwell in booths:

43 That your generations may know that I made the children of Israel to dwell in booths, when I brought them out of the land of Egypt: I am the LORD your God.

44 And Moses declared unto the children of Israel the feasts of the LORD.

So the fourteenth, at even or sunset, when the Passover lamb was sacrificed, took place just before Jesus was being put into the tomb. Then the fifteenth was the first day of unleavened bread, it would have started at sunset with an annual Sabbath," Isaac was working out the details in his mind as he talked.

"Yes," affirmed Adam. "That is why the Jews wanted the legs, of the three crucified that day, to be broken and their bodies taken down. They didn't want them hanging on their crosses on their high Sabbath day of unleavened bread. It's in John's account of that day."

"I remember reading it, but I never made the connection until you pointed it out now. I wondered why it would have been a 'high Sabbath', but never took the time to find out. Let me quickly look it up," Isaac said, as he starter to type on the lap top's keyboard. "There are two sections of scripture mentioning it being the Passover, and one about it being a high day," enthusiastically Isaac begins to read them to Adam.

John 19:31
The Jews therefore, because it was the preparation, that the bodies should not remain upon the cross on the sabbath day, (for that sabbath day was an high day,) besought Pilate that their legs might be broken, and that they might be taken away.

John 19:14
And it was the preparation of the passover, and about the sixth hour: and he saith unto the Jews, Behold your King!

John 18:28

Then led they Jesus from Caiaphas unto the hall of
judgement: and it was early; and they themselves went
not into the judgement hall, lest they should be defiled;
but that they might eat the passover."

"Ya. See, those verses tell us it was the preparation day for an
annual Sabbath, not a weekly one. These annual Sabbaths could
take place on any day of the week not just Saturday, so the
preparation day doesn't have to be a Friday."

"This is all very new and confusing to me," Isaac complained
"I don't really get it. Friday and Sunday Easter is much easier to
understand."

"OK, let's go through it again and see if I can explain it
better," Adam said, sounding like an elementary school teacher.
"We know that every Sabbath has a preparation day, because you
have to rest from your labour on the Sabbath."

"Ya,ya,ya, I get that part. It's all the mumbo jumbo about what
day you start to count on that gets me," Isaac said, still
complaining. "That's what I don't get."

Smiling broadly Adam Joked, "I bet I can tell you, within
three days, the day you were born."

Thinking he was being made fun off Isaac replied angrily.
"What's that got to do with anything?"

"Wednesday," Adam said confidently, brushing off Isaac's
angry response.

"You're daft, March third." Taking a moment to think about it
Isaac soon saw the significance of Adam's riddle. "Oh I think I get
it now. Because of the number of days in a year, any one day, like
my birthday, might land, depending on the year, on a different day
of the weak."

"Exactly," Adam said calmly. "Preparation day could be any
day of the weak for one of the annual Sabbaths. It was also a
'special' preparation day, because on the afternoon of that

preparation day, the Passover lamb was sacrificed before the first Sabbath of unleavened bread."

Scratching his head slowly Isaac looked at Adam with new eyes, uttering a slow, "Yyaaa. I think I get it now. Why does it have to be so confusing?"

"Why should it be simple?" Adam questioned. "Like you said earlier, you're not all that familiar with Old Testament Holy Days.

So let's start again. We should be able to have all of the scriptures fit into place after adding up the six, day and night segments, revealing the preparation day," Adam speculates. "Going by the idea of any portion of a day could count for a day and by Jesus using three days and nights as his sign we can count backwards three light and three dark segments to find the day he was crucified on."

"OK, that would work," Isaac added. "So we have Sunday before sunrise, or Saturday night to us, that's the first dark part, because the first day of the weak starts at sunset, not at midnight."

"Saturday light part," chimed in Adam. "I'll count the daylight portions, you count the nights."

"That will help make it easy to keep track. Friday dark is two," agreed Isaac.

"Friday daylight is two," Said Adam, taking his turn.

"Thursday night makes three," Isaac says, holding up three of his fingers.

"And some portion of Thursday late afternoon completes at least some of each of the day and night parts, of the three days and three nights Jesus had given as a sign," Adam says.

Going on Adam ads speculatively, "It also allows for Sunday to be the third day as a figure of speech, since everything took place. The disciples wouldn't have been finished taking care of Jesus until they rolled the stone sealing the tomb, which would have been after sunset. They probably didn't start counting until they were finished with their work."

Isaac nods his head in agreement. "That would make for two Sabbaths in a row. Thursday at even of the fourteenth for the preparation day Passover, then Friday the fifteenth for the first day of Unleavened Bread Sabbath, followed by the weekly Saturday Sabbath. The Women show up Sunday before daylight only to find an empty tomb and that Jesus has already risen. That should satisfy all of the scripture references we found," Isaac stops talking and a pondering look comes over his face. "I wonder why we don't keep it like that?" he says softly to himself.

"What does it matter when we celebrate?" Adam says loudly. Speaking passionately Adam continues. "We are free to worship at any time. Being tied up in laws and time schedules misses the whole point of grace. Jesus freed us from all of that, we can't let ourselves get tied up in the legalism of, one size fits all. I may not believe all that you believe and vice-versa. But it doesn't really matter as long as we believe in and receive Jesus as our Savior.

That's why I disagreed with your statements about when Jesus died and was resurrected. Your statements left no room for any other possibilities, or beliefs. You said it had to be a Friday burial, with a Sunday morning resurrection. We shouldn't deny the power of God because our traditions don't fully reflect God's truth in every way. Jesus was resurrected just as he said he would be. After three days. We need to give others their freedom of thought as to how they add it up and to follow God's calling in their lives.

We can rest assured that Jesus did rise as he said he would and fulfilled his prophesy. Otherwise the Pharisees would not have tried to make it look like the disciples stole the body of Jesus. They would have just said he didn't come back to life as he had predicted and didn't fulfill his proof of messiah-ship. Why bother bribing the Roman guards? The Pharisees would have kept their beloved money."

Isaac is thoughtfully quiet for a moment, then speaks. "I suppose I should have said, I believe, or that, Christians choose to celebrate the death and resurrection of Jesus on these days."

"How about, some Christians choose to celebrate," interrupted Adam.

"Oh ya, I guise that would be better," said Isaac respectfully. "It's all about making your communication inclusive isn't it?"

"It's all about making your thoughts inclusive," corrected Adam. "If your heart is there, your words will reflect it. Legalism is exclusive and divisive. Love is inclusive and covers a multitude of sin."

"I guess I could work on my subtleties," declared Isaac. "I wonder why the Church ever started keeping Friday and Sunday to commemorate the resurrection."

"Probably because the Jews persecuted them for not keeping the Law of Moses," Adam Guesses. "I would have wanted to get as far away from that Jewish legalism as I could. Paul talks about Jewish converts telling others they had to be circumcised and follow the laws of Moses. It seems like, not everyone fully understood the grace Jesus brought to us. It wasn't until in the three hundreds, with Constantine, that the dates for Easter and a Sunday Sabbath were instituted.

Easter isn't practiced when it is because that's the biblical story, any more than the Christmas story. Our Christmas traditions are totally accurate to the birth of Jesus. The ancient corporate Christian church set out the traditions most modern Christians keep today. Most Christians don't know their own church history; they think their religious holidays are prescribed in the Bible by God. When in actual fact today's Christian traditions were thought up by Christian leaders for a variety of reasons. After all if you are going to leave one set of traditions behind, you need another set of traditions to replace them with."

Reaching down to the floor Adam picks up a grubby half empty plastic water bottle. Twisting off the cap using the fingers from the same hand he held it with, he takes a sip of water from it, threading the cap back on in reverse order, he drops the bottle back to the floor.

"But that doesn't make keeping them wrong. You said yourself Jesus freed us from the law and it's through grace we are saved, we are free to worship God whenever we think best," Isaac sharply pointed out.

"Yes, we are free and it isn't important when we worship God, only that we do," Adam points out. "If it was important to God that we celebrate the death and resurrection of Jesus at a specific time, he would have told us how and when to do it, like he did with the Holy Days. The fact that we can come up with three likely scenarios for how things played out at the resurrection, show that it has been left as a bit of a mystery. God has shown that he can be very precise on how and when to worship him in the past. It seems to me that he isn't looking for people to follow external rules and laws, but follow his spirit, growing in the fruit of love."

Continuing, Adam says forcefully. "So now that you agree that it isn't important the day or time we worship and you understand some of the history around the days kept as special, STOP being legalistic and judgmental of those who don't believe the same way as you.

Oh and before I forget, John was is the spirit, on the Lord's day, refers to the day that Jesus returns to the earth at his second coming. Not Sunday," Adam's voice is animated as he talks to Isaac. His head twisting back and forth, taking quick glances at the empty highway in front of him.

Isaac squirms in his seat as if he was a hot stove. His face starts to redden as the reality of his religiously superior attitudes start to become clear to him. He is not ready to admit defeat to this trucker quite yet though. He still had some spiritual ammo left to fire and he was sure that it would be accurate.

CHAPTER 4
GAME ON

Sitting quietly Isaac formulates strategy for his next foray. His thoughts become hard to formulate and disjointed, as the gentle rocking of the truck once again overwhelms his consciousness with its soothing affect and he is overcome with slumber. His rest is only partial and fleeting as his mind is filled with the thoughts of how to set up his next point of debate. Waking with a new challenge in mind, Isaac starts another sparring round with a pointed question shot at Adam.

"Are you saying that it doesn't matter what you believe as long as you believe in and accept Jesus?

Startled by Isaac's sudden attentiveness, Adam pauses for a moment considering his reply. He adjusts the cab heat and simultaneously checks for traffic in his mirrors. "It depends what you understand the plan of God to be," replies Adam. "Do you believe that accepting Jesus as your Savior and eternal life in heaven, is the extent of God's plan for humanity? Or do you believe we are called to receive eternal life, as well as rewards in God's kingdom as true sons of God. We receive those rewards by developing our talents and by growing in the Spirit of God during this life.

I believe God will reward us for how well we overcome now, in this life. It does matter what you believe, because not fully understanding God or his plans for humanity, will affect how you interact with people around you. It will affect how you show the love of God to the world. Even though you may be saved, you could be misleading others about the Kingdom of God.

As Christians we are to develop the fruit of the spirit and become more like God. We do this by wrestling with our human nature, now is our time for growth. The better we know the Bible the better we will know God." Adam throws in a quote from the Bible. "'Do your best to win full approval in God's sight, as a worker who is not ashamed of his work, one who correctly teaches the message of God's truth'."

"Yes!" Isaac exclaims. "So we must preach to this sinful world so that they will be able to repent and save their souls from eternal torment in the fires of Hell?" Isaac says expanding on Adam's thought. "We should preach Jesus to the world to win those lost souls for the Lord and gain a better reward for ourselves."

Adam shoots a glance at Isaac and says with a frown. "That's not what I was getting at. I was talking about Christians being rewarded by God, for their personal growth, once they are in the kingdom. We need to be skillful in correctly teaching the word of God to others so that we won't be ashamed of our workmanship of proclaiming the Kingdom of God."

Isaac responds impatiently. "As long as people hear the message of Jesus and accept him as their Savior to gain eternal life, that is all that is needed to save them from eternal torment in Hell. That is the prime work of the faithful."

Defiant, Isaac leans back in his chair where he is again overcome by the trucks gentle rocking motion and the heat of the cab. Another wave of exhaustion and relaxation washes over him like an narcoleptic wave. Without warning he is suspended in a jittery, twitchy sleep, his head tipped against the passenger door window in what has now become a familiar pose.

Having plenty of time to formulate his rebuttal, Adam waits patiently as he keeps the truck safely rolling down the highway. "It appears to me that you believe Satan's lie." Adam loudly picks up the conversation where they had left off when Isaac finally awakens with a snort.

"What lie is that?" Isaac replies groggily, wiping the drool from his chin. "Why would I believe anything that Satan tells me?" Isaac demands sharply.

"Well, your statement that those who don't accept Jesus will be tortured eternally in the fires of hell. Or did I misunderstand you? It leads me to believe that you have been duped by Satan along with the majority of mankind," explained Adam.

"Yes, that is what I meant. The unsaved will be tormented in Hell for all eternity, but that is not a satanic lie. It's a biblical fact." Isaac said certifying his beliefs, as the true biblical record.

"Then yes, you do believe the lie Satan told Eve in the Garden of Eden. 'You shall not surely die.' That was the original lie, told by the father of lies and mankind has believed it ever since," Adam said confidently.

"What lie? What are you talking about? We all die physically, but our souls live on. 'The Spirit goes back to God who gave it'. Our spirits are entrusted to be with God when we die, our spirit is immortal, many Bible verses explain that to us. Haven't you ever read them in the Bible?" Isaac asks Adam in mocking sarcasm, astonished with Adam's ignorance of basic Christian doctrine.

"No, actually I never could find that taught in my bible. Maybe you could help me find where it's written. I've heard it being taught in sermons and I know people talk about that notion, but I have not read that anywhere in the Bible," Adam was speaking with a slight hint of sarcasm himself; his eyes were wide giving him a lost puppy look.

"Well OK, let's start with the verse that I have already referred too. The spirit goes back to God. I'll look it up." Isaac's fingers are in a flurry over the key board. "Here it is,

Ecclesiastes 12:7 KJV. Then shall the dust return to the earth as it was: and the spirit shall return unto God who gave it.

48

This is telling us that when we die our Spirit goes back to God. That is strait forward to understand. Don't you see? Man was created as a body out of the ground and then God breathed into him, the spirit, and he became a living soul. We have two separate parts, body and soul. Soul is also referred to as the spirit and here we are told it goes back to God when we die," Isaac is trying to use his best professorial voice.

"I do see the words your reading, however I don't think you got the proper meaning for them," Adam retorts.

"What do you mean? What other possible explanation could there be," Isaac inquires.

"It all goes back to the beginning," said Adam, doing his best to explain. "If your understanding is wrong just a bit at the start, then you will not understand other things correctly later on.

Like surveying land, if you're half a degree off to start with, after a thousand miles you will be a long way from the intended mark. That's what Satan did, he mislead mankind at the start about ourselves and that has led mankind away from God and the plans God has for us ever since."

"Your big on conspiracy theories aren't you?" Isaac says, jokingly sarcastic this time.

"Not normally, but this is the biggest one ever," Adam admits. "It all started in the Garden of Eden. Satan lies to Eve. He tells her she would not die. He misdirects her away from god, by framing his lie in the truth that the tree of knowledge would make her wise. You can read this in Geneses."

Isaac looks up the passage. He starts to read just as Adam finishes speaking. "I will read the entire story for context." Isaac starts to read animatedly for affect.

"Genesis 3:1-7

Now the serpent was more subtil than any beast of the field which the LORD God had made. And he said unto the woman, Yea, hath God said, Ye shall not eat of every tree of the garden?

2 And the woman said unto the serpent, We may eat of the fruit of the trees of the garden:

3 But of the fruit of the tree which is in the midst of the garden, God hath said, Ye shall not eat of it, neither shall ye touch it, lest ye die.

4 And the serpent said unto the woman, Ye shall not surely die:

5 For God doth know that in the day ye eat thereof, then your eyes shall be opened, and ye shall be as gods, knowing good and evil.

6 And when the woman saw that the tree was good for food, and that it was pleasant to the eyes, and a tree to be desired to make one wise, she took of the fruit thereof, and did eat, and gave also unto her husband with her; and he did eat.

7 And the eyes of them both were opened, and they knew that they were naked; and they sewed fig leaves together, and made themselves aprons.

Ya." Isaac said out loud as if reading the story for the first time. "So the lie was in verse 4. He told her she would not die contrary to what God had told her in verse 3," Reverting to traditional teaching Isaac continues. "But God meant that she would not die physically. They could have lived in Eden forever without sin. God created Adam with an immortal soul at creation. Here I will read it to you.

Genesis 2:7 KJV. And the LORD God formed man of the dust of the ground, and breathed into his nostrils the breath of life; and man became a living soul.

See? Man was made physical and with an immortal soul."

Confidently Adam counters the point and directs Isaac to find more information. "If you already had the idea that we have an immortal soul you might believe that, but if you analyze that verse you will find it doesn't say what you think it does. The word Soul is translated from the Hebrew word nephesh. That is the same word used to describe all the rest of the animals created on the fifth day. Look up the meaning and usage in the Strong's Concordance."

Finding the requested material Isaac starts to read the dry subject matter methodically out loud.

" nephesh *neh'-fesh*
From H5314; properly a *breathing* creature, that is, *animal* or (abstractly) *vitality*; used very widely in a literal, accommodated or figurative sense (bodily or mental)
KJV Usage: any, appetite, beast, body, breath, creature, X dead (-ly), desire, X [dis-] contented, X fish, ghost, + greedy, he, heart (-y), (hath, X jeopardy of) life (X in jeopardy), lust, man, me, mind, mortality,"

Isaac says with a loud yawn.

"There! See." Adam quickly interjects, silencing Isaac. "The King James translators used nephesh to mean MORTAL. Not Immortal." He places emphasis on the word mortal. "The KJV translators knew that the verse was not saying man had an Immortal soul as most Christians think."

Thoughtfully Isaac continues reading the concordance.

"one, own, person, pleasure, (her-, him-, my-, thy-) self, them (your) -selves, + slay, soul, + tablet, they, thing, (X she) will, X would have it. Brown-Driver-Briggs' Hebrew Definitions

1. soul, self, life, creature, person, appetite, mind, living being, desire, emotion, passion
   a. that which breathes, the breathing substance or being, soul, the inner being of man
   b. living being
   c. living being (with life in the blood)
   d. the man himself, self, person or individual
   e. seat of the appetites
   f. seat of emotions and passions
   g. activity of mind
   1. dubious
   h. activity of the will
   1. dubious
   i. activity of the character
   1. Dubious

That covers it. It did talk about Soul being our inner man, and the seat of our apatite's, desires, emotions and passions." Isaac points out for clarity, trying to ignore Adam's point about humans being created mortal.

Noticing the vibrations coming from the passenger seat he was sitting in were intensifying rapidly, along with the shrill howl of the wind from the cabs windows, and the deafening rumble of the Jake brake becoming overbearing, Isaac is forced to take notice of the old trucks increasing speed.

He couldn't see it clearly through the steering wheel spokes, but thought he saw the speedometer needle pointing towards the two o'clock position. Looking up he could see the freeway dropping down before them in a steep decline. Nervously clutching onto the armrest of his chair, he looks at Adam calmly resting his elbow on the window ledge, lightly touching two fingers on the steering wheel.

Having reached the top of the engines RPM range, Adam casually skip-shifts into his highest gear. The barking of the exhaust is quietened, but Isaac is alarmed that now the old truck is picking up speed even faster, as if they were in free-fall towards the bottom of the hill that Isaac could see stretched out more than a mile away below them. The calmness of Adam gives him no comfort as beads of sweat form on his brow. Soon the Jake brake is once again screaming out its rumbling song and the speedo needle was pointing towards where five o'clock would be.

Isaac is pushed hard to the left against his armrest as they round a sweeping right hand curve. Shaking violently they bounce onto a wide four lane bridge at the bottom of the hill. Looking out the side window he recognizes the river below them, as the old truck crosses over the bridge at a frantic pace. Trying to be as calm as Adam, Isaac nonchalantly asks. "Wow this trip is really going by fast. Isn't that the river just west of Merit?"

"It sure is. You have been either asleep or busy typing the whole trip. Don't you remember pulling up Snow Shed hill? We flew up it, passing all the other trucks. This old girl has got lots of legs," Adam says proudly. "It's been a real roller coaster run, 'up to slow, down to fast'. Being empty like today though, it's just been fast and then faster."

Soon after crossing the bridge the speed of the truck is lost as Adam presses lightly on the throttle, letting the truck coast most of the way up the next hill. "See it all averages out." Adam says smiling. "Fuel efficiency, let gravity work for you." The truck is soon back to making its usual tremors and groans that Isaac had become accustomed too.

Yet again Isaac is confounded by Adam's trucker slang. "What is he talking about? Well at least he isn't swearing," he thinks to himself. Faking a smile and nodding knowingly, Isaac waits for

Adam to get back to their biblical conversation that had him gripped and seemed to be consuming him.

"Yes soul is that for sure, those things make us different than animals. In that sense, it could be referred to as our human spirit, personality, or will. However those things don't give us eternal life." Adam continues to push his point. "The soul refers to our body just as readily. Beast, body, creature, things with breath, they are all referred to with the same word nephesh. We are lumped together with all creatures that have the breath of life, but those other creatures aren't thought to have an immortal soul. This verse in no way teaches that man has an immortal soul, only that we are no better than an animal. We are told later on in the Bible that we all go to the same place and have no preeminence over a beast."

Checking the reference, Isaac types hurriedly then starts to read.

"Ecclesiastes 3:19-21 KJV.
19 For that which befalleth the sons of men befalleth beasts; even one thing befalleth them: as the one dieth, so dieth the other; yea, they have all one breath; so that a man hath no preeminence above a beast: for all is vanity.
20 All go unto one place; all are of the dust, and all turn to dust again.
21 Who knoweth the spirit of man that goeth upward, and the spirit of the beast that goeth downward to the earth?

This is talking about our bodies being the same, not our souls! And see the man's spirit is going up," contends Isaac.

"It is asking a question, who knoweth, not making a statement. Plus you keep referring to our soul as if it were something special." Adam points out. "Where do you get that belief and teaching from in the Bible. Where are your scriptural references for proof? It wasn't in Genesis 2:7 like you thought." Adam continues to press for confirmation. "If there is any doubt about Adam being created with eternal life or immortality then the account of him being driven out of the Garden of Eden should dispel it."

Again Isaac is finding and preparing to scrutinize the reference as he reads them aloud.

"Genesis 3:22-24
And the LORD God said, Behold, the man is become as one of us, to know good and evil: and now, lest he put forth his hand, and take also of the tree of life, and eat, and live for ever:
23 Therefore the LORD God sent him forth from the garden of Eden, to till the ground from whence he was taken.
24 So he drove out the man; and he placed at the east of the garden of Eden Cherubims, and a flaming sword which turned every way, to keep the way of the tree of life.

What's your point? I don't see it. They were driven out from the garden because of their sin, that's all I get," Isaac declares, giving Adam a curious look.

"Don't you see it? They were like God knowing good from evil but they were kept away from the tree of life by Cherubims. That means they did not possess eternal life at that time. Otherwise it would have done God no good to keep them from the tree of life as they would have no need of its fruit. They would already be able to live forever if they had an immortal soul. That's what immortal means," Adam states emphatically.

They go on for a few more miles quietly pondering their thoughts in silence. Then Adam again starts to talk. "The spirit that goes back to God is his own spirit. We need God's spirit to live and breathe, it makes us alive. When we die and don't need it any more, it goes back to him. It's not the spirit of man going to God. The spirit shall return unto God who gave it, that's God's spirit going back to him. As well, this text is talking about the way it is for all of humanity. Are you comfortable saying that everyone, including the wicked, will go off to be with God at death?"

Fully alert and wide eyed Isaac sits unresponsive, silently going over memorized scriptures to use in the conversation and occasionally typing out a few Google searches for clarification. Eventually Isaac speaks. "So you are saying that mankind has no eternal soul, they just stay in their grave when they die. That idea goes against what the New Testament tells me."

Adam speaks up quickly. "No. I'm not saying that. I am trying to faithfully read what the Bible tells me and not add things to it. Now before we move onto other verses. What is your conclusion for the verses we just covered in Genesis and Ecclesiastes? Do they tell us man has an immortal soul or spirit innately within us? Were we created immortal by God in Eden?"

Isaac shifts uncomfortably in his seat. "Well I guise they don't spell it out completely there, you have to look at the subject with other verses in mind. Take all of the verses as a whole, rather than each one on their own."

Adam encapsulates his thoughts. "Well if there are no verses that say definitively that man has eternal life within himself, how can looking at a lot of verses that don't say we are immortal, lead us to believe we are? To me, that seems to be circumstantial at best and completely self-deluding. There are many verses that tell us we are flesh and blood. 'And the Lord said. My spirit shall not always strive with man, for that he also is flesh: yet his days shall be an hundred and twenty years'. Aren't verses like that telling us the truth?"

"Well take for example King David's infant son that died," Isaac begins a rebuttal. "When the baby died he went to heaven because David said that the baby couldn't come back to him, but that he would be going to the baby. You need a soul or spirit to go to heaven."

"Oh, I think you better look that one up and read it." Adam advises.

Finding the passage Isaac reads it to Adam.

"2 Samuel 12:21-23

21 Then said his servants unto him, What thing is this that thou hast done? thou didst fast and weep for the child, while it was alive; but when the child was dead, thou didst rise and eat bread.

22 And he said, While the child was yet alive, I fasted and wept: for I said, Who can tell whether GOD will be gracious to me, that the child may live?

23 But now he is dead, wherefore should I fast? can I bring him back again? I shall go to him, but he shall not return to me.

See? David will be joining his dead son in heaven. The baby couldn't come to David, but David would be going to him. Why are these ideas so hard for you to grasp? Don't you want to go to heaven when you die?"

"Again, the scripture does not tell us the baby went to heaven, only that the baby could not return to David and that David would be joining the baby where ever it was," Adam says.

"Yes, that is right, David was going to join the baby," Isaac agrees, expecting David to be in Heaven by now.

Adam volleys the ball back to Isaac in their verbal tennis match. "The Bible tells us David is asleep with his fathers. Paul also tells us in Acts that David has seen corruption and is still in his grave. If David was expecting to go to his grave and sleep which is also supported in the New Testament, then it only stands to reason that the baby was in its own grave as well. Yes, David would be going to his son when he died. They would be metaphorically sleeping together in their graves."

Pulling some food out of a soft cooler bag on the floor by the stick shift, Adam makes his points as he chews on a granola bar. With his free hand Adam offers one of the foil wrapped delights to Isaac as he spoke. Isaac looks at it curiously then nods his thanks. Taking it, he unwraps the chocolate covered nut bar hungrily and devours it veraciously.

"That's better," Adam says jokingly. "You're just not yourself when you're hungry."

Isaac gets the joke, having seen the Snickers commercials.

"Oh! Marsha, Marsha, Marsha," he replies grinning broadly.

"I'm not sure. This is not how we covered it in class," Isaac states referring to their discussion.

"Well you have probably always been told what those verses mean, haven't you? When you were in college did you have a lot of free time to think about what you read in the bible?" Adam inquirers.

"No, I had a full course load like everyone else. With sports and the clubs after school we all had to cram in study to get it all done. There wasn't a lot of free time. I took good study notes from the class lectures and would go over them for tests and essays. I got good marks. I know the Bible," Isaac said defensively.

"I have little doubt that you were very diligent with your schooling Isaac. The teachers would have been happy with your test results because you gave them the answers they wanted. You memorized the material they covered very well. But did you scrutinize the validity of that material before you believed it? Did you have time to sit and ponder about what the bible said? A lot of people think that driving a truck is a boring no mind kind of a job, but this job gives me lots of time to think and ponder," said Adam. "So, what new testament scriptures should we look at?" Adam asks.

"I got one ready," Isaac says confidently. "2 Corinthians 5:8." He starts to read but Adam interrupts.

"Let's use the entire passage to get the context, rather than just one verse," Adam suggests.

"OK I will also use the New King James for a change." Isaac makes the changes on the lap top and begins to read.

"2 Corinthians 5:1-8
Assurance of the Resurrection
1 For we know that if our earthly house, *this* tent, is destroyed, we have a building from God, a house not made with hands, eternal in the heavens. 2 For in this we groan, earnestly desiring to be clothed with our habitation which is from heaven, 3 if indeed, having been clothed, we shall not be found naked. 4 For we who are in *this* tent groan, being burdened, not because we want to be unclothed, but further clothed, that mortality may be swallowed up by life. 5 Now He who has prepared us for this very thing *is* God, who also has given us the Spirit as a guarantee. 6 So *we are* always confident, knowing that while we are at home in the body we are absent from the Lord. 7 For we walk by faith, not by sight. 8 We are confident, yes, well pleased rather to be absent from the body and to be present with the Lord.

There you go, we will be pleased to be absent from our bodies and be present with the Lord when we die. We go to heaven to be with Jesus when we die. It is very plain and easy to understand," Isaac contends.

Adam pauses for a moment, then slowly starts to talk. "In order for what you say to be true, mankind would already have to have an immortal soul, which we didn't find supported throughout the Old Testament. Otherwise when you die you would be dead.

Also notice that we are given the Spirit as a guarantee that what God has promised will come true and this Spirit is not given to all of humanity. We don't receive the Spirit to give us immortality, but to give us guidance and comfort. The heading that started the passage was Assurance of the Resurrection. This passage is talking about the resurrection of the believers. Jesus told his disciples 4 times when this resurrection would take place in John 6.30-54"

"Wait. I want to look that up." Isaac interrupts. "We did a class on John and I don't recall that." Typing, Isaac finds the Chapter. Reading quickly Isaac comes to the verses Adam referred to.

"John 6:30-54 KJV
30 They said therefore unto him, What sign shewest thou then, that we may see, and believe thee? what dost thou work?
31 Our fathers did eat manna in the desert; as it is written, He gave them bread from heaven to eat.
32 Then Jesus said unto them, Verily, verily, I say unto you, Moses gave you not that bread from heaven; but my Father giveth you the true bread from heaven.
33 For the bread of God is he which cometh down from heaven, and giveth life unto the world.
34 Then said they unto him, Lord, evermore give us this bread.
35 And Jesus said unto them, I am the bread of life: he that cometh to me shall never hunger; and he that believeth on me shall never thirst.
36 But I said unto you, That ye also have seen me, and believe not.
37 All that the Father giveth me shall come to me; and him that cometh to me I will in no wise cast out.

38 For I came down from heaven, not to do mine own will, but the will of him that sent me.

39 And this is the Father's will which hath sent me, that of all which he hath given me I should lose nothing, but should raise it up again at the last day.

40 And this is the will of him that sent me, that every one which seeth the Son, and believeth on him, may have everlasting life: and I will raise him up at the last day.

41 The Jews then murmured at him, because he said, I am the bread which came down from heaven.

42 And they said, Is not this Jesus, the son of Joseph, whose father and mother we know? how is it then that he saith, I came down from heaven?

43 Jesus therefore answered and said unto them, Murmur not among yourselves.

44 No man can come to me, except the Father which hath sent me draw him: and I will raise him up at the last day.

45 It is written in the prophets, And they shall be all taught of God. Every man therefore that hath heard, and hath learned of the Father, cometh unto me.

46 Not that any man hath seen the Father, save he which is of God, he hath seen the Father.

47 Verily, verily, I say unto you, He that believeth on me hath everlasting life.

48 I am that bread of life.

49 Your fathers did eat manna in the wilderness, and are dead.

50 This is the bread which cometh down from heaven, that a man may eat thereof, and not die.

51 I am the living bread which came down from heaven: if any man eat of this bread, he shall live for ever: and the

bread that I will give is my flesh, which I will give for the life of the world.

52 The Jews therefore strove among themselves, saying, How can this man give us his flesh to eat?

53 Then Jesus said unto them, Verily, verily, I say unto you, Except ye eat the flesh of the Son of man, and drink his blood, ye have no life in you.

54 Whoso eateth my flesh, and drinketh my blood, hath eternal life; and I will raise him up at the last day.

"There, at the last day," Adam draws attention to the text. "Verse 39, 40, 44 and 54, the last day is when Jesus returns to earth. 'At the last day' is when we will be, 'well pleased rather to be absent from the body and to be present with the Lord'. At the last day, is when we will receive our immortality. 'So *we are* always confident, knowing that while we are at home in the body we are absent from the Lord'. We are confident of our future resurrection for we walk by faith, not by sight. We have the Holy Spirit until then as our guide and guarantee of Gods promise to us," continuing, Adam presses his point.

"Besides, 2 Corinthians doesn't state that we have a soul that lives on after we die. You have to believe we have an immortal soul ahead of time to understand those verses like you say. It's not cut and dry like in Acts when it says. 'There is salvation in no one else! Under all heaven there is no other name for men to call upon to save them'. If there was a verse forthright like that saying we had an immortal soul, it would be simpler to prove we all have eternal life innately within us. But there isn't and we don't."

Isaac's thoughts are whirling inside his head. "Oh. I don't know." He says cautiously slow. "I need to think about this for a bit."

"Take your time," Adam says. "Would you like to stop for a while and stretch your legs? We will be in Merit soon; we can get something to drink."

"That sounds good to me," Isaac replies, and stares out the window. He starts typing again and soon asks. "What about in

Philippians 1:20-24. Paul says that to die is gain.

20 According to my earnest expectation and my hope, that in nothing I shall be ashamed, but that with all boldness, as always, so now also Christ shall be magnified in my body, whether it be by life, or by death.

21 For to me to live is Christ, and to die is gain.

22 But if I live in the flesh, this is the fruit of my labour: yet what I shall choose I wot not.

23 For I am in a strait betwixt two, having a desire to depart, and to be with Christ; which is far better:

24 Nevertheless to abide in the flesh is more needful for you.

He looks forward to death so he can be with Jesus. So he will be with Jesus at his death."

Adam formulates his response as he passes a camper driving in the slow lane. Checking his mirrors to see that it is safe, he pulls back into the right hand lane in front of the vacationers, their image growing steadily smaller as the distance increases between them. "I like the KJV version but sometimes it can be hard to understand what is being said. Try an easier to read version, just for clarity."

"OK. I can do that. How about this?

'Easy-to-Read Version'.

20 I am full of hope and feel sure I will not have any reason to be ashamed. I am certain I will continue to have

the same boldness to speak freely that I always have. I will let God use my life to bring more honor to Christ. It doesn't matter whether I live or die. 21 To me, the only important thing about living is Christ. And even death would be for my benefit. 22 If I continue living here on earth, I will be able to work for the Lord. But what would I choose—to live or to die? I don't know. 23 It would be a hard choice. Sometimes I want to leave this life and be with Christ. That would be much better for me; 24 however, you people need me here alive.

See, Paul says that it would be better for him if he was to die and be with Christ. When he dies he believes he will be with Jesus, that part is straight forward." Isaac explains.

"Well if we remember Paul's life, he was always getting beat-up by unbelievers and the Jews. His life as a disciple was a hard one. So like he said, 'But what would I choose—to live or to die'? I don't know. It would be a hard choice. He knows that people need him to help them with their faith, yet he says. 'Sometimes I want to leave this life and be with Christ'.

It doesn't say, when, he would be with Christ. It only shows that he had faith that he would be with Jesus. John 6 tells us Paul will be with Jesus, at the last day, when Jesus returns. He explains this hope of the resurrection in 1 Thessalonians when he talks about the brethren that are asleep. Can you find it?" Adam asks, glancing over to his right at Isaac.

"Ya. I think so," responds Isaac. "Yes here it is.

1 Thessalonians 4:13-17
But I would not have you to be ignorant, brethren, concerning them which are asleep, that ye sorrow not, even as others which have no hope.

14 For if we believe that Jesus died and rose again, even so them also which sleep in Jesus will God bring with him.

See they return with Jesus, so they must be in heaven with him now," Isaac points out excitedly.

Adam quickly responds dramatically. "Just keep reading and you'll see."

Isaac continues.

"15 For this we say unto you by the word of the Lord, that we which are alive and remain unto the coming of the Lord shall not prevent them which are asleep.
16 For the Lord himself shall descend from heaven with a shout, with the voice of the archangel, and with the trump of God: and the dead in Christ shall rise first:"

"There did you get it? At the descent of the Lord is when the dead in Christ rise first. Just like we read in John, at my return, that's when everyone which seethe the Son, and believeth on him, may have everlasting life," Adam interrupts abruptly.

Isaac continues with the last verse.

"17 Then we which are alive and remain shall be caught up together with them in the clouds, to meet the Lord in the air: and so shall we ever be with the Lord."

"Do you see it now? It all starts with a resurrection at the return of Jesus. That is when we get our new life. Until Jesus returns, those believers who die, are asleep in their graves. Paul thinks, I want to leave this life and be with Christ. That would be much better for him. He would escape a lot of violent persecution if he was dead. He would be in peaceful sleep, knowing nothing of the world or its cares. His next conscious thought would be when he rises with his new body at the return of Jesus. After he dies, he will be with Jesus, just as he knew he would be. It doesn't happen though until the resurrection, on the day of the Lord, along with all of the other believers that have died. There is another verse that is similar at the end of Hebrews 11. See if you can find it."

Isaac is familiar with what is commonly called the faith chapter. He is curious about the verse Adam was referring to, as he didn't remember any verse there that talked about a resurrection from the dead. He finds the chapter and starts to scan through it.

"How far down is your verse Adam?" He questions.

"Right at the end, the last 3 or 4 verses," Adam assures him.

"OK. I will read the last 6 verses for context.

Hebrews 11:35-40

35 Women received their dead raised to life again: and others were tortured, not accepting deliverance; that they might obtain a better resurrection:

36 And others had trial of cruel mockings and scourgings, yea, moreover of bonds and imprisonment:

37 They were stoned, they were sawn asunder, were tempted, were slain with the sword: they wandered about in sheepskins and goatskins; being destitute, afflicted, tormented;

38 (Of whom the world was not worthy:) they wandered in deserts, and in mountains, and in dens and caves of the earth.

39 And these all, having obtained a good report through faith, received not the promise:

40 God having provided some better thing for us, that they without us should not be made perfect."

Isaac finishes reading the chapter.

"There, the last 2 verses. They received not the promise, the promise of eternal life. None of them received it. Why not? They're all dead. Why weren't they changed and taken off to heaven? The next verse tells us why.

They didn't receive it, the promise of eternal life, because God had something better for, all of us, 'so that they, without us, should not be made perfect'. We are all made perfect at the same time. We all will receive eternal life together at the same time, at the return of Jesus, at the last day. That is when we are changed and made perfect. That is when we are to be resurrected from the dead and receive our new bodies. Remember, according to the Old Testament, we don't have an immortal soul."

"You know I have read that chapter since I was little and I've never thought of it that way before, you make some interesting points for sure," Isaac admits.

"Well it's not me," Adam says modestly. "It's the Bible scriptures speaking, would you expect anything less than for them to be consistent? It is the word of God, he will not lie, nor will he contradict himself. If the Bible appears to be contradictory then it is us who don't understand the text properly. I think there is another passage that tells us about the resurrection of the believers in their order. Can you look it up?" Adam questions Isaac.

"I'll give it a try. Not much to go on, but we'll see what comes up." Isaac starts doing a search on the net. "Here it is. That was easy, got it on the first try. There is a lot of semi related verses, I will read it all just for context"

1 Corinthians 15:12-26
Now if Christ be preached that he rose from the dead, how say some among you that there is no resurrection of the dead?
13 But if there be no resurrection of the dead, then is Christ not risen:

14 And if Christ be not risen, then is our preaching vain, and your faith is also vain.

15 Yea, and we are found false witnesses of God; because we have testified of God that he raised up Christ: whom he raised not up, if so be that the dead rise not.

16 For if the dead rise not, then is not Christ raised:

17 And if Christ be not raised, your faith is vain; ye are yet in your sins.

18 Then they also which are fallen asleep in Christ are perished.

19 If in this life only we have hope in Christ, we are of all men most miserable.

20 But now is Christ risen from the dead, and become the firstfruits of them that slept.

21 For since by man came death, by man came also the resurrection of the dead.

22 For as in Adam all die, even so in Christ shall all be made alive.

23 But every man in his own order: Christ the firstfruits; afterward they that are Christ's at his coming.

24 Then cometh the end, when he shall have delivered up the kingdom to God, even the Father; when he shall have put down all rule and all authority and power.

25 For he must reign, till he hath put all enemies under his feet.

26 The last enemy that shall be destroyed is death.

"Here, I'll read it from the Good News Translation," offed Isaac.

1 Corinthians 15:12-26 Our Resurrection

Now, since our message is that Christ has been raised from death, how can some of you say that the dead will not be raised to life? 13 If that is true, it means that Christ was not raised; 14 and if Christ has not been raised from death, then we have nothing to preach and you have nothing to believe. 15 More than that, we are shown to be lying about God, because we said that he raised Christ from death—but if it is true that the dead are not raised to life, then he did not raise Christ. 16 For if the dead are not raised, neither has Christ been raised. 17 And if Christ has not been raised, then your faith is a delusion and you are still lost in your sins. 18 It would also mean that the believers in Christ who have died are lost. 19 If our hope in Christ is good for this life only and no more, then we deserve more pity than anyone else in all the world.

20 But the truth is that Christ has been raised from death, as the guarantee that those who sleep in death will also be raised. 21 For just as death came by means of a man, in the same way the rising from death comes by means of a man. 22 For just as all people die because of their union with Adam, in the same way all will be raised to life because of their union with Christ. 23 But each one will be raised in proper order: Christ, first of all; then, at the time of his coming, those who belong to him. 24 Then the end will come; Christ will overcome all spiritual rulers, authorities, and powers, and will hand over the Kingdom to God the Father. 25 For Christ must rule until God defeats all enemies and puts them under his feet. 26 The last enemy to be defeated will be death.

Adam affirms the scripture choice with an excited, "Ya! That was it! Verse 23 is where it tells us people will be raised in proper order. Jesus is first, then the believers when he returns. Believers don't go to heaven when they die. They sleep in their graves until Jesus comes back to get them. That's when we all receive our promised eternal life, together, at his return."

CHAPTER 5
BUT OTHERS SAY

Adam finishes talking just in time to signal and steer the truck onto
the off ramp leaving the freeway. Staying to the right at the cross
road, Adam smoothly shifts the transmission into a lower gear,
checking for traffic he cruising past the yield sign. Adam presses
the throttle and the engine torques the right front corner of the
truck upwards slightly as they quickly head towards the big truck
stop sign, HUSKY it read, glittering in the sun about a quarter mile
away. Turning onto the access road he drives behind the buildings
to the truck parking area. Making wide arching turns, Adam
maneuvers the long trailer between two other units in the parking
lot.

Coming to a stop, Adam turns the ignition key off and for the
first time since getting into the truck, Isaac is in complete
tranquility and silence. Gone is the roar of the engine, the whistling
of the wind, tires and drive line whine, but most of all, gone is the
harsh barking of the Jake brake. The constant vibration and
bouncing was gone as well. Closing his eyes he sinks slightly into
the passenger seat relishing the calm. Slowly, his hearing and
feeling start to become adjusted to the lack of noise and movement.
The subtle sounds from outside the cab begin to register with him
and his elbow is sore from repeatedly bouncing it on the metal
window ledge. But for a fleeting moment he was in the warm
blanket of sensory deprivation. It felt as though he was insulated
from the world, adrift on a sea of bliss.

"I don't want to stop too long, just long enough for a drink and
a pee," Adam says opening his door to get out. "Don't bother
locking your door; if you do we can't unlock it from the outside.
Things are safe around here anyway. Thieves tend to pick on the
new pretty trucks, the chances of finding good stuff is better than it

is in ruff looking old trucks. You'd never think I had a lap top in here, even if it's an old hand-me-down one. Kids old cast off junk, but it works for me." With that said, Adam turned and launched himself out of the door as before with his left hand squeezing the grab rail controlling his decent to the ground.

Isaac pulled the inside door latch while giving the door a shove with his right shoulder to get it to open. He cautiously climbed down the fuel tank steps holding tightly to the hand rails attached to the cab in convenient spots. Once his feet were planted firmly on the ground he pushed the door to close it. It barely managed to latch and remained partially open. He tugged the door handle to open it again and this time with a continued push it closed firmly. Looking at the door and shaking his head in disgust he looked towards the truck stop building for Adam. He didn't see him anywhere in the parking lot and it was too far for him to already be inside. Isaac's eyes darted around the mostly empty lot looking for his new companion. Not seeing him, he stood in front of the truck looking back and forth hoping to catch a glimpse of Adam somewhere.

"Where could he have gone," Isaac thought to himself. Startled by a touch on his right arm, Isaac turns to see Adam standing behind him.

"Are you ready to go in?" Adam gestures towards the Husky station. "I always like to walk around the truck and check the tires and stuff when I stop. It helps me to stay on top of any developing problems," Adam explains.

"Well your passenger door doesn't close very well. You might put that on your, to do list," Isaac points out in aggravation.

"Oh, that's nothing. It's just that the cab is to air tight with the windows up. Once they are down an inch or so the doors close much better." Adam is smiling craftily as he explains the door problem to Isaac who is skeptically listening with growing disbelief.

"Well let's go get a drink and I really have to pee," Adam is still talking as he starts to head towards the truck stop. "I don't know why, but once I stand up and it's a bit cooler, I really got to go," his pace quickens as he gets caught up in a light breeze that swirls the dust and bits of garbage at his feet. Isaac follows just behind him, sticking his hands deep into his front jean pockets and hunching his shoulders to help guard against the cool wind.

Once inside the glass doors Adam heads directly to the men's room with Isaac in tow. Emerging through the same bathroom door a short time later both Isaac and Adam are drying their hands on their pant legs. Adam gets the attention of the cashier behind the counter.

"You're out of paper hand towel in the bathroom." He said slightly grumpily. He didn't mean to sound that way. His mood often got reflected in his tone of voice without him noticing and he had never been successful at speaking with a loud happy voice. It always sounded a bit angry just because of the volume. His mostly deaf mother had thought he was always mad at her until he explained himself to her one day.

"Mom, I am not mad! I can't shout happily?" He told her. After that his Mom felt better, but no one had explained these subtleties to the truck stop clerk.

"Oh yaa. I'll be sure to get right on that." She said sarcastically while twirling her long bangs. "And by the way, the bathrooms are for paying customers," the gum snapping in her mouth as she chewed it hard.

"We will be customers in a minute," Replied Adam bewildered by the girls crabbiness. Remembering his wife's encouraging to make other people's day nicer. Adam makes sure his tone is pleasant when he speaks again to the bleach blond clerk.

Isaac picks himself a bottle of Dr. Pepper from the cooler. Adam notices the small sign advertising buy one get the second one 75% off. Thinking that Dr. Pepper would be good, he gets a bottle for himself and grabs a couple of Eat More from the chocolate bar rack. Only having his pop to pay for, Isaac is standing at the till when Adam comes up beside him and says, "Here I'll get that for you."

Taking the pop out of Isaac's hand Adam places the items on the counter then pulls out his wallet. The cashier rings up the total coming to $4.37. Adam passes her a new blue five and waves off the change and receipt.

"Don't need that." Adam told her smiling, making sure to have a pleasant tone. "Have a good day." Adam said turning to go.

"Thanks. You too," The girl also had a sweeter tone to her voice. "Come again."

"Here you go." Adam said as he handed Isaac back his pop and the bonus Eat More. "That should keep you going for a while. There's some ripe fruit in the truck we can eat as well. Benefits from hauling produce and groceries. If it's not visually perfect then the retailers don't want it. I hardly ever have to buy food. It may not look the best, but it is tasty."

"Thank you." Isaac replies, twisting the plastic lid off of his pop and taking a drink.

"Don't through the lid away unless you're going to drink that all at once. Those bottles tend to fall over in the truck with all of the bouncing," admonishes Adam.

"OK. Good point. This should last me a while." Isaac replies, replacing the lid back onto the bottle.

They walk slowly around the building towards the back and the parked trucks. A cattle liner comes into the parking lot a bit fast off of the frontage road. Taking the corner hard, the air ride trailer leans its bawling load of cows to the ditch side of the road. Streams of brown clumpy water pour out of the large ventilation holes down the sides and back of the aluminum E.coli wagon.

"Nothing like the smell of money," Jokes Adam.

"I'm glad that it wasn't pigs," Quips Isaac. "That smell can really stay with you all day."

They detour around the stinky spots on the road stretching their appendages as they go, heading back to the old Western Star. When they get close Adam instinctively starts to check for wet spots under his truck and trailer. Isaac follows him counter clock wise around the old semi kicking tires and checking hubs for heat. Adam half crawls under the trucks rear duels and then again under the trailer axles.

"What are you checking under there?" asks Isaac.

"The brakes," Adam replies.

Smiling nervously Isaac stammers. "Hope they're OK. Will they make it all the way home?"

"Ya, they're fine. They have to be checked all the time. All trucks have to be routinely checked during a long trip. That's why I do my walk-rounds whenever I make stops. It keeps me aware of problems that might come up during the trip and lets me chose when to fix things, before they become problems." Adam says wiping his now dirty hands on his lower pant legs.

Nodding as if he understood, Isaac follows behind Adam as he continues up the passenger side of the trailer towards the cab. Aware of his shadow Adam makes his checks more elaborate than necessary. Sensing Isaac's nervous naivety to the world of trucks, Adam displays worried scrutiny by rubbing and touching seemingly vital parts of the semi. Slowly shaking his head and scrunching his brow he quietly utters distressed phrases like, ah I don't know, that doesn't look too good, and his favorite, ewww, I forgot about that, to even the most unimportant component. Arriving back at the passenger door Adam gives the handle a knowing flip and the door pops open for Isaac to climb in.

"There you go, don't forget to buckle up," Adam says not letting Isaac see his smile. He heads around the front of the truck to the driver's door, opening it and springing into the cab from off the tank steps. Once in, he closes his door just in time to see Isaac role his window down an inch before he pulls the passenger door shut.

It closes tight with little effort. Isaac then rolls his window back up.

"Now you're getting it," Adam says encouragingly. "It won't take long and you'll be wanting to drive." Holding the parking brake valves in the released position, Adam waits until the hissing sound of moving air subsides before taking his hand off of them. Checking his mirrors he puts the transmission into gear and pulls ahead, then gives the spike a small tug. The back end of the trailer dips as its brakes slow the truck's forward movement. Letting go of the spike, air hisses at the steering wheel as the trailer brakes release and the truck lurches forward. Adam then jabs lightly at the brake pedal with his right foot and again the forward movement of the semi is momentarily hindered.

Smiling his approval and without thinking Adam picks up the pace of the truck with a quick series of shifts recorded in his muscles memory from years of practice, accelerate shift, accelerate shift, accelerate shift. The route towards the highway is quickly retraced. Turning to the left after crossing the overpass Adam now heads west, back a few miles to the Connector overpass that will take him and Isaac home.

It felt good to have been out in the fresh air and stretch his legs with some walking around. Now that he was back in the cab of the truck Isaac was eager to pick up the discussion where they had left off. Having some time to think things over, a few new thoughts came to mind and Isaac was anxious to share them with Adam. They were barely back on the Coquihalla heading west towards the Okanagan Connector overpass, when Isaac starts to talk.

"At school we used a book as a guide to find ancient reference material. It was written by a scholar, professor and church leader from England. It had to do with the Resurrection of Jesus, what the apostles, Paul and the early church believed and why. It went into great detail about pagan ideas and how the beliefs of Paul and the Jews differed from them. It contained a lot of very good documented research. All of which was peer reviewed. I wish I had a copy of it with me. I remember that in it, the professor author believed, that after death we went to be with Jesus, before we were resurrected into our new bodies, an intermediate stage. I always thought he had an interesting explanation for how it all worked."

Adam takes a quick glance at Isaac then replied. "You said the ground rules were to only use the King James Bible. That the thoughts of men couldn't be trusted and we had to rely solely on the word of God. Are you thinking of changing those parameters?"

"No, No, not at all. I was only thinking of what he said and how it made sense to me at the time. I would like to see the scriptures he used to come up with his conclusions. There must be some verses that we, or I'm not thinking of. He did a lot of well documented research; he must have used some verses that I am missing."

Believing Isaac's words are sincere, Adam instructs him to check under the plywood on the passenger front side of the sleeper bunk mattress. The leg was broken off and in its place he would find a thick tattered book on top of a tool box holding up the bed's corner from disjointedly dangling in mid-air. It took a lot of squirming but Isaac retrieved the book before they turned onto the Connector off ramp.

Wiping off the dusty cover Isaac smiles in amazement, "This is it, it's the book that I was talking about. The Resurrection Of The Son of God, by N.T. Wright. Did you read it all? We didn't have the time, it's so long. We only used it as a reference book to find material that was hard to source. If I can find the places where he talked about what I remember him saying, then we could read the verses he used to support his beliefs."

Taking short glances at Isaac, Adam answers. "Well yes, I did read it all. It took a long time too. The history was good, but I found myself disagreeing with some of his speculation. I thought some of the conclusions had no scriptural support. I wrote notes on the mostly blank front pages when I didn't agree, or I wanted to refer to his research later and needed to find the page."

Isaac opens the cover to find the first six pages covered in tiny hand writing, each line documenting a random thought provoked by the book and its corresponding page number. Isaac turned to the bibliography section at the back of the book. He looks up where Ecclesiastes 12:7 is used. Turning to a few pages before the first page referenced, squinting, he starts to scan silently to himself to understand the context. "It's hard to read the fine print with all of this bouncing" He complained.

"We'll soon be going up a long steep hill and things will smooth out." Adam assured him as he held the steering wheel hard to the right as they careened around a seemingly endless 270 degree cornered off ramp that was leading them onto the Okanagan Connector. "Oh no, bad luck. We caught a red light," Adam declared slowing to a stop.

Isaac wasn't paying attention. Taking advantage of the brief refrain from the constant movement, Isaac reads aloud from the small font the book was printed in. Listening intently to Isaac's oratory as the traffic light turned green, Adam smoothly and repetitively shifts his way up the long arduous hill that stretched out before them.

"Page 96-99. N.T. Wright is talking about the nature of humans and animals and the Old Testament belief that death was a one way street and the grave is a land of no return, Isaac sums up. He has a part about Ecclesiastes I wanted to read, since we had already been discussing it." Isaac reads from the worn paperback book.

"'Ecclesiastes, too, insists that death is the end, and there is no return. Though nobody can be sure what precisely happens at death, as far as we can tell humans are in this respect no different from beasts: The fate of humans and the fate of animals is the same; as one dies, so dies the other. They all have the same breath, and humans have no advantage over the animals; for all is vanity. All go to one place; all are from dust, and all turn to dust again. Who knows whether the human spirit [or: 'breath', rauch] goes upwards and the spirit of animals goes downward to the earth? No: to die is to be forgotten for good. Death means that the body returns to the dust, and the breath to God who gave it; meaning not that an immortal part of a person goes to live with God, but that the God who breathed life's breath into human nostrils in the first place will simply withdraw it into his own possession.'

Then he goes on about how the Old Testament was focused on the hope of the nation of Israel, rather than on each individual. So it appears as though N.T. favours your understanding over mine. Let's see what he has to say about Philippians 1."

Isaac is again searching through Mr. Wright's book. Scanning the preceding pages for context he picks up at the end of the first paragraph on page 226.

"'Paul believes that what this God has already done in the present life through the gospel and Spirit is the guarantee of the final salvation which he will describe more fully in 3.20-21.

This leads him to some extended reflections on his own situation, in which he thinks through the issues that face him, and which indeed are out of his control: will he die, presumably through being condemned to death by the Roman authorities, or will he live and continue his apostolic work? He turns the matter this way and that, revealing almost casually the way in which he looks at death in the most telling of cases, namely his own:

Phil. 1.18b-26

Well, but I shall go on celebrating. 19 because I know that this will result in my deliverance, through your prayers and the continued working of the Spirit of Jesus the Messiah, 20 in accordance with my eager expectation and hope, that I won't be ashamed in any way, but that with all boldness, as always and so now, the Messiah will be honoured in my body, whether by life or by death.

21 To me, you see, living means the Messiah, and death means gain. 22 If it is to be living in the flesh, that means fruitful work for me; so I don't know which to choose. 23 I am pulled hard by both at once: I badly want to make my departure and be with the Messiah; that would be better by far. 24 But to stay on in the flesh is more necessary for your sake. 25 Since I am convinced of this, I know that I shall remain, and continue on with all of you, for your benefit and the joy of your faith, 26 so that your celebration may abound in me in the Messiah, Jesus, through my coming to you again.

If this was the only passage of Paul, or even of Philippians, which addressed the question of what happens to Christians after they die, we could be forgiven for thinking that Paul held a one-stage view of life after death: Christians depart and go to be with the Messiah (verse 23). We know from the other letters that this is not his position; but, more importantly, we know from Philippians itself that he believed in a two-stage view: final resurrection will follow 'life after death' (3.20-21). What we have here, therefor, is a reinforcement of what we saw in 1 Thessalonians 4: between death and resurrection, Christians are 'with the Messiah'.'

See, we do go to be with Jesus when we die," Isaac adds enthusiastically.

"Well, apparently that is what N.T. Wright thinks. Keep reading to see if he uses any scripture to support his belief," Adam suggests

Isaac continues reading.

"Paul describes this in such glowing terms ('better by far') that it is impossible to suppose that he envisaged it as an unconscious state."

"Conjecture," Adam protests as if he was a lawyer in court. "I can easily suppose that he did plan to be asleep. Is Mr. Wright's only proof left to supposition?"

"I'm not done the thought yet. Let me finish reading this part!" exclaimed Isaac.

"He looks forward to being personally present with the one who loved him and whose love will not let him go. This is the clearest answer we ever get from Paul to question 1b, the question of an intermediate state. He does not speak of 'going to heaven', though he would presumably have given that as the present location of the Messiah."

"Now are you done? Adam asks forcefully. Isaac nods his head yes. "That's it? That's the proof that we have a spirit or something that goes to be with God when we die? Three words, Better by far, is the clearest answer we ever get! And as N.T. points out, Paul does not speak of going to heaven. It is left for us to, presume, that is his destination. Presumption and supposition, is not what I want to build my understanding of the afterlife on.

We just read the Old Testament does not support the thought of having an immortal soul, that the Spirit we live by is God's, not ours. That it goes back to God when we die. If we have some kind of an entity that lives on consciously after we die, where and when did we receive it? Did it come to all of mankind or do only Christians have it? If Christians go to be with Jesus immediately after death, what happens to non-Christians when they die, where do they go? Mr. Wright does not supply any supporting scriptures for his presumptions and suppositions," Adam loudly complained.

Isaac picks up the defense of Mr. Wright. "Well we would only have to read the parable of Lazarus to see what happens to bad people when they die. It tells us plainly what awaits both the good and the bad." Isaac has the parable cued up and was reading loudly before Adam had time to reply.

"Luke 16:19-31
19 There was a certain rich man, which was clothed in purple and fine linen, and fared sumptuously every day:
20 And there was a certain beggar named Lazarus, which was laid at his gate, full of sores,
21 And desiring to be fed with the crumbs which fell from the rich man's table: moreover the dogs came and licked his sores.
22 And it came to pass, that the beggar died, and was carried by the angels into Abraham's bosom: the rich man also died, and was buried;

23 And in hell he lift up his eyes, being in torments, and seeth Abraham afar off, and Lazarus in his bosom.

24 And he cried and said, Father Abraham, have mercy on me, and send Lazarus, that he may dip the tip of his finger in water, and cool my tongue; for I am tormented in this flame.

25 But Abraham said, Son, remember that thou in thy lifetime receivedst thy good things, and likewise Lazarus evil things: but now he is comforted, and thou art tormented.

26 And beside all this, between us and you there is a great gulf fixed: so that they which would pass from hence to you cannot; neither can they pass to us, that would come from thence.

27 Then he said, I pray thee therefore, father, that thou wouldest send him to my father's house:

28 For I have five brethren; that he may testify unto them, lest they also come into this place of torment.

29 Abraham saith unto him, They have Moses and the prophets; let them hear them.

30 And he said, Nay, father Abraham: but if one went unto them from the dead, they will repent.

31 And he said unto him, If they hear not Moses and the prophets, neither will they be persuaded, though one rose from the dead.

There, that should help put an end to your conspiracy theory. It is plain that Lazarus went to heaven and it tells us explicitly that the rich man was being tormented by the flames of hell. How much more plain does the Bible need to be on the subject before you are convinced?

Adam replies to the questions by agreeing. "Yes it is very plain that Lazarus is in luxury with Abraham and that the rich man is in the tormenting fires of Hell. The crucial point that you are missing, is that this story, is just that, a story. That is why it is called, a parable. It wasn't told to reveal the afterlife destination of mankind. Any more than the parable of the yeast tells us that heaven is a fluffy place made out of flour, or the parable of the mustard seed means that the kingdom of God is one big garden.

The meaning to the parable of Lazarus comes at the end of the story. If they hear not Moses and the prophets, neither will they be persuaded, though one rose from the dead. He told this parable shortly before he brought, not coincidentally, a real life Lazarus, back to life after he had been dead for more than three days. Jesus resurrected Lazarus out of his grave to fulfill the last of the messianic miracles the Jews had devised to identify the Messiah. True to the parable the Jews still denied Jesus and from then on they actively perused a pretense to kill him.

So yes, it plainly tells us where both the rich man and Lazarus were and what happens to them, but it is in the context of a story used to show how far the Jews would go to reject Jesus. Even when Jesus came back from the dead fulfilling his sign to them, they still would not accept him. That is the meaning of the parable. It's not given to us as a literal description of heaven and hell."

Isaac responds indignantly, "Well you're the only one who believes that. You'd be hard pressed to find anyone credible to support that interpretation of those scriptures."

"Oh, you think so? Adam said coolly. "Well you seem to hold N.T. Right in high regard, look through my notes there and find what he has to say about it."

Isaac starts to scan through the scrawled notations in the front of the thick well-worn book. He finds a note that could apply and looks it up.

"Here at the bottom of page four hundred and thirty seven is something." He says, nervous to find out that he once again overstated his argument.

"Well let's hear what it says," Adam grins knowingly. "I'm sure no one credible would support my interpretation of those scriptures."

Isaac clears his throat and starts to read out loud the words of N.T. Right.

" 'I stressed in the earlier volume that the parable of the rich man and Lazarus is to be treated precisely as a parable, not as a literal description of the afterlife and its possibilities. It is therefore inappropriate to use it as prima facie evidence for Jesus' own sketching (or Luke's portrait of Jesus' sketching) of a standard post-mortem scenario. It is, rather, an adaptation of a well-known folk-tale, projecting the rich/poor divide of the present on to the future in order to highlight the present responsibility, and culpability, of the careless rich. However, while the parabolic nature of the story prevents us from treating it as Jesus' own description of how the afterlife is organized, it does not prevent us from saying that for Jesus himself, and/or for those who handed on the tradition, this story indicates, in standard Jewish style, a clear belief in continuity between the present life and the future one. As it stands it is impossible to say whether it belongs with the 'resurrection' strand in second-Temple Judaism, or with a 'disembodied immortality' strand;'

See," Isaac said excitedly. "N.T. says that you can't tell if it supports the Jewish notion of resurrection, or the notion of going to heaven when you die."

"You mean the pagan notion of becoming a disembodied spirit?" Adam interjects. "It was the Greek philosophers who promoted that belief."

"Let me finish reading," Isaac complained. "Let's hear the rest of it." Picking up where he left off Isaac continues, hoping for more support of his belief. "Continuing on page four hundred and thirty eight.

The possibility is envisaged that Lazarus might return from the dead, but Abraham forbids that it should happen. It does, however, highlight one of the many metaphors current in Judaism for the abode of the blessed, either in perpetuity or prior to their possible rising again: Lazarus has gone to 'Abraham's bosom'. Luke's intention in placing the story here (soon after the 'inaugurated eschatology' of 15.24, 32, and soon before the apocalyptic warnings of 17.22-37) is at least clear: things done and decided in the present are to be seen in the light of the promised future. 'Resurrection' is coming forwards into the present in Jesus' ministry, but those who cannot see it and reorder their lives accordingly are in danger of loosing all. Significantly, this message of resurrection is clearly linked to the call for justice, which remains a closely related theme throughout early Christianity."

"So he supports my belief that the parable is just that, a parable about the hard hearted Jews and not a description of what it is like in heaven or hell," Adam was forceful in his assertion.

"Well let me check that out later," Isaac says. "I still agree with the idea that we go to our final destination as soon as we die. That we have something innately in us that lives on."

"Why? We don't need it, God has a perfect memory. He is quite capable of resurrecting us back into who we are now. He knows everything about us. Our moods, emotions and memories are stored inside our brains through electrical connections that we develop while we live and think. When we are resurrected back to life with the same brain connections we have now, all of our emotions, memories, moods and habits will still be the same as when we died. We will be the same people as before our resurrection. We lose nothing by sleeping in death. We don't have to be conscious somewhere else, we will be with God, safe and sound in his memory, waiting for our resurrection to take place. As Christians our next thought after death, will be our first thought in our reinvigorated spirit bodies," After pausing for a moment Adam goes on.

"What do you suppose the most quoted verse in the Bible is, the one you would most likely see at a sporting event? Adam asks Isaac.

"Probably John 3:16, I'm not really sure," Isaac responded, puzzled by the question.

"I don't know for sure either, but that's the one I would pick as well," Adam said nodding his head. "I believe that the two verses of 15 and 16 are the sum total of salvation truth. Those two verses are the truth, the whole truth and nothing but the truth. They are the bedrock of the Christian faith, to disagree with them; one would be straying away from what it is to be Christian. That whosoever believeth in him should not perish, but have eternal life. For God so loved the world that he gave his only begotten Son, that whosoever believeth in him should not perish, but have everlasting life."

"Yes! Now you're talking. I couldn't agree with you more," Isaac said wholeheartedly.

"That's what I thought, we can agree on these basics," Adam said smiling. Then with his smile fading into a frown, he asks Isaac. "So why do you agree that eternal life can be found only in Jesus, yet you say that all of humanity has an eternal soul, or spirit, apart from Jesus? Why do you think we are born with immortality, if we can only obtain eternal life, if, we believe in Jesus.

The fate of those who don't believe in Jesus is the opposite of life, they will perish. The opposite of eternal life is eternal death; they will be dead for the rest of time. Not be tortured for the rest of eternity in the fires of Hell. To be tortured for all of eternity would require an eternal life which can only be gained from having a belief in Jesus. Having this faith in Jesus not only brings eternal life, but will also spare you from ever being in Hell. How can John 3:15-16 be the truth if everyone is born with eternal life, whether they believe in Jesus or not?"

"If that is true and we do sleep in our graves, then why does God say that all souls belong to him in Ezekiel 18:4? Here I'll read it," Isaac protests. He finds the scripture quickly and begins to read.

"4 Behold, all souls are mine; as the soul of the father, so also the soul of the son is mine:

See, this section of scripture is talking about the righteous that follow the laws of God; all of their souls belong to God. We do have souls that belong to God." Isaac can't understand Adam's failure to understand the straight talking scripture.

"Again you are giving a definition to soul that is unbiblical. We went through the definitions for soul and found that it means,

Mortal! Every time you read soul you seem to think it means Immortal," Adam points out aggressively. "This verse seems familiar to me. Does it say anything else?" he questions Isaac further.

"I'm not sure. I've only ever read this much of it in the context of the righteous followers of God." Isaac admits.

"Well let's read all of it," Adam said encouragingly.

"OK. Here it is.

4 Behold, all souls are mine; as the soul of the father, so also the soul of the son is mine: the soul that sinneth, it shall die,"

Isaac reads out loud.

"How can the soul die if it's immortal? That's a conflict of terms," Adam asks exasperatedly.

"Well I have never read it with those thoughts in mind. I need to do some research for a while before I give you an answer." Isaac turns back to the lap top, questions flowing out of his fingertips as they peck at the keys.

CHAPTER 6
ROAD HAZARD

Adam says nothing, letting Isaac work things out for himself with the help of the lap top programs and the web. Something on the road ahead of them catches Adam's eye. Paying close attention, Adam sees what looks like a cylindrical object in their lane a short distance in front of them. With the truck moving slowly up the steep grade Adam prepares to drive around the dangerous looking obstacle by changing lanes. Seeing only one dark car a long way behind them and no traffic in the lane on his left, he signals and then starts to move his rig over the white dotted line.

A quarter of the way into the fast lane he checks his passenger mirror to make sure he will miss the jagged end of a large broken pipe. The sound of a blaring horn coming through the driver's door window startles him. Looking to his left, he sees a dark car overtaking the truck at a rapid pace. The driver fingers him out of the sunroof opening as he flies past, going at least sixty clicks over the buck ten speed limit.

Instinctively steering to his right to avoid a collision with the speeding car, Adam is unable to avoid the sharp end of the pipe with his trailer tires. He watches in his mirror with a grimace as the front right outside duel tire's sidewall scrubs hard on the pipe's broken end, sending it spinning wildly off into the ditch. Immediately, the sound of escaping air reaches Adam. Slight plumes of dust fly off the pavement and into the air each time the tire's rupture rotates to the ground. A few revolutions later and with the hiss of escaping air stopped, the now flat tire is left flopping as it continues to role beside its mate.

"Damn! Stupid Jerk!" Adam yelled at the vanishing car.

Startled, Isaac looked up from the lap top screen, "What's wrong! What's that noise!"

"That's the sound of about four hundred dollars escaping from my pocket," Adam said angrily. "And about an hour of extra time, if I'm lucky. At least we are almost at the top of the hill. I'll pull a U-turn into the brake check lane on the other side of the road and can put on the spare tire there." Adam was still fuming but he felt better that at least he had a plan. "Good thing I got a spare along," he said out loud. While silently in his head he was still heaping curses on the dark car's driver.

Pulling over onto the highways paved shoulder, He waited with his four ways flashing. A couple of cars whizzed past. Seeing no traffic from either direction he cranked the steering wheel to the left as hard as he could. Guiding his truck across all four lanes of the highway and onto the brake check lane they exited off the highway before going down the long steep hill they had just climbed. Staying to his right, Adam pulls about halfway down the empty brake check lot where he dynamites all of the brakes and parks the truck at the top of the long steep hill they had just climbed.

"I've never changed a tire before," said Isaac excitedly. "This, will, be a trip to remember."

"Ya, it seems like you always try to have a pleasant uneventful trip, but you only remember the ones that were crappy and you had trouble. The only good thing is that the aggravation usually diminishes with time. You can even find yourself laughing about the troubles later," Adam tells him with almost half a smile. "Well let's get started and we can get it done while the weather is nice."

Using the small outside storage door, Adam gets the wheel tools and a beat-up red hydraulic bottle jack out from the sleeper storage bin along with a small cloth tool bag. Handing them to Isaac, he pulls a six foot long two inch wide hollow chrome pipe out from its resting place between the truck frame and fuel tank. The two of them wrestle the heavy tools to the back of the truck by the trailers flat tire.

Crawling under the trailer, Adam positions the jack so that it will lift on the axle picking the flat tire up off the ground. Getting part way back out from under the trailer, Adam makes his way forward to the spare tire cradle. Unhooking the safety chain that was keeping the spare tire from escaping its confines, Adam slides the tire out of the rest and roles it back to the flat.

Isaac mostly watches but tries to help when he sees the opportunity. Adam explains how the tire tool works by putting it together with the pry-bar and getting it ready to loosen off the first wheel lug nut. Picking up the five foot snipe Adam slides it over the pry-bar; the free end of the snipe is about six feet off the ground. Holding onto the end of the snipe Adam puts all of his weight on the end by dangling under the snipe with his knees bent. Nothing happens so Adam starts to make bouncing movements and slowly the snipe starts to lower towards the ground as the wheel nut begrudgingly turns counter clockwise.

"Well that's one loose, only nine more to go," Adam says a bit out of breath.

"If there is anything that I can do let me know. So far I haven't been much help," Isaac said earnestly.

"That's OK. You look a bit light to break these nuts free, but you can loosen them the rest of the way off. They are supposed to be torqued on from five to five hundred and fifty foot pounds, but a little bit of rust in the threads can make them even harder to get off. If we can't break them all free, we may have to drive back to town and find a tire shop. Check in the cloth tool bag and pass me the can of WD40 would you." After liberally spraying all of the lug nut studs Adam relaxes, sitting on the ground with his back resting against the trailer tires. "We'll let that work on the nuts for a bit, it should make them easier to get off."

Isaac sits cross legged on the warm pavement. He silently contemplates his thoughts for a moment, then expresses them to Adam. "The primary desire of God is to heal the relationship between himself and mankind, broken by sin at the Garden of

Eden. Nothing is more important to him, he loves us. So much in fact that he sent his son Jesus to die for us, so our sins could be forgiven and we could be with him. As Christians, our job is to tell people about Jesus so they can be saved from their sins and join with God as his children. There is no other way for our sins to be forgiven, we must go through Jesus. If a person doesn't accept Jesus they are doomed."

Adam nodded his head in agreement while Isaac spoke. "Now with that I can wholeheartedly agree. But tell me, when does this accepting of Jesus need to take place?

Isaac was perplexed by the question. "Well, now, while they're alive and able to. Once they've passed on, it'll be too late for them."

Frowning, Adam shakes his head slightly. "That way of thinking stems from the conspiracy. It's only to late if this present life is the only time that humans can come to Jesus to be saved. Believing the conspiracy has blinded mankind to the potential they possess and has diminished the privilege and blessings shown by God to those, who do, come to Jesus in this life. Not everyone is capable of coming to Jesus during this life. What if they never heard about Jesus due to a lack of preachers? What if the gospel never made sense to them? People must be drawn to Jesus by God. Christians are called out of this world to follow Jesus, by God himself, but we must choose to follow."

Adam stands up and starts to undo the lug nuts on the wheel. He doesn't notice Isaac get up and head towards the truck. He soon returns and resumes his position on the pavement. Only this time he has the lap top set up and has started typing.

"What about these verses?" Isaac questions demandingly.

"2 Corinthians 6:1-2 KJV
We then, as workers together with him, beseech you also that ye receive not the grace of God in vain.

2 (For he saith, I have heard thee in a time accepted, and in the day of salvation have I succoured thee: behold, now is the accepted time; behold, now is the day of salvation.)

2 Peter 1:10
Wherefore the rather, brethren, give diligence to make your calling and election sure: for if ye do these things, ye shall never fall:

It is in this present life that we have to be faithful in following Jesus. We aren't given any other time to be saved. We have only this life to follow Jesus and we must not turn away," Isaac continues to read and question.

"Luke 9:62
And Jesus said unto him, No man, having put his hand to the plough, and looking back, is fit for the kingdom of God.

If we do we will be tossed into the fires of Hell like in the parable of the tares and wheat.

Matthew 13:24-30 New KJV
Another parable He put forth to them, saying: "The kingdom of heaven is like a man who sowed good seed in his field; 25 but while men slept, his enemy came and sowed tares among the wheat and went his way. 26 But when the grain had sprouted and produced a crop, then the tares also appeared. 27 So the servants of the owner came and said to him, 'Sir, did you not sow good seed in your field? How then does it have tares?' 28 He said to

them, 'An enemy has done this.' The servants said to him, 'Do you want us then to go and gather them up?' 29 But he said, 'No, lest while you gather up the tares you also uproot the wheat with them. 30 Let both grow together until the harvest, and at the time of harvest I will say to the reapers, "First gather together the tares and bind them in bundles to burn them, but gather the wheat into my barn."'

We need to accept Jesus now while we can and not put it off. We don't know how much time we will have before the Lord will return for us and we are raptured away."

Adam stops working the heavy tools long enough to agree with Isaac. "Those points are all very accurate. God's greatest desire is to repair the relationship that mankind has abandoned. His plan is to give everyone the opportunity to accept the salvation brought by Jesus. All will have that chance, but not necessarily during their present life in this world. The majority of mankind has not lived their lives with the ability to learn about Jesus, to become saved. Your belief would place them all in hell, tormented for the rest of eternity. They would be all lost children to God. Aborted out of son-ship before they had the opportunity to even hear of Jesus and the deliverance he brings them.

Christians are individually called out of this world by God, to come to Jesus during this life. If God does not draw us, we cannot come to Jesus. God has shown us love while we still hated him, all of humanity has been blinded to Jesus so that 'seeing they cannot see and hearing they cannot perceive'. Most Christians don't realize the special gift we have been given through our calling.

Look up the verses that say how we are called or predestined to come to Jesus. God specifically chooses to call the foolish and weak of the world to confound the mighty. The ones that God doesn't call cannot come to Jesus at this time, but they will have their opportunity, when God's time is right."

Isaac starts to go through Bible references and dutifully reads them out loud as Adam continues to undo wheel nuts.

"Here are some of the scriptures that you referred to, in the KJV" Isaac announced before he started to read the located texts out loud.

"John 12:40
He hath blinded their eyes, and hardened their heart; that they should not see with their eyes, nor understand with their heart, and be converted, and I should heal them.

Matthew 13:13-15
Therefore speak I to them in parables: because they seeing see not; and hearing they hear not, neither do they understand. 14 And in them is fulfilled the prophecy of Esaias, which saith, By hearing ye shall hear, and shall not understand; and seeing ye shall see, and shall not perceive: 15 For this people's heart is waxed gross, and their ears are dull of hearing, and their eyes they have closed; lest at any time they should see with their eyes and hear with their ears, and should understand with their heart, and should be converted, and I should heal them.

Luke 8:10
And he said, Unto you it is given to know the mysteries of the kingdom of God: but to others in parables; that seeing they might not see, and hearing they might not

understand.

Mark 4:12
That seeing they may see, and not perceive; and hearing
they may hear, and not understand; lest at any time they
should be converted, and their sins should be forgiven
them.

Romans 11:7-11
What then? Israel hath not obtained that which he
seeketh for; but the election hath obtained it, and the rest
were blinded. 8 (According as it is written, God hath given
them the spirit of slumber, eyes that they should not see,
and ears that they should not hear;) unto this day. 9 And
David saith, Let their table be made a snare, and a trap,
and a stumblingblock, and a recompence unto them: 10
Let their eyes be darkened, that they may not see, and
bow down their back alway. 11 I say then, Have they
stumbled that they should fall? God forbid: but rather
through their fall salvation is come unto the Gentiles, for
to provoke them to jealousy.

Romans 9:18
Therefore hath he mercy on whom he will have mercy,
and whom he will he hardeneth.

Acts 28:26
Saying, Go unto this people, and say, Hearing ye shall
hear, and shall not understand; and seeing ye shall see,
and not perceive:

John 9:39

And Jesus said, For judgment I am come into this world, that they which see not might see; and that they which see might be made blind.

Matthew 22:14

For many are called, but few [are] chosen.

2 Timothy 1:9

Who hath saved us, and called [us] with an holy calling, not according to our works, but according to his own purpose and grace, which was given us in Christ Jesus before the world began,

John 6:44. No man can come to me, except the Father which hath sent me draw him: and I will raise him up at the last day.

Romans 8:28-30

And we know that all things work together for good to them that love God, to them who are the called according to [his] purpose.29 For whom he did foreknow, he also did predestinate to be conformed to the image of his Son, that he might be the firstborn among many brethren.30 Moreover whom he did predestinate, them he also called: and whom he called, them he also justified: and whom he justified, them he also glorified."

Pausing briefly for a few deep breaths and a sip from the pop he pulled from his hoodie pouch, Isaac continues to read out loud.

"1 Corinthians 1:25-29

Because the foolishness of God is wiser than men; and the

weakness of God is stronger than men. 26 For ye see your
calling, brethren, how that not many wise men after the
flesh, not many mighty, not many noble, are called: 27
But God hath chosen the foolish things of the world to
confound the wise; and God hath chosen the weak things
of the world to confound the things which are mighty; 28
And base things of the world, and things which are
despised, hath God chosen, yea, and things which are not,
to bring to nought things that are: 29 That no flesh should
glory in his presence.

Ephesians 1:3-4
Blessed be the God and Father of our Lord Jesus Christ,
who hath blessed us with all spiritual blessings in
heavenly places in Christ:4 According as he hath chosen
us in him before the foundation of the world, that we
should be holy and without blame before him in love:

1 Peter 2:20-21
For what glory is it, if, when ye be buffeted for your faults,
ye shall take it patiently? but if, when ye do well, and
suffer for it, ye take it patiently, this is acceptable with
God. 21 For even hereunto were ye called: because Christ
also suffered for us, leaving us an example, that ye should
follow his steps:

Hebrews 3:1
Wherefore, holy brethren, partakers of the heavenly
calling, consider the Apostle and High Priest of our
profession, Christ Jesus;

John 17:24

Father, I will that they also, whom thou hast given me, be with me where I am; that they may behold my glory, which thou hast given me: for thou lovedst me before the foundation of the world.

John 6:37

All that the Father giveth me shall come to me; and him that cometh to me I will in no wise cast out.

1 Peter 2:9

But ye are a chosen generation, a royal priesthood, an holy nation, a peculiar people; that ye should shew forth the praises of him who hath called you out of darkness into his marvellous light;

1 Peter 1:15-16

But as he which hath called you is holy, so be ye holy in all manner of conversation; 16 Because it is written, Be ye holy; for I am holy.

2 Thessalonians 2:13-14

But we are bound to give thanks alway to God for you, brethren beloved of the Lord, because God hath from the beginning chosen you to salvation through sanctification of the Spirit and belief of the truth: 14 Whereunto he called you by our gospel, to the obtaining of the glory of our Lord Jesus Christ.

1 Thessalonians 4:7

For God hath not called us unto uncleanness, but unto

holiness.

Ephesians 1:11
In whom also we have obtained an inheritance, being
predestinated according to the purpose of him who
worketh all things after the counsel of his own will:"

Wiping his forehead with the palm of his hand Isaac sits back
on his elbows questioning Adam. "Those are interesting scriptures,
but where does it say that God is not calling everyone when they
are alive?" Isaac Quotes

Romans 1:20,
"For the invisible things of him from the creation of the
world are clearly seen, being understood by the things
that are made, even his eternal power and Godhead; so
that they are without excuse:

See people are without excuse not to know God." Isaac says
contemptuously. "God has made himself available to everyone
from the beginning, but mankind has sinfully turned their backs on
God, not wanting to follow him." With eyes narrowing and his
face looking stern, Isaac ads. "Sinners deserve to suffer in Hell for
the sins that they do in their lives. They must choose to follow God
now. That is why Christians have to teach the world about Jesus, as
he is the only way to salvation."
Adam has all of the lug nuts off and has started removing the
flat tire off of the axle. Pulling the wheel in a jerky motion he gets
it to slide off the hub and free of the axle end. Rolling it off to the
side he wipes the sweat from his forehead with a fairly clean rag.
Taking a few deep breaths he rests, leaning against the side of the
trailer and addresses Isaac, "I think you should read more of that

passage in Romans 1, as it will make what Paul is talking about, more clear."

Isaac obliges quickly, smug in his thoughts of accuracy. "OK, how about this?" he asks sharply.

"Romans 1:18-21.
18 For the wrath of God is revealed from heaven against all ungodliness and unrighteousness of men, who hold the truth in unrighteousness;
19 Because that which may be known of God is manifest in them; for God hath shewed it unto them.
20 For the invisible things of him from the creation of the world are clearly seen, being understood by the things that are made, even his eternal power and Godhead; so that they are without excuse:
21 Because that, when they knew God, they glorified him not as God, neither were thankful; but became vain in their imaginations, and their foolish heart was darkened."

"That should do" Adam says, stretching out the muscles in his arms and upper body. "Notice that the wrath of God is against the willful sins of the people. They knew right from wrong, but they were willfully sinning, they actively sought out sin. God is revealed through his creation to the world. People are without excuse, but without excuse for what? If we refer to what Paul is talking about at the beginning, we see that it is referring to God's wrath. People are without excuse for encoring the wrath of God by sinning. Later on in Romans, Paul tells us that all have sinned and fall short of the glory of God. He also goes on to tell us that the wages of sin is death, not eternal torment. The point Paul is making, is that we all need a Savior, Jew or Gentile and the only one who can save us is Jesus."

Adam wrestles the spare tire into its proper position on the axle. Reaching for the tool bag he pulls out a small tin of never seize, spreading it sparingly onto the threads of each wheel stud with the little brush built into the lid. "That should keep them from rusting on again," Adam audibly says to himself.

"What?" Isaac says. "It's hard to hear you when your head is turned away."

"Oh, I was just talking to myself about the studs. Talking to yourself, dangers of the job and old age," Adam says laughingly.

Picking up where he left off Adam goes on with his thoughts, turning his head more towards Isaac, so as to be better heard as he starts the lug nuts onto the wheel studs. "This visual display of God, through creation, lets people know there is a God. The knowledge of knowing there is a God however is not what is needed for salvation, as you so rightly pointed out, we can only have our sins forgiven if we accept, Jesus, as our Savior.

That is why Paul was not ashamed of the gospel of Jesus, as it is through that message all must be saved. Christians need to share this message about Jesus and the coming kingdom of God with as many people we can. It's through hearing the gospel message that people can learn about Jesus. But it's by seeing the gospel lived out in people's lives that the world is drawn to Jesus by God. God reaches out to the world through Christians, calling those he has chosen. Those who don't hear the gospel for whatever reason, or who God does not call, have no chance to follow after Jesus during this life."

Picking up the wheel wrenches Adam laboriously starts to install and tighten the lug nuts back up.

"Just knowing there is a creator God will not save anyone. Like you said, we can only be saved by going through Jesus. The resurrections provide the only time-frame when those, not called by God in this life, can have a chance to learn about Jesus. Coming back to a physical life through a resurrection is the only way most people will have their eyes opened to Jesus and the love of God.

Free from the influence of Satan, everyone who has ever lived will have their turn to accept or reject Jesus."

CHAPTER 7
ONE CHANCE FOR SALVATION

"That means people who aren't called during this life, would get a second life and a second chance later on. That's just wrong," Isaac boldly states angrily. Looking up scripture for his proof he reads

Hebrews 9:27.
"And as it is appointed unto men once to die, but after this the judgment,"

With his intensity rising Isaac goes on to say. "Man will only live one life, then the judgement of God, with either Heaven or Hell to follow. We don't get second chances at salvation."

Clearly seeing he has hit a nerve, Adam calmly formulates his response by questioning Isaac. "Did God create people so they could live with him as a family, with God as our father and Jesus our older brother?"

Isaac thinks warily, looking for an ecclesiastical trap. "Yes, I believe that statement could be scripturally supported. Jesus is said to be our older brother, he is the first born of many brethren. We are told repeatedly in the bible we are heirs, God is our father and we will be his children."

"Will God force us into following him, or do we have freedom of choice?" Adam asks, as he strains down on the snipe, putting the final torque on each lug nut.

Becoming calmer Isaac answers with less apprehension, "Oh yes. We are free moral agents. God is love, he wants us to love him and choose his ways of love because we willingly want to be with him. If he forced himself on us and gave us no choice, he would be a spiritual rapist. He is so dedicated to free will, he even allowed the angels to decide their own destiny. That is when Lucifer became Satan and one third of the angels turned into demons."

Pausing for a moment Isaac asks. "If I can use a Star Trek expression, Free moral agency would be one of God's prime directives. He won't violate the principle of personal choice, in fact he can't because he is love, it is part of his makeup, it's in his DNA. Being made of love he always has others best interest first and foremost above his own. It wouldn't be love to force people into being with him. God wants us to love him freely with our whole hearts."

Adam pauses from tightening the lug nuts and adds, "I suppose you could say another prime directive would be that no human can be saved without going through the blood of Jesus." After making his statement Adam returns to tighten the remaining lug nuts.

Isaac nods his head. "Ya, that would make two basic unbreakable rules of God. He will allow everyone to choose and we can only be forgiven of our sins by going through Jesus, for there is no other name by which we can be saved."

Having finished with the lug nuts, Adam starts to put things back into the tool bag while asking Isaac. "So with the your traditional thoughts of man's fate, while adhering to those two unbreakable rules and keeping in mind that we can only learn about Jesus and the salvation he alone brings by being taught and called, when do those who lived on the wrong continent, or in the wrong century, get to learn about Jesus so they can be saved?

Isaac thinks about his answer as Adam removes the jack from under the trailer axle. Not until Adam was out from under the trailer and they were carrying tools back to put away in the truck, did Isaac finally answer. "You know, I have never given much thought to the people who haven't heard the gospel. Other than the fact they need to hear about Jesus to be saved and those not saved, will be condemned. I have always believed we need to accept God at some time in this life now."

"Yes people will be condemned if they don't accept Jesus, but shouldn't they at least have an opportunity to hear about Jesus and his salvation before they are written out of eternity? After all, if God wants all who love him to become his children, for he is no respecter of people and treats all repentant sinners the same, shouldn't everyone be given the opportunity to repent? Adam asks as he puts the tools and snipe back into their storage spaces.

Isaac seemed puzzled by the questions when he stated, "I suppose that some things need to be left up to God. This is just one of those unfathomable mysteries of God where we just have to trust and have faith. But you can't argue with the scripture that tells us man is to only live once."

Adam is quick to reply. "No, I will not argue with the words that scripture says, but I will argue with the context in which you are framing them. Let's read the entire passage to see if we can get the context that is used. After all, there are several people in the Bible that have lived more than once. All those who were resurrected back to a physical life, like the young man who fell from the window. He would have lived more than once."

"OK, I will look it up and read it in the truck," Isaac agrees. "But first, let's get that flat tire put into the spare tire cradle under the trailer."

"You took the words right out of my mouth," Adam sang, being careful not to sing the next line of the song. Adam hums the rest of the tune while he and Isaac struggle with the heavy tire carcass. Sliding it safely back to where the spare tire belongs, they secure it with the safety chain. Taking one last look for any stray tools or equipment, they head back to the truck.

Adam was getting back into the truck when a police car pulled up alongside of the old Western Star and parked. A tall thin officer stepped out of the cruiser. Putting on his hat, he approached Adam, who was standing beside the driver's door with one foot on the tank step.

"I'd like to ask you a few questions," the constable said as he strolled up to Adam. "I have received a complaint about an old blue truck cutting off a car by recklessly changing lanes. There aren't that many old blue trucks on the road, so maybe it was you."

"Well I don't know. Who was the complainant and what are the details?" Adam responded. Being careful not to incriminate himself by saying too much.

"I had a radar trap set up a few miles down the way, when a fellow officer on his way to Kelowna stopped to complain about getting cut off in the passing lane coming up this hill out of Merit. He gave me a description of the truck as old and blue. He said it all happened so fast that he didn't get a very good look at the truck, but he was very mad at the careless driver."

"Well I've been here for a while now changing a flat tire. Don't recall any old blue truck going past here. But I was on the other side of the trailer changing a tire, so I couldn't see much traffic. I did see a dark car going like a rocket though. I say see, but I heard it more than I saw it. By the time I looked around, it had already gone by and I was looking at its back end. All I could see was this dark object disappearing down the road. He must have been going Mach two. If you had a trap set up, it's funny you didn't pick him up on your radar when he got close to you?" Adam said curiously.

"Well I did have to extend him some professional courtesy, after I pulled him over. He said he was going to be late for a court appointment in Kelowna," the wiry red headed constable said with a grin.

"Ya, I'd bet you get all kinds of excuses. It is odd there would be court on a Sunday, don't you think?" said Adam suspiciously. "Anyway, it seems as though I am headed in the wrong direction to have gotten in his way. And besides," Adam said, walking over to the side of his trailer pointing towards the naked lady mural. "If you were only half paying attention to things, would you describe my truck as, just, old and blue?"

Looking up at the huge painting the constable nodded his head. "Yes I see your point. Perhaps I didn't get the whole story."

"No doubt, we seldom do," Adam said as the officer returned towards his car. With the closing of the car door, the cruiser was soon speeding off down the hill, leaving Adam alone as he climbed into his truck and prepared to leave.

"What was that all about? Isaac asked, once Adam had the brakes released and the truck in gear. "What did the police want?"

"Oh it was nothing; he was just looking for some information. I helped him out the best I could. But you know, everything you say, will be used against you, so you dare not say too much."

"I suppose," Isaac half-heartedly agreed, thinking Adam must be using more trucker talk. "I found those scriptures," he said, cheerily changing the subject. "Should I read them now?"

"No, could you wait till I get back onto the road and headed in the right direction. It's hard to listen attentively and do much other stuff." Adam was checking his mirrors and looking down the hill for traffic. Seeing none, he turns the steering wheel hard to the left when he gets to the freeway entrance. Not wanting to be long crossing all lanes of traffic Adam accelerates the truck as it leaves the on ramp, picking up a gear as he makes the U turn across the four lane highway pointing the truck back up the hill towards Kelowna.

He pins the throttle hard to the floor causing an eruption of black smoke to billow out of the exhaust stack. The engine had cooled off while he spent time changing the blown tire. With the engine pulling hard against the steep incline he steers into the slow lane before any traffic approaches. Adam continues to smoothly up shift, picking up speed, the smoke starts to fade away as the engine temperature quickly rises. Isaac begins to read as they roll ever closer to their destination.

Yelling out to be herd, Isaac continues reading scriptures about living only once and there being only a one time sacrifice for all.

"Hebrews 9:20-28 KJV 20
This is the blood of the testament which God hath enjoined unto you. 21 Moreover he sprinkled with blood both the tabernacle, and all the vessels of the ministry. 22 And almost all things are by the law purged with blood; and without shedding of blood is no remission. 23 It was therefore necessary that the patterns of things in the heavens should be purified with these; but the heavenly things themselves with better sacrifices than these. 24 For Christ is not entered into the holy places made with hands, which are the figures of the true; but into heaven itself, now to appear in the presence of God for us: 25 Nor yet that he should offer himself often, as the high priest entereth into the holy place every year with blood of others; 26 For then must he often have suffered since the foundation of the world: but now once in the end of the world hath he appeared to put away sin by the sacrifice of himself. 27 And as it is appointed unto men once to die, but after this the judgment: 28 So Christ was once offered to bear the sins of many; and unto them that look for him shall he appear the second time without sin unto salvation.

Hebrews 10:1-17
For the law having a shadow of good things to come, and not the very image of the things, can never with those sacrifices which they offered year by year continually make the comers thereunto perfect. 2 For then would they not have ceased to be offered? because that the worshippers once purged should have had no more conscience of sins. 3 But in those sacrifices there is a

remembrance again made of sins every year. 4 For it is not possible that the blood of bulls and of goats should take away sins. 5 Wherefore when he cometh into the world, he saith, Sacrifice and offering thou wouldest not, but a body hast thou prepared me: 6 In burnt offerings and sacrifices for sin thou hast had no pleasure. 7 Then said I, Lo, I come (in the volume of the book it is written of me,) to do thy will, O God. 8 Above when he said, Sacrifice and offering and burnt offerings and offering for sin thou wouldest not, neither hadst pleasure therein; which are offered by the law; 9 Then said he, Lo, I come to do thy will, O God. He taketh away the first, that he may establish the second. 10 By the which will we are sanctified through the offering of the body of Jesus Christ once for all. 11 And every priest standeth daily ministering and offering oftentimes the same sacrifices, which can never take away sins: 12 But this man, after he had offered one sacrifice for sins for ever, sat down on the right hand of God; 13 From henceforth expecting till his enemies be made his footstool. 14 For by one offering he hath perfected for ever them that are sanctified. 15 Whereof the Holy Ghost also is a witness to us: for after that he had said before, 16 This is the covenant that I will make with them after those days, saith the Lord, I will put my laws into their hearts, and in their minds will I write them; 17 And their sins and iniquities will I remember no more.

These texts are talking about how the sacrifice of Jesus replaced the law, as a better one time sacrifice, done once and for all. Now we live under a new covenant based on the blood of Jesus."

"Ya, that about covers it," agreed Adam. "However, those verses don't say that man will not be brought back to life a second time in a resurrection. Only that judgement comes sometime after we die the first time. It doesn't specify when that judgement takes place, only that there is a judgement coming after we die.

We are told in other places there is a second death that will not hurt those who love god. If there is a second death it would only stand to reason that mankind would have a second life. Some people speculate that the second death is when our spirit or soul dies. However, they give no scriptural proof to back up the existence of such a soul or spirit possessed by humans. We have gone over the scriptures and have found that man has no eternal soul or spirit. Such is the power of Satan's conspiracy, to blind mankind to the life giving good news of their loving father. God's plans are uplifting for all who understand them."

"Wait, let me look those second death references up," Isaac pleads, as he begins to type. He reads them in the order he finds them.

"Revelation 21:8 King James Version," he announces. "But the fearful, and unbelieving, and the abominable, and murderers, and whoremongers, and sorcerers, and idolaters, and all liars, shall have their part in the lake which burneth with fire and brimstone: which is the second death.

Revelation 2:11
He that hath an ear, let him hear what the Spirit saith unto the churches; He that overcometh shall not be hurt of the second death.

Here is another one.

Revelation 20:6
Blessed and holy is he that hath part in the first
resurrection: on such the second death hath no power, but
they shall be priests of God and of Christ, and shall reign
with him a thousand years.

Last one.

Revelation 20:14
And death and hell were cast into the lake of fire. This is
the second death. 15 And whosoever was not found
written in the book of life was cast into the lake of fire.

OK it does tell us about a second death. But then why does it
say, it is appointed unto men once to die. What do you think it's
talking about?"

Adam tries to explain his understanding. "To start with, the
passage refers to the sacrifices the people made to God trying to
cleanse themselves from their sins. They made these sacrifices
throughout the year, every year. There was no end to the sacrifices
for sin.

Then Jesus came and made one sacrifice, the sacrifice of his
life. He only had to make it once for all of mankind, for all of the
ages. Once to die, is talking about the normal course of our human
existence, to live and then die. Jesus didn't have to keep repeating
his sacrifice with a new body for every generation. He lived his
one life and that was all that was needed, 'as in Adam all died, so
in Christ shall all be made alive'."

"That's a lot to take in. I need to think about your ideas, I'm
not sure they are completely accurate," Isaac said skeptically.

"Hey, that's not a problem," Adam said smiling. "A man
convinced against his will, is still of the same mind still. My
interpretation may not be a hundred percent accurate, but using, 'it

is appointed unto men once to die', to say that humans can only live one life, can't be right. It contradicts other Bible scriptures, as many people in the Bible were brought back to life after having died. Like I always say, the Bible will not contradict itself, if it seems to be, then we are not understanding the scriptures properly. Let God be true and every man a liar."

CHAPTER 8
PROVE ALL THINGS

"How do these resurrections you talk about fit in with the rapture? Do they take place before the tribulation, when Jesus comes and takes all of the Christians out of this world?" Isaac inquires. "Did you know that rapture is derived from the Latin verb rapere? It means to carry off, or, to catch up. That's what Jesus is going to do with all of the Christians. He is going to come back and get us Christians and leave all the sinners on earth to go through the tribulation. Do you know about the tribulation? When God punishes all sinners left on the earth, with dreadful punishments. It will be the worst time in the history of mankind."

"Ya, I have heard about it. The 'Left Behind' books were based on the belief," Adam states skeptically. "Are you familiar with the verses that support the belief of being raptured away?"

"You don't sound all that enthusiastic about it. Oh let me guess. You don't think the verses say what I think they say. You probably think I am taking them, out of context," Isaac says with a dramatic flair and a wave of his hand.

"Talk about a conspiracy addict. You don't seem to believe in anything that normal Christians believe in. Is there an anti-establishment conspiracy that you're caught up in? Isaac says, frustrated by Adam's nonstop demand for scriptural proof of his religious beliefs and doctrines.

Adam speaks bluntly to Isaac. "Well, has my skepticism been unwarranted so far?
Was mankind created immortal in Genesis as you had thought? How about Sunday, is it commanded to be kept holy? Or, how strongly do the scriptures support the notion that Christians go to heaven once they die? Are you bothered that my questions challenge your beliefs, or that your beliefs aren't as scripturally

supported as you had thought? What's better, being faithful to the Bible, or to denominational doctrines?"

Isaac pauses for a moment and then sheepishly answers. "Ya, you're somewhat right. Your points have made me re-evaluate some of my beliefs. The meaning you bring out of the scriptures is definitely different from what I have ever heard before. It's just that, no matter what belief I talk about, you seem to disagree with it."

"It's all not that bad," Adam says encouragingly. "We agree on the essential lifesaving beliefs. People must accept Jesus in order to be saved from their sins and gain eternal life. You and I have the same desire to follow God where ever he may lead us. We both want to live our lives as if Jesus was alive in us. The rest is peripheral. Like the story with Paul and the believers that didn't know about the baptism of the Holy Ghost. God used them with the knowledge they had, and he led them into greater wisdom as they followed him.

Making sure people know all mysteries at the start isn't that critical to God, if it were, he would have made things more obvious and given us a test before we could become a Christian. The most important thing is the love people have inside of them and displaying it to others. Love will be what's most important in the Kingdom. After we are in the Kingdom it won't be important how we got there. Prophesies, discernment of spirits, healing powers, things that we think are important now, won't be of much use or value once we are living in the Kingdom with God as our father."

"What story about Paul are you talking about? I'm not familiar with it. I'll have to look it up." Doing a few searches Isaac finds the passage. "Here it is.

Acts 19:1-7

1 And it came to pass, that, while Apollos was at Corinth, Paul having passed through the upper coasts came to Ephesus: and finding certain disciples,
2 He said unto them, Have ye received the Holy Ghost since ye believed? And they said unto him, We have not so much as heard whether there be any Holy Ghost.
3 And he said unto them, Unto what then were ye baptized? And they said, Unto John's baptism.
4 Then said Paul, John verily baptized with the baptism of repentance, saying unto the people, that they should believe on him which should come after him, that is, on Christ Jesus.
5 When they heard this, they were baptized in the name of the Lord Jesus.
6 And when Paul had laid his hands upon them, the Holy Ghost came on them; and they spake with tongues, and prophesied.
7 And all the men were about twelve."

"That's the one," Adam says. "They were believers without even knowing about being baptized into the name of Jesus, how long they were in the dark we can only guess, but God led them to where he wanted them in his time. There is a similar story about a preacher, I think it was Apollos. He was instructed by other believers into a better understanding of baptism."

Isaac starts to type right away. "I think I remember this one," he says. Finding it quickly Isaac starts to read.

"Acts 18:24-28
And a certain Jew named Apollos, born at Alexandria, an eloquent man, and mighty in the scriptures, came to Ephesus.

25 This man was instructed in the way of the Lord; and being fervent in the spirit, he spake and taught diligently the things of the Lord, knowing only the baptism of John.
26 And he began to speak boldly in the synagogue: whom when Aquila and Priscilla had heard, they took him unto them, and expounded unto him the way of God more perfectly.
27 And when he was disposed to pass into Achaia, the brethren wrote, exhorting the disciples to receive him: who, when he was come, helped them much which had believed through grace:
28 For he mightily convinced the Jews, and that publicly, shewing by the scriptures that Jesus was Christ.

OK I get it. We don't have to know everything right away, we grow in our understanding as God directs."

"Yes, we learn by following where God leads us," Adam agrees. "Usually through people we come into contact with. It is by talking about scripture with others that we can grow in the knowledge of God. Iron sharpens iron, our beliefs and doctrines mean nothing if we can't support them from the Bible.

We need to be discerning, judging good from evil, for it's our salvation that is at stake. We need to prove our beliefs for ourselves and not outsource them to others. Like the Bereans did, proving what was true. Once we have the basics understood the Holy Spirit will guide us into more important areas of our Christian faith. We need to worship God in spirit and in truth, and then we can show the full love of Jesus to our fellow man, so that they might praise God because of that love."

"Are there references for that? Who were the Bereans anyway? Isaac asked as he started typing. "I will try to get your references in order but you made several points all at once."

Isaac mumbles to himself before he reads aloud. "God teaches us through other people.

Romans 10:12-17
For there is no difference between the Jew and the Greek: for the same Lord over all is rich unto all that call upon him.
13 For whosoever shall call upon the name of the Lord shall be saved.
14 How then shall they call on him in whom they have not believed? and how shall they believe in him of whom they have not heard? and how shall they hear without a preacher?
15 And how shall they preach, except they be sent? as it is written, How beautiful are the feet of them that preach the gospel of peace, and bring glad tidings of good things!
16 But they have not all obeyed the gospel. For Esaias saith, Lord, who hath believed our report?
17 So then faith cometh by hearing, and hearing by the word of God.

We sharpen our beliefs by discussing scripture with other people.

Proverbs 27:17
Iron sharpeneth iron; so a man sharpeneth the countenance of his friend.

2 Timothy 3 KJV
16 All scripture is given by inspiration of God, and is profitable for doctrine, for reproof, for correction, for

instruction in righteousness: 17 That the man of God may be perfect, thoroughly furnished unto all good works."

Finding more proof, Isaac continues. "Need to have our beliefs supported by the Bible.

Hebrews 5:12-14
For when for the time ye ought to be teachers, ye have need that one teach you again which be the first principles of the oracles of God; and are become such as have need of milk, and not of strong meat. 13 For every one that useth milk is unskilful in the word of righteousness: for he is a babe. 14 But strong meat belongeth to them that are of full age, even those who by reason of use have their senses exercised to discern both good and evil.

Our salvation depends on how we respond," Isaac calls out.

Philippians 2:12
Wherefore, my beloved, as ye have always obeyed, not as in my presence only, but now much more in my absence, work out your own salvation with fear and trembling.

Who were the Bereans?" Isaac answers his own question.

"Acts 17. 10
And the brethren immediately sent away Paul and Silas by night unto Berea: who coming thither went into the synagogue of the Jews. 11 were more noble than those in Thessalonica, in that they received the word with all readiness of mind, and searched the scriptures daily, whether those things were so.

Basics first, then go on to perfection.

Hebrews 6:1-3
Therefore leaving the principles of the doctrine of Christ, let us go on unto perfection; not laying again the foundation of repentance from dead works, and of faith toward God, 2 Of the doctrine of baptisms, and of laying on of hands, and of resurrection of the dead, and of eternal judgment. 3 And this will we do, if God permit.

Then, worship God in Spirit and truth.

John 4:24
24 God is a Spirit: and they that worship him must worship him in spirit and in truth.

Dut da da du." Isaac sings a vocal fan fair. "And lastly, love is the best.

1 Corinthians 13
1 Though I speak with the tongues of men and of angels, and have not charity, I am become as sounding brass, or a tinkling cymbal.
2 And though I have the gift of prophecy, and understand all mysteries, and all knowledge; and though I have all faith, so that I could remove mountains, and have not charity, I am nothing.
3 And though I bestow all my goods to feed the poor, and though I give my body to be burned, and have not charity, it profiteth me nothing.
4 Charity suffereth long, and is kind; charity envieth not; charity vaunteth not itself, is not puffed up,

5 Doth not behave itself unseemly, seeketh not her own, is not easily provoked, thinketh no evil;

6 Rejoiceth not in iniquity, but rejoiceth in the truth;

7 Beareth all things, believeth all things, hopeth all things, endureth all things.

8 Charity never faileth: but whether there be prophecies, they shall fail; whether there be tongues, they shall cease; whether there be knowledge, it shall vanish away.

9 For we know in part, and we prophesy in part.

10 But when that which is perfect is come, then that which is in part shall be done away.

11 When I was a child, I spake as a child, I understood as a child, I thought as a child: but when I became a man, I put away childish things.

12 For now we see through a glass, darkly; but then face to face: now I know in part; but then shall I know even as also I am known.

13 And now abideth faith, hope, charity, these three; but the greatest of these is charity.

"Are you going to look up all of my references?" Adam questions bewilderedly.

"Sure am. Like you said, I need to prove all things to see if it's true or not," Isaac replied with a smile. "It's my salvation and I need to be sure that I'm on the right path. Just like a Berean."

CHAPTER 9
LEFT BEHIND

"I can't argue with that," Adam said. "You do need to be sure that you're following the word of God to be at your best. But we have gotten distracted a bit. We were going to talk about the rapture and the return of Jesus."

"Yes. It seemed as though you don't believe in the rapture," Isaac stated.

"Well I just thought we should look up the scriptures and read them. That's the best way to be sure you are getting the wisdom of God and not just what others want you to believe," Adam said sincerely. "I think the foundational scriptures for the belief talked about one taken and the other left behind."

"I have read these scriptures a lot, I don't think they have been misunderstood," Isaac boldly stated.

"I'm sure your right, but let's read through them anyway, just to stay consistent with the rest of our discussions. You never know, we may learn something," Adam said casually.

"I suppose it wouldn't hurt," Isaac starts to look up scriptures and reads them out loud. "I found a site that lists verses that talk about the rapture and the return of Jesus. I will read through them first and then we can discuss them. It starts with;

1 Thessalonians 4:16-17
For the Lord himself shall descend from heaven with a shout, with the voice of the archangel, and with the trump of God: and the dead in Christ shall rise first: 17 Then we which are alive [and] remain shall be caught up together with them in the clouds, to meet the Lord in the air: and so shall we ever be with the Lord.

1 Corinthians 15:52
In a moment, in the twinkling of an eye, at the last
trump: for the trumpet shall sound, and the dead shall be
raised incorruptible, and we shall be changed.

Daniel 12:1-2 King James Version
And at that time shall Michael stand up, the great prince
which standeth for the children of thy people: and there
shall be a time of trouble, such as never was since there
was a nation even to that same time: and at that time thy
people shall be delivered, every one that shall be found
written in the book.
2 And many of them that sleep in the dust of the earth
shall awake, some to everlasting life, and some to shame
and everlasting contempt.

Matthew 24:27-44
For as the lightning cometh out of the east, and shineth
even unto the west; so shall also the coming of the Son of
man be.
28 For wheresoever the carcase is, there will the eagles be
gathered together.
29 Immediately after the tribulation of those days shall
the sun be darkened, and the moon shall not give her
light, and the stars shall fall from heaven, and the powers
of the heavens shall be shaken:
30 And then shall appear the sign of the Son of man in
heaven: and then shall all the tribes of the earth mourn,
and they shall see the Son of man coming in the clouds of
heaven with power and great glory.

31 And he shall send his angels with a great sound of a trumpet, and they shall gather together his elect from the four winds, from one end of heaven to the other.

32 Now learn a parable of the fig tree; When his branch is yet tender, and putteth forth leaves, ye know that summer is nigh:

33 So likewise ye, when ye shall see all these things, know that it is near, even at the doors.

34 Verily I say unto you, This generation shall not pass, till all these things be fulfilled.

35 Heaven and earth shall pass away, but my words shall not pass away.

36 But of that day and hour knoweth no man, no, not the angels of heaven, but my Father only.

37 But as the days of Noah were, so shall also the coming of the Son of man be.

38 For as in the days that were before the flood they were eating and drinking, marrying and giving in marriage, until the day that Noe entered into the ark,

39 And knew not until the flood came, and took them all away; so shall also the coming of the Son of man be.

40 Then shall two be in the field; the one shall be taken, and the other left.

41 Two women shall be grinding at the mill; the one shall be taken, and the other left.

42 Watch therefore: for ye know not what hour your Lord doth come.

43 But know this, that if the goodman of the house had known in what watch the thief would come, he would have watched, and would not have suffered his house to be broken up.

44 Therefore be ye also ready: for in such an hour as ye think not the Son of man cometh.

Luke 12:40

Be ye therefore ready also: for the Son of man cometh at an hour when ye think not.

Mark 13:32-37

But of that day and that hour knoweth no man, no, not the angels which are in heaven, neither the Son, but the Father.

33 Take ye heed, watch and pray: for ye know not when the time is.

34 For the Son of Man is as a man taking a far journey, who left his house, and gave authority to his servants, and to every man his work, and commanded the porter to watch.

35 Watch ye therefore: for ye know not when the master of the house cometh, at even, or at midnight, or at the cockcrowing, or in the morning:

36 Lest coming suddenly he find you sleeping.

37 And what I say unto you I say unto all, Watch.

Luke 17:34-37

34 I tell you, in that night there shall be two men in one bed; the one shall be taken, and the other shall be left.

35 Two women shall be grinding together; the one shall be taken, and the other left.

36 Two men shall be in the field; the one shall be taken, and the other left.

37 And they answered and said unto him, Where, Lord? And he said unto them, Wheresoever the body is, thither will the eagles be gathered together.

1 Thessalonians 1:10

And to wait for his Son from heaven, whom he raised from the dead, [even] Jesus, which delivered us from the wrath to come.

1 Thessalonians 5:2

For yourselves know perfectly that the day of the Lord so cometh as a thief in the night.

2 Thessalonians 2:3-7

Let no man deceive you by any means: for that day shall not come, except there come a falling away first, and that man of sin be revealed, the son of perdition;
4 Who opposeth and exalteth himself above all that is called God, or that is worshipped; so that he as God sitteth in the temple of God, shewing himself that he is God.
5 Remember ye not, that, when I was yet with you, I told you these things?
6 And now ye know what withholdeth that he might be revealed in his time.
7 For the mystery of iniquity doth already work: only he who now letteth will let, until he be taken out of the way.

Mark 14:62

And Jesus said, I am: and ye shall see the Son of man sitting on the right hand of power, and coming in the clouds of heaven.

Revelation 3:10

Because thou hast kept the word of my patience, I also will keep thee from the hour of temptation, which shall come upon all the world, to try them that dwell upon the earth.

Revelation 20:2-5

And he laid hold on the dragon, that old serpent, which is the Devil, and Satan, and bound him a thousand years, 3 And cast him into the bottomless pit, and shut him up, and set a seal upon him, that he should deceive the nations no more, till the thousand years should be fulfilled: and after that he must be loosed a little season. 4 And I saw thrones, and they sat upon them, and judgment was given unto them: and I saw the souls of them that were beheaded for the witness of Jesus, and for the word of God, and which had not worshipped the beast, neither his image, neither had received his mark upon their foreheads, or in their hands; and they lived and reigned with Christ a thousand years. 5 But the rest of the dead lived not again until the thousand years were finished. This is the first resurrection.

Revelation 11:15-19

15 And the seventh angel sounded; and there were great voices in heaven, saying, The kingdoms of this world are become the kingdoms of our Lord, and of his Christ; and he shall reign for ever and ever. 16 And the four and twenty elders, which sat before God on their seats, fell upon their faces, and worshipped God,

17 Saying, We give thee thanks, O LORD God Almighty, which art, and wast, and art to come; because thou hast taken to thee thy great power, and hast reigned.
18 And the nations were angry, and thy wrath is come, and the time of the dead, that they should be judged, and that thou shouldest give reward unto thy servants the prophets, and to the saints, and them that fear thy name, small and great; and shouldest destroy them which destroy the earth.
19 And the temple of God was opened in heaven, and there was seen in his temple the ark of his testament: and there were lightnings, and voices, and thunderings, and an earthquake, and great hail."

Adam paraphrases the scriptures that Isaac just read, "Some of those verses talk about the noisy, obvious return of Jesus, At some unexpected time, to establish the Kingdom of God. The dead believers rise from their graves, just before those who are alive are changed in the twinkling of an eye, according to Jesus in John, 'on the last day', at his second coming, the day of the Lord.

Other verses tell us about Satan, being bound for a thousand years, the lake of fire, and all mankind being judged. These versus are all used by people who believe Jesus will return for his believers. There were two sections of verses that are commonly used to support a pe-tribulation rapture. Luke 17:34-37 is one of them, could you read it again?" Adam asked.

"Sure let me find it. OK here it is," Isaac responded.

34 I tell you, in that night there shall be two men in one bed; the one shall be taken, and the other shall be left.
35 Two women shall be grinding together; the one shall be taken, and the other left.

36 Two men shall be in the field; the one shall be taken, and the other left.

37 And they answered and said unto him, Where, Lord? And he said unto them, Wheresoever the body is, thither will the eagles be gathered together."

"Now read the other one. Matthew 24:27-44," Adam directed.

"Got it," said Isaac before starting to read.

27 For as the lightning cometh out of the east, and shineth even unto the west; so shall also the coming of the Son of man be.

28 For wheresoever the carcase is, there will the eagles be gathered together.

29 Immediately after the tribulation of those days shall the sun be darkened, and the moon shall not give her light, and the stars shall fall from heaven, and the powers of the heavens shall be shaken:

30 And then shall appear the sign of the Son of man in heaven: and then shall all the tribes of the earth mourn, and they shall see the Son of man coming in the clouds of heaven with power and great glory.

31 And he shall send his angels with a great sound of a trumpet, and they shall gather together his elect from the four winds, from one end of heaven to the other.

32 Now learn a parable of the fig tree; When his branch is yet tender, and putteth forth leaves, ye know that summer is nigh:

33 So likewise ye, when ye shall see all these things, know that it is near, even at the doors.

34 Verily I say unto you, This generation shall not pass, till all these things be fulfilled.

35 Heaven and earth shall pass away, but my words shall not pass away.

36 But of that day and hour knoweth no man, no, not the angels of heaven, but my Father only.

37 But as the days of Noah were, so shall also the coming of the Son of man be.

38 For as in the days that were before the flood they were eating and drinking, marrying and giving in marriage, until the day that Noe entered into the ark,

39 And knew not until the flood came, and took them all away; so shall also the coming of the Son of man be.

40 Then shall two be in the field; the one shall be taken, and the other left.

41 Two women shall be grinding at the mill; the one shall be taken, and the other left.

42 Watch therefore: for ye know not what hour your Lord doth come.

43 But know this, that if the goodman of the house had known in what watch the thief would come, he would have watched, and would not have suffered his house to be broken up.

44 Therefore be ye also ready: for in such an hour as ye think not the Son of man cometh.

These are the passages that my profs taught from at school. We will have no notice before Jesus comes to get us. That's why we have to be saved as soon as possible, and not put accepting Jesus off till later. My mom and dad led me to the Lord when I was five. I didn't want to be left behind with all of the sinners after Jesus came back to get his faithful believers. We have to warn everyone and help them see their need for Jesus, so they too can escape the tribulation. I've heard it described as being almost as bad as the torments of Hell," Isaac passionately recounted.

"Let's read some verses before and after the passages in Luke to see if we can get complete understanding," Adam suggested.

"OK," Agreed Isaac. "If you think it will help. How about if we read from,

Luke 17:22-37?

22 And he said unto the disciples, The days will come, when ye shall desire to see one of the days of the Son of man, and ye shall not see it.

23 And they shall say to you, See here; or, see there: go not after them, nor follow them.

24 For as the lightning, that lighteneth out of the one part under heaven, shineth unto the other part under heaven; so shall also the Son of man be in his day.

25 But first must he suffer many things, and be rejected of this generation.

26 And as it was in the days of Noe, so shall it be also in the days of the Son of man.

27 They did eat, they drank, they married wives, they were given in marriage, until the day that Noah entered into the ark, and the flood came, and destroyed them all.

28 Likewise also as it was in the days of Lot; they did eat, they drank, they bought, they sold, they planted, they builded;

29 But the same day that Lot went out of Sodom it rained fire and brimstone from heaven, and destroyed them all.

30 Even thus shall it be in the day when the Son of man is revealed.

31 In that day, he which shall be upon the housetop, and his stuff in the house, let him not come down to take it away: and he that is in the field, let him likewise not return back.

32 Remember Lot's wife.

33 Whosoever shall seek to save his life shall lose it; and whosoever shall lose his life shall preserve it.

34 I tell you, in that night there shall be two men in one bed; the one shall be taken, and the other shall be left.

35 Two women shall be grinding together; the one shall be taken, and the other left.

36 Two men shall be in the field; the one shall be taken, and the other left.

37 And they answered and said unto him, Where, Lord? And he said unto them, Wheresoever the body is, thither will the eagles be gathered together.

Let's start at the beginning," Isaac said, enthusiastically starting to describe the texts. "Verses 22-24 tells us that the disciples will miss being with Jesus and some people will try to trick them about the return of Jesus, but don't believe them because the return of Jesus will be obvious, like lightning in the dark sky."

"That's good. You summed up the thoughts nicely," Adam agrees. "Go on."

Bolstered by the encouragement, Isaac continues. "25, refers to the Crucifixion and the rejection of Jesus by the Jewish leaders. 26-30 tells us that people won't be expecting the return of Jesus, that it will catch them off guard like in the times of Noah and Lot. Going on 31-33 reminds us to be vigilant in preserving our spiritual lives and not our physical ones. 34-36 are the verses that describe the believers being raptured away to be with Jesus. 37, Jesus tells his disciples, where those left behind can be found. The Eagles are the vultures gathered around the spiritually dead false religious teachers or false saviours. The ones left behind will be with the antichrist and the false ministers of God."

Adam has a questioning look as he drives, then he says. "I wonder if we could expand on the section of 26-30. It seems like

Jesus was very specific about the two examples he used. Both stories involved people dying on a large scale and he does say that, as it was in those days, so it will be when the son of man is revealed. I wonder if there is anything in those stories that we can learn from."

Isaac ponders the question. "I don't know. I have never thought about it past the fact that destruction took them by surprise. Let's overlap Mathew 24:37. Let me see here," Isaac looks up the scriptural texts and scans over the verses. "Mathew 24:37 to 39 should do it.

37 But as the days of Noah were, so shall also the coming of the Son of man be.

So again the end time will be like it was in the days of Noah. 38 For as in the days that were before the flood they were eating and drinking, marrying and giving in marriage, until the day that Noe entered into the ark,"

"They were going about their lives like normal until Noah entered the ark," Adam interjects."

Isaac nods and continues to read without hardly a pause.

"39 And knew not until the flood came, and took them all away; so shall also the coming of the Son of man be.

That's when they were taken by surprise, God took them all away and they perished in the flood, leaving behind only Noah and his family alive to repopulate the earth. It will be the same when Jesus returns," Isaac elaborates his point.

Adam looks puzzled when he exclaims. "Hey wait a minute, who was taken away? In the rapture scenario, those that love Jesus are supposed to be taken and the evil ones left behind alive on the earth, not the other way around. That happens in the story of Lot as well, the evil people are taken away with fire and brimstone, destroying them all. The evil ones were destroyed and taken away. Lot was left behind alive. The rapture doctrine seems to have it backwards."

Isaac looks puzzled as well, staring in disbelief at the scriptures on the screen. "I have read these verses countless times and I have never thought of them that way before. Luke 17:30 says.

Even thus shall it be in the day when the Son of man is revealed.

And in

Mathew 24:39
and knew not until the flood came, and took them all away; so shall also the coming of the Son of man be.

If the coming of Jesus is to be like it is in those stories, then, the righteous are the ones left behind, not the ones taken away. What about the Eagles or vultures and the body or carcass. What could they represent?" Isaac questioned out loud.

Adam offered a thought. "Maybe the Eagles are not Vultures, but are the majestic chosen of God. As well a body doesn't have to be dead; there are many verses that talk positively about Eagles. Perhaps each story has a slightly different meaning? There are many interpretations for what Jesus said."

"Ya, there are good Eagle references," Isaac said, starting to type on the keyboard looking up scripture and reviewing commentaries for differing opinions.

"Here are some verses where the Bible refers to people as eagles, not that they explain the meaning of the other verse, just that eagles, aren't always used in a negative term and can be positively positive." Isaac joked with a grin. Then read some more.

"Psalm 103:5.
Who satisfieth thy mouth with good things; so that thy youth is renewed like the eagle's.

And in;

Isaiah 40:31.
But they that wait upon the LORD shall renew their strength; they shall mount up with wings as eagles; they shall run, and not be weary; and they shall walk, and not faint.

Another positive reference is in Ezekiel 1:10, where Cherubim are described.

As for the likeness of their faces, they four had the face of a man, and the face of a lion, on the right side: and they four had the face of an ox on the left side; they four also had the face of an eagle.

The commentaries have different opinions for the meaning of 'where the eagles gather'. Some say the eagles are the wicked, some say they could be church members like in the Pulpit Commentary. The dead body (the carcass), according to these interpreters, is the body of Christ, and the eagles are his saints, who flock to his presence and who feed upon him, especially in the act of Holy Communion.

Others believe Jesus was just telling the disciples where it would take place. Like here in

Jamieson-Fausset-Brown Bible Commentary
37. Where—shall this occur?
Wheresoever, etc.—"As birds of prey scent out the carrion, so wherever is found a mass of incurable moral and spiritual corruption, there will be seen alighting the ministers of divine judgment," a proverbial saying terrifically verified at the destruction of Jerusalem, and many times since, though its most tremendous illustration will be at the world's final day.

There is a great variety of opinion. How can they all be right?" Isaac wonders out loud.

"Let's look at this through the lens of mankind not being in possession of an eternal soul. If, as we have read, mankind actually dies when they die, how would that affect the interpretation?" Adam asks. "After all, the faithful in Hebrews did not receive the promise; they have to wait for something better, when all the believers are resurrected at the same time. How has the lie of Satin affected the understanding of those Christians who promote all of these differing opinions?"

"Ah yes, back to the conspiracy," Isaac teases.

"Well, how would it affect your understanding? If you believed we are only mortal?" Adam asks defensively.

"I suppose to start with," Isaac starts to talk tentatively. "The dead saints would rise from their graves at the return of Jesus to the earth at his second coming. I think that was somewhere in John. Let me find the verses, ya here they are. John 6. Jesus told them they would be raised at his return, at the last day.

39 And this is the Father's will which hath sent me, that of all which he hath given me I should lose nothing, but should raise it up again at the last day.

40 And this is the will of him that sent me, that every one which seeth the Son, and believeth on him, may have everlasting life: and I will raise him up at the last day. 44 No man can come to me, except the Father which hath sent me draw him: and I will raise him up at the last day. 54 Whoso eateth my flesh, and drinketh my blood, hath eternal life; and I will raise him up at the last day.

So if all of the faithful from the Old Testament didn't receive the promise of eternal life, separate from those under the new covenant, that means they are still in their graves. I have it here." Isaac reads the scriptures from the lap top screen.

"Hebrews 11: 39
And these all, having obtained a good report through faith, received not the promise:
40 God having provided some better thing for us, that they without us should not be made perfect.

Those Christians that are still alive, and those who are dead, will be raised all at the same time. Or very close to it, as there is an order to them being made perfect. The dead in Christ shall be raised first, at his return. Like it tells us in 1 Thessalonians 4:13-17," Reading off of the screen Isaac rereads more previously covered material.

"13 But I would not have you to be ignorant, brethren, concerning them which are asleep, that ye sorrow not, even as others which have no hope.
14 For if we believe that Jesus died and rose again, even so them also which sleep in Jesus will God bring with him.

15 For this we say unto you by the word of the Lord, that
we which are alive and remain unto the coming of the
Lord shall not prevent them which are asleep.
16 For the Lord himself shall descend from heaven with a
shout, with the voice of the archangel, and with the trump
of God: and the dead in Christ shall rise first:
17 Then we which are alive and remain shall be caught
up together with them in the clouds, to meet the Lord in
the air: and so shall we ever be with the Lord."

Isaac leans back in his bucket seat and is quiet. He stares
blankly out the window at the passing scenery deep in thought.
Several minutes go by before he speaks again.

CHAPTER 10
SHOW ME

Isaac sits up straight in his chair, looking intently at Adam.

"Not having an immortal soul does change how the end time events would play out. It also changes how mankind relates to God, as well as my understandings of how we come to be with God. These beliefs would all need to be re-thought. I'm just not sure I agree with your belief about our souls dying.

Why is it that N.T. Wright or my professors don't believe anything like what you propose? They have diligently studied the subject for decades. All of N.T.'s material is thoroughly researched, documented and peer reviewed. How is it that an old trucker should know more about the subject that all of the scholars that have devoted their entire lives to the subjects of God and religion? Your ideas are intriguing and interesting to discus, but how can I take you seriously when you have no formal background in the study of God. You just aren't credible."

Adam pays attention to his driving as he rounds a long sweeping left hand corner and is forced to do several down shift as he ascends a steep hill. Considering Isaac's rebuffs, he does some slow deep breathing to calm himself before responding further. He starts to talk just as the truck starts to pick up speed on the backside of the hill.

"I suppose then, I am the living proof for the verse that says, God calls the foolish and the week to confound the wise and mighty, for I am the most foolish of all, just a dumb old trucker. Wasn't Jesus rejected by the Jews for basically the same reason? Because he was a nobody, the son of a carpenter from a small town, in a backwater part of the country."

Isaac was quick to respond with sarcasm. "Oh, so now you are comparing yourself to Jesus?"

"No," Adam said forcefully. "I am not nearly as Jesus like as I should be. I am only pointing out that having credentials and schooling isn't what one needs to understand the plans of God. In fact, having lofty credentials probably hinders your understanding of God. If you have your time and energy invested in those credentials, you could have years of work and a career to lose if you should come to any new understanding.

My first rule in buying things is, never believe the salesman. I like to prove their claims through an unbiased third party. My source for Godly wisdom is, as we agreed on at the start, the word of God as recorded in the Bible. The King James is good, but I find it helpful to use the Strong's concordance to find the proper word used in the original manuscript, like we did to find the proper usage for the word soul in Genesis.

Besides the disciples were not chosen from the elite of society, but from the bottom and despised. My points of view come from the Bible, not from books written by learned men. I do my best not to have any non-biblical preconceived ideas or agendas. Like we said, if it doesn't come from the word of God, it cannot be relied on."

"We did say that," Isaac responded reluctantly. "I better look up your references just to be safe." He finds what he thinks they are and reads them loudly.

"Mark 6:1-6 KJV.
And he went out from thence, and came into his own country; and his disciples follow him.
2 And when the sabbath day was come, he began to teach in the synagogue: and many hearing him were astonished, saying, From whence hath this man these things? and

what wisdom is this which is given unto him, that even
such mighty works are wrought by his hands?
3 Is not this the carpenter, the son of Mary, the brother of
James, and Joses, and of Juda, and Simon? and are not
his sisters here with us? And they were offended at him.
4 But Jesus, said unto them, A prophet is not without
honour, but in his own country, and among his own kin,
and in his own house.
5 And he could there do no mighty work, save that he laid
his hands upon a few sick folk, and healed them.
6 And he marvelled because of their unbelief. And he
went round about the villages, teaching.

And here in 1 Corinthians 1:18-31.

For the preaching of the cross is to them that perish
foolishness; but unto us which are saved it is the power of
God.
19 For it is written, I will destroy the wisdom of the wise,
and will bring to nothing the understanding of the
prudent.
20 Where is the wise? where is the scribe? where is the
disputer of this world? hath not God made foolish the
wisdom of this world?
21 For after that in the wisdom of God the world by
wisdom knew not God, it pleased God by the foolishness of
preaching to save them that believe.
22 For the Jews require a sign, and the Greeks seek after
wisdom:
23 But we preach Christ crucified, unto the Jews a
stumblingblock, and unto the Greeks foolishness;

24 But unto them which are called, both Jews and Greeks, Christ the power of God, and the wisdom of God.
25 Because the foolishness of God is wiser than men; and the weakness of God is stronger than men.
26 For ye see your calling, brethren, how that not many wise men after the flesh, not many mighty, not many noble, are called:
27 But God hath chosen the foolish things of the world to confound the wise; and God hath chosen the weak things of the world to confound the things which are mighty;
28 And base things of the world, and things which are despised, hath God chosen, yea, and things which are not, to bring to nought things that are:
29 That no flesh should glory in his presence.
30 But of him are ye in Christ Jesus, who of God is made unto us wisdom, and righteousness, and sanctification, and redemption:
31 That, according as it is written, He that glorieth, let him glory in the Lord.

Are those the verses you were referring to?" Isaac asks, wanting to get the right references.

"I think so, there might be others, but those give us a pretty good picture of what I am referring too," Adam agrees.

Smiling broadly, not wanting to let the opportunity to tease Adam pass, Isaac says with a laugh. "Well you're certainly right. You do resemble those verses about the weak and foolish."

"HA. HA," Adam smiles. "And as far as N.T. Wright is concerned, his book The Resurrection Of The Son Of God, was to prove that Jesus was bodily resurrected from the dead. He was proving the resurrection story wasn't just fantasy made up by the disciples. He didn't like the distorted resurrection teachings that modern scholars and clergy were bringing into mainstream

Christianity. If you look in my copy I have the page references of him saying that."

Isaac picks up Adam's worn copy of the book and checks the hand written notes scrawled on the first few pages. "I think this is it here on page 7 and 8." Reading silently he then sums up what was written. "It basically states what you said; he wanted to set the discussion on a historically accurate footing."

"That's right," Adam said. "He had a narrow agenda based on proving the resurrection of Jesus in history. N.T. wasn't looking at how all of the covered material showed God's plan of salvation for the world. He doesn't even let the facts he uncovers affect his belief in an intermediate state after death, he seems to believe our conscious souls go to heaven to be with God. Even though his research shows this to be a pagan belief, not held by Paul or the Pharisee sect that Paul came out of. Mr. Wright fails to connect the facts that his research highlights to his own beliefs, instead he stays mired in his trust of conjecture and speculation."

"Whoa, that is a pretty bold statement. I'd like to see you prove that!" Isaac says with astonishment. "His book has been scrutinized by many professionals; I doubt they would have missed something as glaring as that."

"They would miss it if they weren't looking for it; because they have similar beliefs as N.T. It was a surprise to you that man was mortal in the Garden of Eden. Other thoughts never occurred to you either. That's why I say Satin has deceived the whole world with his, 'though shall not surely die' lie. Take any faith, with the exception of an evolutionary atheist; they all will have some kind of a belief in an afterlife. The belief that mankind possesses an eternal soul is universal and has been with us from our collective beginnings."

"Don't try and change the subject, we have been through all of that. I want to see your proof about N.T. Wright's book," Isaac demands.

"OK. I have the notes there on the first pages. You'll need to look them up as I can't do that and drive at the same time." Adam explained as he corrected the trucks currant trajectory from off of the highway's paved shoulder.

Isaac checks the books front cover for Adam's scrawling notes. "Here is a prospect. You have the middle of page 31 flagged as, resurrection belief. Let's see what it says." Isaac starts to read out of the well-worn paperback book.

"Thus, when the ancients spoke of resurrection, whether denying it or affirming it, they were telling a two-step story. Resurrection itself would be preceded (and was preceded even in the case of Jesus) by an interim period of death-as-a-state. Where we find a single-step story death-as-event being followed at once by a final state, for instance of disembodied bliss – the texts are not talking about resurrection. Resurrection involves a definite content (some sort of re-embodiment) and a definite narrative shape (a two-step story, not a single-step one). This meaning is constant throughout the ancient world, until we come to a new coinage in the second century.

The meaning of 'resurrection' as 'life after "life after death"' cannot be overemphasized, not least because much writing continues to use 'resurrection' as a virtual synonym for 'life after death' in the popular sense. It has sometimes been proposed that this usage was current even for the first century, but the evidence is simply not there. If we are to engage in history, rather than projecting the accidents of (some) contemporary usage on to the remote past, it is vital to keep these distinctions in mind.

So what's your point? It talks about the definition and understanding for the word resurrection."

Adam looks bewildered at Isaac's lack of ability to see what was so plain to him. "You read it without understanding. The part that said:

'Where we find a single-step story death-as-event being followed at once by a final state, for instance of disembodied bliss – the texts are not talking about resurrection.'

That is telling us the belief in a disembodied state is not referred to as resurrection in the Bible," Adam explains.

"'Resurrection involves a definite content (some sort of re-embodiment) and a definite narrative shape (a two-step story, not a single-step one). This meaning is constant throughout the ancient world, until we come to a new coinage in the second century,'"

Adam continues to explain what was just read. "The idea that resurrection meant a disembodied state didn't show up till the second century. At least a hundred years after Jesus died. After the apostles were dead and the texts inspired by God were completed. When the scriptures talk about the resurrection of the dead for mankind they are referring to a two-step story. Take a look and see."

"You mean like in 1 Corinthians 15:20-23." Isaac brakes into the conversation and starts to read aloud a verse he had on another tab.

"20 But now is Christ risen from the dead, and become the firstfruits of them that slept.
21 For since by man came death, by man came also the resurrection of the dead.
22 For as in Adam all die, even so in Christ shall all be made alive.
23 But every man in his own order: Christ the firstfruits; afterward they that are Christ's at his coming."

"Exactly, mankind is to be resurrected as Jesus was, a two-step story. We follow the example of Jesus, into our new lives with God," added Adam agreeably. "The idea that we become a disembodied spirit immediately after death is not a biblical teaching, but a pagan one. We need to believe what God tells us if we want to worship him in Spirit and truth."

"I have that verse.

John 4:24
God is a Spirit: and they that worship him must worship him in spirit and in truth.

We read that one before, but I just like it," quipped Isaac.

Adam nods. "Yes it is a good one and it highlights the importance of knowing the truth about God and his word to the best of our ability. We need to take care to prove that what we believe comes from the word of God. I know Christians that won't do any yoga poses, or use acupuncture for healing, because the origins of those arts stem from paganism. Yet they believe they go to heaven and become a disembodied spirit as soon as they die, wrongly believing it to be a Christian truth. Continue with my notes and see what history Mr. Wright uncovers in his book."

"OK," agrees Isaac. He had a lot of respect for Mr. Wright and his research. Isaac was starting to become curious as to what he and his professors missed in N.T.'s large book.

Adam continued to explain further. "N.T. goes into great detail on the pagan beliefs of death and where people end up after they die. These pagan beliefs have a lot in common to the Christian beliefs of today. Their ideas did not come from God or his written word."

Isaac gets busy at finding more pertinent points out of Adam's scrawled notes. As he finds them he reads them out loud so they can be explored further. "Page 49.

Since for many Greeks 'the immortals' were the gods, there is always the suggestion, at least by implication, that human souls are in some way divine. Because the soul is this sort of thing, it not only survives the death of the body but is delighted to do so. If it had known earlier where its real interests lay it would have been longing for this very moment. It will now flourish in a new way, released from the prison that had hitherto enslaved it. Its new environment will be just what it should have wanted. Popular opinion would attempt to bring the dead back if that were possible, but this would be a mistake. Death is frequently defined precisely in terms of the separation of soul and body, seen as something to be desired.

Hades, in other words, is not a place of gloom, but (in principle at least) of delight. It is not terrifying, as so many ordinary people believe, but offers a range of pleasing activities - of which philosophical discourse may be among the chief, not surprisingly since attention to such matters is the best way, during the present time, of preparing the soul for its future. The reason people do not return from Hades is that life is so good there; they want to stay, rather than to return to the world of space, time and matter. Plato suggests that the word 'Hades' itself is derived, in terms both of etymology and basic meaning, either from the word for 'unseen', or from the word for 'knowledge'.

What happens to souls in Hades - at least, to souls who go there to begin with - is then far more interesting than anything envisaged in Homer. Judgement is passed according to the person's previous behaviour: we see here the philosophical roots of those judgement scenes that became so familiar in the, Page 50. Platonized Christianity (or was it Christianized Platonism?) of the Middle Ages."

"Here!" Adam breaks in energetically. "N.T. describes Christianity's belief in the punishment of, sinful souls in Hell, as originating in the philosophies of Plato. These pagan ideas had already been embraced and taught by Christianity in the middle Ages, becoming Platonized Christianity, beliefs that are still prevalent and taught as fact today."

Isaac nods and then continues to read.

"Three judges are appointed, one each from Europe and Asia and one (Minos, conveniently from Crete, poised as it were between the two continents) as the judge of appeal. At last, after all the botched earthly attempts at justice, truth will win out and judgement will be just; the virtuous will find themselves sent to the Islands of the Blessed, and the wicked will be put in Tartarus." From here it is a short step to the view of Cicero and others, that virtuous souls go to join the stars. Plato needs to be careful here, since he wants simultaneously to deny the normal gloomy view of the entire underworld (hence the censorship mentioned earlier) and to develop a strong theology of post-mortem punishment for the wicked. His way round this dilemma, clearly, is to emphasize the blessings that await the virtuous - not just the philosophers, but those who exhibit courage in battle and sundry other civic virtues. And the central point is important: judgement, even when negative, is emphatically a good thing, because it brings truth and justice to bear at last on the world of humans."

Isaac finished the section then adds. "Yes this belief of a soul being rewarded for their actions after death appears to have been taught by Plato, but that might just mean that he took the idea from the Old Testament."

"That's a stretch, but let's keep reading about the Greek philosophers, then we'll see what N.T. tells us about the Jewish concept of death," Adam suggests.

"OK. Your next note is for page 52." Isaac finds the page and a logical place to start reading.

"Plato did not sweep the board of subsequent opinion at either a popular or an intellectual level. Socrates' own followers were clearly unable to sustain the master's cheerfulness about his departure into the next world; if even they, with his own example, teaching and specific exhortation, could not refrain from inconsolable grief, it was perhaps unwise to suppose that anyone else would manage it either. In any case, other conflicting ideas were on offer as well. We glanced at Democritus and Epicureanism earlier; Stoic philosophers continued to debate such matters. Plato's ideas on the soul (and much else besides) were, in addition, severely modified by his equally influential pupil Aristotle. He took the view that the soul was the substance, or the species-form, of the living thing; this represents a turning away from, Page 53, the lively Platonic view of the soul as a more or less independent, and superior, entity to the body. Aristotle did allow, however, that 'the highest aspect of reason might be immortal and divine'. These exceptions do not, however, damage the general rule, followed with innumerable variations over the succeeding centuries: in Greek philosophy, care for and cure of the soul became a central preoccupation. And - this is, after all, the point for our present enquiry - neither in Plato nor in the major alternatives just mentioned do we find any suggestion that resurrection, the return to bodily life of the dead person, was either desirable or possible."

Adam voices his interpretation. "Ya, this section show that the Pagans had many different ideas about the soul, but none of them believed that it was possible to come back with any kind of a physical body. Only the Christians believed in a bodily resurrection after death and only because they had seen it happen to Jesus," Adam contends. "The first Christian converts did not believe they would be in a disembodied state after death. They believed they would be following the example of their Savior Jesus and be bodily resurrected after sleeping in their graves."

"Let me finish these points first, then we can talk," Isaac complains. "The next point that your notes talk about, picks up on page 54. A quarter ways down the page and it's underlined.

The similar testimony of Seneca, from a different social and cultural background, is itself evidence that such views were not confined to one cultural stream but made their way widely in the greco-roman world. For Seneca, the immortal human soul has come from beyond this world - from among the stars, in fact - and will make its way back there. Though one might hold that it simply disappeared, it is more likely that it will go to be with the gods. Death is either the end of everything, in which case there is nothing to be alarmed about, or it is a process of change, in which case, since the change is bound to be for the better, one should be glad. The soul, in fact, is at present kept as a prisoner within the body, which is both a weight and a penance to it. One should not, then, fear death; it is the birth day of one's eternity.' As long as one ceases to hope, one may also cease to fear." Once again, though the thought has developed somewhat, we are still clearly within the broad stream of Platonism, carrying Cicero and others along with it. And if death is to be welcomed, it follows that an early death is a good thing, despite popular opinion. 'Those whom the gods love die young'; few who quoted this at the death of Princess Diana will have realized that it goes back to the forth-century BC poet Menander, with echoes in other ancient plays.

I wondered where that saying came from. Just like the Billy Joel song, 'Only The Good Die Young'," Isaac states. "I knew it wasn't from the Bible, but I had no idea it was so old. I thought it might have been from Shakespeare or something."

"No, it originates from a Pagan belief," Adam states. "Just like the belief of the immortal soul, or spirit, being an innate part of man."

CHAPTER 11
OLD TESTAMENT SPEAKS

"Your next point is on page 90, it refers to the Old Testament beliefs of what it was like to be dead." Isaac runs his finger under the words to keep his place with the constant bouncing of the truck cab. Carefully he reads them out loud. "Page 90.

This combination of themes is taken up and repeated in what becomes the regular formula for dying kings. David 'slept with his ancestors, and was buried in the city of David', which is the more interesting since his ancestors were not buried there. 'Sleeping with one's ancestors', in other words, was not simply a way of saying that one was buried in the same grave or cave, but that one had gone to the world of the dead, there to be reunited with one's forebears. The minimal sort of 'life' that the shades had in Sheol, or in the grave, approximated more to sleep than to anything else known by the living. They might be momentarily aroused from their comatose state by an especially distinguished newcomer, as in Isaiah 14, or (as we shall see) by a necromancer; but their normal condition was to be asleep. They were not completely non-existent, but to all intents and purposes they were, so to speak, next to nothing.

Then more on page 93

This explicit link of life with the land and death of exile, coupled with the promise of restoration the other side of exile, is one of the forgotten roots of the fully developed hope of ancient Israel. The dead might be asleep; they might be almost nothing at all; but hope lived on within the covenant and promise of YHWH.

"See," Isaac sneers. "The dead aren't nothing at all, like you make them out to be. N.T. says that they could be woken up from their slumber, or brought back to life. What about that, your theory doesn't appear to be as strong as you say it is," Isaac protests. "You were right though, about having to be careful who you believe and trust," Isaac said with a distrustful tone in his voice as he looks at Adam warily.

"Yes, we do have to be prudent about where we get our information," Adam agreed. Not acknowledging Isaac's sarcasm. "Let's hear exactly what Isaiah 14 says."

Surprised by Adam's response, Isaac finds and then reads Isaiah 14.

"Isaiah 14 King James Version
1 For the LORD will have mercy on Jacob, and will yet choose Israel, and set them in their own land: and the strangers shall be joined with them, and they shall cleave to the house of Jacob.
2 And the people shall take them, and bring them to their place: and the house of Israel shall possess them in the land of the LORD for servants and handmaids: and they shall take them captives, whose captives they were; and they shall rule over their oppressors.

3 And it shall come to pass in the day that the LORD shall give thee rest from thy sorrow, and from thy fear, and from the hard bondage wherein thou wast made to serve,

4 That thou shalt take up this proverb against the king of Babylon, and say, How hath the oppressor ceased! the golden city ceased!

5 The LORD hath broken the staff of the wicked, and the sceptre of the rulers.

6 He who smote the people in wrath with a continual stroke, he that ruled the nations in anger, is persecuted, and none hindereth.

7 The whole earth is at rest, and is quiet: they break forth into singing.

8 Yea, the fir trees rejoice at thee, and the cedars of Lebanon, saying, Since thou art laid down, no feller is come up against us.

9 Hell from beneath is moved for thee to meet thee at thy coming: it stirreth up the dead for thee, even all the chief ones of the earth; it hath raised up from their thrones all the kings of the nations.

10 All they shall speak and say unto thee, Art thou also become weak as we? art thou become like unto us?

11 Thy pomp is brought down to the grave, and the noise of thy viols: the worm is spread under thee, and the worms cover thee.

12 How art thou fallen from heaven, O Lucifer, son of the morning! how art thou cut down to the ground, which didst weaken the nations!

13 For thou hast said in thine heart, I will ascend into heaven, I will exalt my throne above the stars of God: I will sit also upon the mount of the congregation, in the sides of the north:

14 I will ascend above the heights of the clouds; I will be like the most High.

15 Yet thou shalt be brought down to hell, to the sides of the pit.

16 They that see thee shall narrowly look upon thee, and consider thee, saying, Is this the man that made the earth to tremble, that did shake kingdoms;

17 That made the world as a wilderness, and destroyed the cities thereof; that opened not the house of his prisoners?

18 All the kings of the nations, even all of them, lie in glory, every one in his own house.

19 But thou art cast out of thy grave like an abominable branch, and as the raiment of those that are slain, thrust through with a sword, that go down to the stones of the pit; as a carcase trodden under feet.

20 Thou shalt not be joined with them in burial, because thou hast destroyed thy land, and slain thy people: the seed of evildoers shall never be renowned.

21 Prepare slaughter for his children for the iniquity of their fathers; that they do not rise, nor possess the land, nor fill the face of the world with cities.

22 For I will rise up against them, saith the LORD of hosts, and cut off from Babylon the name, and remnant, and son, and nephew, saith the LORD.

23 I will also make it a possession for the bittern, and pools of water: and I will sweep it with the besom of destruction, saith the LORD of hosts.

24 The LORD of hosts hath sworn, saying, Surely as I have thought, so shall it come to pass; and as I have purposed, so shall it stand:

25 That I will break the Assyrian in my land, and upon my mountains tread him under foot: then shall his yoke depart from off them, and his burden depart from off their shoulders.

26 This is the purpose that is purposed upon the whole earth: and this is the hand that is stretched out upon all the nations.

27 For the LORD of hosts hath purposed, and who shall disannul it? and his hand is stretched out, and who shall turn it back?

28 In the year that king Ahaz died was this burden.

29 Rejoice not thou, whole Palestina, because the rod of him that smote thee is broken: for out of the serpent's root shall come forth a cockatrice, and his fruit shall be a fiery flying serpent.

30 And the firstborn of the poor shall feed, and the needy shall lie down in safety: and I will kill thy root with famine, and he shall slay thy remnant.

31 Howl, O gate; cry, O city; thou, whole Palestina, art dissolved: for there shall come from the north a smoke, and none shall be alone in his appointed times.

32 What shall one then answer the messengers of the nation? That the LORD hath founded Zion, and the poor of his people shall trust in it."

"I don't think you need to read quite as many verses to get to the point. The scripture I heard about the dead being woken up was around eight or ten. Could you read that part again," Adam asks Isaac.

"Ya but I don't want to miss the context, or anything important. Apparently I have made that mistake before and I want to get it right." says Isaac with a sneer.

"8 Yea, the fir trees rejoice at thee, and the cedars of Lebanon, saying, Since thou art laid down, no feller is come up against us.

9 Hell from beneath is moved for thee to meet thee at thy coming: it stirreth up the dead for thee, even all the chief ones of the earth; it hath raised up from their thrones all the kings of the nations.

10 All they shall speak and say unto thee, Art thou also become weak as we? art thou become like unto us?

11 Thy pomp is brought down to the grave, and the noise of thy viols: the worm is spread under thee, and the worms cover thee."

"That was it," Adam said aggressively. "The language of this chapter is very poetic. It wouldn't be such a good idea to build a doctrine about the state of dead people from it. There are plenty of verses that tell us the dead know nothing, or that they are silent and can't even praise God. I'm surprised that N.T. hasn't come up with a theory that tells us, the trees of the forest can have rational thought and talk, using verse 8 as proof.

And you say that I can't be taken seriously as a credible source on what the Bible has to say. Do you call these verses credible as describing the true state of the dead, or are they poetic allegory and metaphor? Are these some of the verses you were talking about? Where you had to look at them as a whole, to understand how mankind has an eternal soul, verses that are taken out of their contextual meaning!"

Isaac defensively responds. "No! I hadn't thought of these verses, I can see how they seem poetic, the first verses were talking about Israel being re-established in their own land and how Babylon will be punished for its sins. I don't agree with N.T. that these verses are a description of the grave."

"Oh," Adam said sheepishly. "Well let's hear the story about the necromancer. Maybe it will be more accurate in its description of dead people."

"Got it coming," Isaac said brightly. He scans the text to find the proper verse. "Let's see, ya, this is it. 1 Samuel 28:6-25 KJV. I'll read the whole story for context, if that's all right?

6 And when Saul enquired of the LORD, the LORD answered him not, neither by dreams, nor by Urim, nor by prophets.

7 Then said Saul unto his servants, Seek me a woman that hath a familiar spirit, that I may go to her, and enquire of her. And his servants said to him, Behold, there is a woman that hath a familiar spirit at Endor.

8 And Saul disguised himself, and put on other raiment, and he went, and two men with him, and they came to the woman by night: and he said, I pray thee, divine unto me by the familiar spirit, and bring me him up, whom I shall name unto thee.

9 And the woman said unto him, Behold, thou knowest what Saul hath done, how he hath cut off those that have familiar spirits, and the wizards, out of the land: wherefore then layest thou a snare for my life, to cause me to die?

10 And Saul sware to her by the LORD, saying, As the LORD liveth, there shall no punishment happen to thee for this thing.

11 Then said the woman, Whom shall I bring up unto thee? And he said, Bring me up Samuel.

12 And when the woman saw Samuel, she cried with a loud voice: and the woman spake to Saul, saying, Why hast thou deceived me? for thou art Saul.

13 And the king said unto her, Be not afraid: for what sawest thou? And the woman said unto Saul, I saw gods ascending out of the earth.

14 And he said unto her, What form is he of? And she said, An old man cometh up; and he is covered with a mantle. And Saul perceived that it was Samuel, and he stooped with his face to the ground, and bowed himself.

15 And Samuel said to Saul, Why hast thou disquieted me, to bring me up? And Saul answered, I am sore distressed; for the Philistines make war against me, and God is departed from me, and answereth me no more, neither by prophets, nor by dreams: therefore I have called thee, that thou mayest make known unto me what I shall do.

16 Then said Samuel, Wherefore then dost thou ask of me, seeing the LORD is departed from thee, and is become thine enemy?

17 And the LORD hath done to him, as he spake by me: for the LORD hath rent the kingdom out of thine hand, and given it to thy neighbour, even to David:

18 Because thou obeyedst not the voice of the LORD, nor executedst his fierce wrath upon Amalek, therefore hath the LORD done this thing unto thee this day.

19 Moreover the LORD will also deliver Israel with thee into the hand of the Philistines: and to morrow shalt thou and thy sons be with me: the LORD also shall deliver the host of Israel into the hand of the Philistines.

20 Then Saul fell straightway all along on the earth, and was sore afraid, because of the words of Samuel: and there was no strength in him; for he had eaten no bread all the day, nor all the night.

21 And the woman came unto Saul, and saw that he was sore troubled, and said unto him, Behold, thine handmaid hath obeyed thy voice, and I have put my life in my hand, and have hearkened unto thy words which thou spakest unto me.

22 Now therefore, I pray thee, hearken thou also unto the voice of thine handmaid, and let me set a morsel of bread before thee; and eat, that thou mayest have strength, when thou goest on thy way.

23 But he refused, and said, I will not eat. But his servants, together with the woman, compelled him; and he hearkened unto their voice. So he arose from the earth, and sat upon the bed.

24 And the woman had a fat calf in the house; and she hasted, and killed it, and took flour, and kneaded it, and did bake unleavened bread thereof:

25 And she brought it before Saul, and before his servants; and they did eat. Then they rose up, and went away that night.

11-19 are the verses mostly talking about bringing the dead back to life," Isaac gives his overview of the scriptures he just read. "Now I must say, N.T. seems to have these verses in context."

"Yes it does seem that way," Agreed Adam. "It is a story about the dead. But was Samuel actually brought back to life? Or was Saul beguiled by the woman with the familiar spirits? In verse 13 we see that Saul didn't see Samuel, but took the woman's word for what she saw. We need to keep in mind that she had a familiar satanic spirit. These spirits are real; they are the ones who lead us away from the truths of God. She was often in contact with this spirit and was known for her visions. Verse 14 explains to us, Saul perceived that what she was describing was Samuel. He didn't actually see Samuel."

"Yes but in verse 15 Saul talks to Samuel," Isaac contends. "That would make Samuel alive, brought back from the dead."

"I am surprised you think Satan has the power to raise the dead," Adam says to Isaac as he steers around an upcoming pot hole. "I thought God was the only one capable of giving life. I'm sure I read that somewhere."

Isaac pauses for a moment then nods his head as he searches the lap top files. Moments later he triumphantly says with a smile. "Here are a few places,

1 Samuel 2:6.
The LORD killeth, and maketh alive: he bringeth down to the grave, and bringeth up.

Deuteronomy 32:39.
See now that I, even I, am he, and there is no god with me: I kill, and I make alive; I wound, and I heal: neither is there any that can deliver out of my hand.

John 1:3-4.
All things were made by him; and without him was not any thing made that was made.
4 In him was life; and the life was the light of men."

"Well then," Adam states matter of factually. "If it is only God who can raise the dead and God wasn't talking to King Saul, then what the woman saw couldn't have been Samuel the prophet of God, but was her familiar spirit giving her a message, that Saul perceived to be Samuel. Going by the scripture, when Saul bowed down, he would have been bowing to the woman who was seeing the vision. The familiar spirit may have been audibly talking through the woman directly to Saul. But to say that Samuel was brought back from the dead, by Satan, to speak to Saul using this passage as proof, displays a superficial understanding of what is actually going on.

As we have already found out, mankind is completely mortal. There is no part of us that lives on beyond our physical lives. God, who has a perfect memory, will re-create us within his time frame through a resurrection process. Once God resurrects us, we will be the same people we were before we died. Our neurological contacts and brain chemistry is what holds our emotions, memories, thoughts and personality. Once they are restored to their original state, we will be back to life as if we had never died.

The Bible does not tell us we have a conscious life after death, but rather tells us the opposite; it tells us we will have no thoughts or ambitions at all in the grave. We will sleep the slumber of death. That is why Christian's incorruptible inheritance that is undefiled and doesn't fade away, is reserved in heaven for us and will be revealed at our resurrection. Christians are resurrected into immortality, receiving their inheritance of eternal life at the return of Jesus, just as Jesus told us in John 6."

"Let me read that last reference," Isaac was quick to start a search. After reading a couple of sites, Isaac finds the verses and reads them out loud. "I think this is it,

1 Peter 1:3-5.
Blessed be the God and Father of our Lord Jesus Christ, which according to his abundant mercy hath begotten us again unto a lively hope by the resurrection of Jesus Christ from the dead,
4 To an inheritance incorruptible, and undefiled, and that fadeth not away, reserved in heaven for you,
5 Who are kept by the power of God through faith unto salvation ready to be revealed in the last time.

I can see how you think that you're right," Isaac confesses. "But N.T. Wright, my professors and virtually all the published Bible scholars say you're wrong. Why don't they agree with you if you are so right? They have studied the Bible more than you."

Adam replies quickly. "I don't know why others that read the Bible fail to see what I see so clearly. Maybe that would be a good question for them," Adam leans forward, resting his elbows on the large steering wheel as he stares ahead through the windshield. "I may not know much, but I do know what I read. Does the Bible contradict itself? I don't believe it will and I thought you believed that as well."

"I do believe that," Isaac asserted forcefully. "The Bible will not contradict its self."

"Well then, can Satan raise the dead? Does he have power to bring the dead back to life here on the earth? If he does, show me you scriptural proof," Adam pressed Isaac for scriptural proof. "As we have learned, assuming what the bible says is often a lot different than understanding what the scriptures have to say on a subject.

We agreed at the start, it isn't what people say that matters, it's what God tells us through the Bible that's important. After reading the scriptures N.T. used to describe the dead in the grave I have to conclude that Mr. Wright was incorrect in his assessment of those verses. I agree with Paul and the Pharisees that the dead are just that, dead, with no attributes of life at all. The best analogy to describe death is the same one used in the Bible. It is like a deep sleep, knowing and thinking nothing."

Adam pauses for a moment of reflection and then states with a hint of sadness in his voice, "It's as though most Christians are living their spiritual lives in a post-truth reality. They think they are following the teachings of the Bible, but never take the time to prove their beliefs against what the Bible actually teaches."

"What's that? Are you making up words now too? Isaac scoffs derisively. "Post-truth? What's that supposed to mean? Isaac is shaking his head in bewilderment.

"It's a word that got used a lot during the Trump presidential campaign. It is was formally recognized as a word that same year, although I liked the Stephen Colbert word 'truthiness' better," Adam responded without hesitation.

"I'd better look that one up for myself," Isaac retorted, starting to type. "OK, so it is a word," Isaac begrudgingly agrees. "Here is what the *oxforddictionaries.com* has to say about it," He reads out loud, thinking the word will not apply to their conversation.

"adjective
Relating to or denoting circumstances in which objective facts are less influential in shaping public opinion than appeals to emotion and personal belief:

'in this era of post-truth politics, it's easy to cherry-pick data and come to whatever conclusion you desire'

'some commentators have observed that we are living in a post-truth age'

This word is meant to be used in a political context, not in a religious one," Isaac protested. "You're taking it out of context."

Adam responds coolly, "No I'm not! Denominations have always tried to shape public opinion with appeals to emotion and personal belief. It's not only a political word. If Christians only use the objective facts from the Bible and if the Bible is the non-contradictory word of God, then why are there so many different denominations, with such a wide range of practice?"

CHAPTER 12
THE SECOND COMING

Isaac retorts back at Adam heatedly. "Well if they are all wrong, what do you believe the plan of God to be? You seem to have definite thoughts on the subject. How is God going to save humanity and have them as his children? It's easy to complain and pick ideas apart. It's far more difficult to give a seamless, Bible based plan where humanity receives salvation."

"I don't have a plan like that," Adam admits.

"I'm not surprised in the least," Isaac says snidely. "Most people can only pick apart ideas of their intellectual superiors, while they don't have a single original thought of their own."

"Yup. You got me figured out," Adam readily admits. "I don't have one original thought about the plans God has for humanity. But I will share with you the plan that God has described in the Bible. I can guarantee that it isn't mine and that it's all God's. But first we need to finish discussing how the immortal soul idea is not anywhere to be found in the Old Testament. If it had been there the Pharisees would have found it, but as N.T. pointed out, they believed in a physical body resurrection that has two distinct parts, death for a while, then a resurrection back to a physical life.

It was the pagans that had the concept of an immortal soul that became a disembodied spirit after death. As Mr. Wright described, they believed in a one step process, just like the belief that Christians go directly to Heaven to be with Jesus when they die and sinners go directly to Hell for torment.

God modified Paul's traditional Pharisaical belief in the two-step resurrection through the example of Jesus, who after being completely dead, was resurrected to a new body that was not just physical, but made up of spirit as well. This spirit-physical body is what those who are called and accept Jesus in this life will be resurrected into, when Jesus returns to the earth. Until then, they sleep in their graves, a two-step process. Just like the example Jesus left us.

You see, N.T. Wright was not out to discover how the plan of God was to unfold. He was looking narrowly at where the idea of a bodily resurrection came from, to set theologians and clergy that taught Jesus wasn't bodily resurrected straight. N.T.'s book also showed the history of the immortal soul belief and how it isn't biblical. A fact that Mr. Wright personally ignores, as he seems to believe in a personal spirit life somewhere after we die. A one step process, just like the Greek philosophers believed in. In his book he talks about going to be with Jesus after death, which is fine if you are a Christian, but he doesn't provide much information, or hope, for those who are not. Where do all the non-Christians go? What hope is there for them?"

"OK!" Isaac exclaims exasperatedly. "N.T. doesn't appear to believe the same as the Pharisees. But Jesus didn't like them either. They were the ones who had Jesus crucified. Why should N.T. agree with what they believed?"

"Because they believed the Old Testament," Adam replied passionately. "They knew the word of God up to that point in time, and having an immortal soul was not included in their beliefs, which proves that if you want to stay true to what the Bible teaches in the Old Testament, you won't either."

"Well the New Testament tells me that I am born again of the Holy Spirit. It tells me that if I believe in Jesus I will never die, that I now have eternal life," Isaac states frantically, growing increasingly red faced.

"Yes," Adam replies. "That is what you will inherit. Those things will come true for you, in the future. You are an 'heir' to the promise, not a 'possessor' of it. You do not have it now, today, in this life." Letting the air out of his driver's seat's suspension, Adam drops within arm's reach of the floor. Bending sideways towards his side window he reaches down to the floor with his left hand. From under his gloves, by the fire extinguisher, he retrieves a razor knife. Returning the seat to its normal ride height, he shuffles the knife to his right hand. Opening it so that about four inches of the blade is exposed, he holds it out to Isaac. Looking Isaac in the eye he states stone-faced, "One way to prove it for sure, cut your throat and we'll see how immortal you are!"

Isaac gives Adam a long look of disdain, then replies, "Weren't you going to tell me God's plan for humanity."

"I suppose you see my point. Feel free to check all of my scriptural references," invites Adam, as he closes the knife and drops it back on the floor by his door.

"Oh don't worry. I'll be checking all of them for accuracy," snarled Isaac.

"I believe you are aware of the fact that humans are mortal and when they die they are dead, with no hope of a future apart from the grace of God. I won't recover that ground," states Adam. "I will start with the resurrections as they occur in order with the return of Jesus to the earth."

"Resurrections?" questions Isaac skeptically. "You mean there are two of them?"

"No. There are not two of them. There are several," Adam says patiently. "One resurrection for each group of people, but you will get me side tracked if I try to explain more now, just wait and you will see how it all works out. God will make sure everyone has an opportunity to accept his offer of life. If anyone willingly refuses his offer of life, he will reluctantly give them what they desire and let them reject eternal life and have death instead."

Exhaling heavily, Isaac reluctantly gets himself ready to look up the scriptures Adam will eventually refer too. "OK. You can start now. I'm listening," Isaac says with a whine.

Clearing his throat noisily, Adam roles down his window and hoping to miss the trailer behind him, spits out of it as far as he could. Wiping his mouth with the back of his hand he turns to

Isaac and without missing a beat says. "Before Jesus returns, the tribulation is in full swing. The church is in a place of safety and the two witnesses are preaching to the world.

There are different thoughts on how long the tribulation lasts, some think seven, others say three and a half years. I think the man of perdition and the beast are in charge for a total of seven years, but they don't start persecuting Christians until the last three and a half years. So the tribulation part is three and a half years long."

"OK. Stop now till I find those references," Isaac interjects. "I have heard about that controversy and have been wondering where people get their time lines from." Doing some word and topic searches on Adam's Bible-program laden lap top, Isaac finds some relevant scriptures and reads them aloud.

"Revelation 12:14-17
14 And to the woman were given two wings of a great eagle, that she might fly into the wilderness, into her place, where she is nourished for a time, and times, and half a time, from the face of the serpent.
15 And the serpent cast out of his mouth water as a flood after the woman, that he might cause her to be carried away of the flood.
16 And the earth helped the woman, and the earth opened her mouth, and swallowed up the flood which the dragon cast out of his mouth.
17 And the dragon was wroth with the woman, and went to make war with the remnant of her seed, which keep the commandments of God, and have the testimony of Jesus Christ.

This is about the church being safe for three and a half years, then some of its, seed, being persecuted. Maybe those seed, are people who herd about Jesus before the church fled. Like real seeds starting to grow, but don't become Christians until after the church is taken to a safe place and they, after becoming Christians, are persecuted during the tribulation."

"That could be. I don't think there are many verses that talk about them other than in the book of Revelations," Adam agreed.

"Here are the two witnesses preaching to the world," Isaac continued.

"Revelation 11:3
And I will give power unto my two witnesses, and they shall prophesy a thousand two hundred and threescore days, clothed in sackcloth.

That sounds like three and a half years, but I'd have to do the math," Isaac approximated.
"Here is a bunch of scriptures that support three and a half years of persecution.

Revelation 11:2
But the court which is without the temple leave out, and measure it not; for it is given unto the Gentiles: and the holy city shall they tread under foot forty and two months.

Revelation 13:5-7
And there was given unto him a mouth speaking great things and blasphemies; and power was given unto him to continue forty and two months.
6 And he opened his mouth in blasphemy against God, to blaspheme his name, and his tabernacle, and them that dwell in heaven.

7 And it was given unto him to make war with the saints, and to overcome them: and power was given him over all kindreds, and tongues, and nations.

Revelation 17:6

I saw that the woman was drunk with the blood of God's holy people, the blood of those who bore testimony to Jesus.

Matthew 24:21-22

For then shall be great tribulation, such as was not since the beginning of the world to this time, no, nor ever shall be.

22 And except those days should be shortened, there should no flesh be saved: but for the elect's sake those days shall be shortened.

Daniel 12:7

Then I heard the man clothed in linen, who *was* above the waters of the river, when he held up his right hand and his left hand to heaven, and swore by Him who lives forever, that *it shall be* for a time, times, and half *a time;* and when the power of the holy people has been completely shattered, all these *things* shall be finished.

Here is the verse that talks about trouble coming in the middle of the week. You have to use a day for a year interpretation. As well, there is debate about when this was to happen, some claim that it has already taken place.

Daniel 9:27

And he shall confirm the covenant with many for one week: and in the midst of the week he shall cause the sacrifice and the oblation to cease, and for the overspreading of abominations he shall make it desolate, even until the consummation, and that determined shall be poured upon the desolate.

All the different time line possibilities can get confusing, but I do agree with you that there will be a tribulation and it will last for three and a half years. It will be a terrible time to be alive for those who are Christians. Things will be so bad, that if God doesn't intervene, no one would be left alive.

Revelation 17:6
I saw that the woman was drunk with the blood of God's holy people, the blood of those who bore testimony to Jesus.

Matthew 24:21-22 King James Version.
For then shall be great tribulation, such as was not since the beginning of the world to this time, no, nor ever shall be.
22 And except those days should be shortened, there should no flesh be saved: but for the elect's sake those days shall be shortened.

Mark 13:19-20
For in those days shall be affliction, such as was not from the beginning of the creation which God created unto this time, neither shall be.

20 And except that the Lord had shortened those days, no flesh should be saved: but for the elect's sake, whom he hath chosen, he hath shortened the days."

"Those are all good verses to highlight my points," Adam agrees. "I don't get all that worried about the seven year thing. It makes sense to me either way, if it's included or not. The three and a half years of tribulation is very straight forward to my understanding."

"Yes I agree with you about that, but it is nice to see where others are getting their ideas from," Isaac pointed out. "OK, I am satisfied with your references, so you can continue with your ideas, what happens next."

"No, no, no, no, uh-uh," Adam said shaking his head while wagging his finger at Isaac. "I told you, this is not my story or ideas. If it isn't from the Bible then it's not worth anything, but if it is accurately understood from the scriptures, then we had better believe it."

"Beeeg your paaardon," Isaac says over dramatically. "Please continue explaining the plaaan of God using, Biiible scriptures."

Adam rolls his eyes and frowns at Isaac. "Just remember, this knowledge is coming from the word of God." Pausing for a moment, Adam picks up the story where he left off.

"Alright, Jesus returns at the end of the tribulation. As he descends from the clouds, the dead believers are resurrected and rise to meet him in the air. Then those that believe in him, who are alive, are changed into their new spirit bodies and they all join him in the air as he continues to descend back to the earth to fight the Beast at the battle of Armageddon."

"Now we have covered the verses that talk about this resurrection before. So I know about them," Isaac states confidently. "But I better find the ones about Armageddon." Typing out his inquiry Isaac gets an almost instantaneous response.

"Here it is describing the battle in Revelation 16.

14 For they are the spirits of devils, working miracles, which go forth unto the kings of the earth and of the whole world, to gather them to the battle of that great day of God Almighty.

15 Behold, I come as a thief. Blessed is he that watcheth, and keepeth his garments, lest he walk naked, and they see his shame.

16 And he gathered them together into a place called in the Hebrew tongue Armageddon.

17 And the seventh angel poured out his vial into the air; and there came a great voice out of the temple of heaven, from the throne, saying, It is done.

18 And there were voices, and thunders, and lightnings; and there was a great earthquake, such as was not since men were upon the earth, so mighty an earthquake, and so great.

19 And the great city was divided into three parts, and the cities of the nations fell: and great Babylon came in remembrance before God, to give unto her the cup of the wine of the fierceness of his wrath.

20 And every island fled away, and the mountains were not found.

21 And there fell upon men a great hail out of heaven, every stone about the weight of a talent: and men blasphemed God because of the plague of the hail; for the plague thereof was exceeding great.

And again, talking about the same battle but not using the name Armageddon.

Revelation 14:14-20

And I looked, and behold a white cloud, and upon the cloud one sat like unto the Son of man, having on his head a golden crown, and in his hand a sharp sickle.

15 And another angel came out of the temple, crying with a loud voice to him that sat on the cloud, Thrust in thy sickle, and reap: for the time is come for thee to reap; for the harvest of the earth is ripe.

16 And he that sat on the cloud thrust in his sickle on the earth; and the earth was reaped.

17 And another angel came out of the temple which is in heaven, he also having a sharp sickle.

18 And another angel came out from the altar, which had power over fire; and cried with a loud cry to him that had the sharp sickle, saying, Thrust in thy sharp sickle, and gather the clusters of the vine of the earth; for her grapes are fully ripe.

19 And the angel thrust in his sickle into the earth, and gathered the vine of the earth, and cast it into the great winepress of the wrath of God.

20 And the winepress was trodden without the city, and blood came out of the winepress, even unto the horse bridles, by the space of a thousand and six hundred furlongs.

Wow it sounds like quite a battle," Isaac says wide eyed. "It's no wonder that every eye will see Jesus when he returns. I'm not sure how the secret rapture fits in with Jesus coming back and snatching his believers away, if this describes his return to the earth."

"That's why we shouldn't be afraid to prove all things against what the Bible tells us. It's easy to get carried away with the popular beliefs of the day, thinking they must be right if everyone else believes them," Adam says. "Finding Bible truth is a bit like panning for gold. You put a shovel full of gravel and dirt in your pan and then you slowly wash away all the light stuff. Soon you only have the heavier bits left. Then you rinse them some more until only the specks of gold are left."

"How is that like reading the Bible?" Isaac questioned irritated.

Adam looked over to see Isaac frowning at him. "The gravel and dirt are Bible verses," Adam said. "You have to inspect each one for bits of truth on the subject you're studying. Then you take all of the verses that pertain to your topic and see what they teach you. As we have found out in our recent conversations, we may think a verse tells us something that it doesn't."

"Oh. I get it now," Isaac grunts contentedly. "It's not a great analogy. Here is more about the battle, only we are given more information as the Beast and false prophet are now thrown into the lake of fire.

Revelation 19:11-21

And I saw heaven opened, and behold a white horse; and he that sat upon him was called Faithful and True, and in righteousness he doth judge and make war.

12 His eyes were as a flame of fire, and on his head were many crowns; and he had a name written, that no man knew, but he himself.

13 And he was clothed with a vesture dipped in blood: and his name is called The Word of God.

14 And the armies which were in heaven followed him upon white horses, clothed in fine linen, white and clean.

15 And out of his mouth goeth a sharp sword, that with it he should smite the nations: and he shall rule them with

a rod of iron: and he treadeth the winepress of the fierceness and wrath of Almighty God.

16 And he hath on his vesture and on his thigh a name written, KING OF KINGS, AND LORD OF LORDS.

17 And I saw an angel standing in the sun; and he cried with a loud voice, saying to all the fowls that fly in the midst of heaven, Come and gather yourselves together unto the supper of the great God;

18 That ye may eat the flesh of kings, and the flesh of captains, and the flesh of mighty men, and the flesh of horses, and of them that sit on them, and the flesh of all men, both free and bond, both small and great.

19 And I saw the beast, and the kings of the earth, and their armies, gathered together to make war against him that sat on the horse, and against his army.

20 And the beast was taken, and with him the false prophet that wrought miracles before him, with which he deceived them that had received the mark of the beast, and them that worshipped his image. These both were cast alive into a lake of fire burning with brimstone.

21 And the remnant were slain with the sword of him that sat upon the horse, which sword proceeded out of his mouth: and all the fowls were filled with their flesh."

"Any more?" Adam asked as he adjusted himself in his driver's seat.

"No, that should prove your point. What's next?" Isaac demanded.

CHAPTER 13
NEW WORLD ORDER

Ready with where he should pick up the thought, Adam continues. "Well as you just read the false prophet and the Beast are thrown into the lake of fire at the return of Jesus. Now we are told, Satan is chained up in there as well. For a thousand years the world will be free of his evil influence to sin. The world will be rebuilt and healed of its wounds with the help of the people that are left alive on the world after the battle of Armageddon. They will repopulate the earth and take care of it under the guidance of the newly resurrected children of God. These people and their offspring will be the first humans to live on the earth without the influence of Satan pulling them towards sin. It will be a thousand years of peace and prosperity."

Isaac nods. "I've heard people talk about this millennial time, but it never fit in with going to heaven. They couldn't figure out how the time line worked, so they supposed it was poetic scripture and not meant to be taken literally."

"Well they were right," Stated Adam confidently. "It doesn't fit in with going to heaven, because we don't go to heaven. God brings his Kingdom to us. Humanity isn't supposed to escape the mess they've made here on the earth, we have to stay and fix our problems, our physical, spiritual and social problems."

Isaac starts typing. "Let me find those scriptures," he says with vigour. "Here is one about Satan being chained up.

Revelation 20:1-3
And I saw an angel come down from heaven, having the key of the bottomless pit and a great chain in his hand.
2 And he laid hold on the dragon, that old serpent, which is the Devil, and Satan, and bound him a thousand years,

3 And cast him into the bottomless pit, and shut him up, and set a seal upon him, that he should deceive the nations no more, till the thousand years should be fulfilled: and after that he must be loosed a little season.

It says that he will be let go after the thousand years is over, why is that?"

"We'll get to it," Adam says.

"OK," Isaac replies. "But I have never heard this story before."

"Is it coming out of the Bible?" Adam questions.

"Ya, whatever," Retorts Isaac. "Here are some more scriptures supporting your story. Oh sorry, I mean the story from, the Bible, about the plan of God."

Adam shoots a look at Isaac but refrains from responding. Isaac is grinning as he looks up more scripture.

"Here are some more.

Ezekiel 47:8-9

Then said he unto me, These waters issue out toward the east country, and go down into the desert, and go into the sea: which being brought forth into the sea, the waters shall be healed.

9 And it shall come to pass, that every thing that liveth, which moveth, whithersoever the rivers shall come, shall live: and there shall be a very great multitude of fish, because these waters shall come thither: for they shall be healed; and every thing shall live whither the river cometh.

And more here in

Romans 8:20-23

For the creature was made subject to vanity, not
willingly, but by reason of him who hath subjected the
same in hope,
21 Because the creature itself also shall be delivered from
the bondage of corruption into the glorious liberty of the
children of God.
22 For we know that the whole creation groaneth and
travaileth in pain together until now.
23 And not only they, but ourselves also, which have the
firstfruits of the Spirit, even we ourselves groan within
ourselves, waiting for the adoption, to wit, the redemption
of our body.

Nature gets rebuilt when the believers get their new bodies."

"Exactly!" Adam says enthusiastically. "We receive our new
bodies and the world gets rebuilt when Jesus returns."

"I have heard these verses put in a different context, but we
can keep going. I want to see how this plays out," Isaac states
curiously. "So you believe that the newly born physical-spirit
children of God are the leaders in this millennial time of
restoration."

"That's Right," Adam nods. "Look it up. We are to become
Kings and Priests. Kings and Priests over who?"

Isaac frowns and types some more. "Revelation 20:6," he
hollers over the truck noise.

"Blessed and holy is he that hath part in the first
resurrection: on such the second death hath no power, but
they shall be priests of God and of Christ, and shall reign
with him a thousand years."

After more searching Isaac finds another section of scripture.
"Here as well, I think it will be on topic.

Isaiah 30:18-22

And therefore will the LORD wait, that he may be gracious unto you, and therefore will he be exalted, that he may have mercy upon you: for the LORD is a God of judgment: blessed are all they that wait for him.

19 For the people shall dwell in Zion at Jerusalem: thou shalt weep no more: he will be very gracious unto thee at the voice of thy cry; when he shall hear it, he will answer thee.

20 And though the Lord give you the bread of adversity, and the water of affliction, yet shall not thy teachers be removed into a corner any more, but thine eyes shall see thy teachers:

21 And thine ears shall hear a word behind thee, saying, This is the way, walk ye in it, when ye turn to the right hand, and when ye turn to the left.

22 Ye shall defile also the covering of thy graven images of silver, and the ornament of thy molten images of gold: thou shalt cast them away as a menstruous cloth; thou shalt say unto it, Get thee hence.

I suppose this will be the first time that mankind has lived without the influence of Satan, because he was in the Garden of Eden at the beginning. It should be such a joyous time for humanity, everyone happily following in the loving ways of God."

"No, I don't think so. Why should people be any better than the angels were?" Adam contends. "They lived with God in piece, but one third of them rejected his ways of love and it ended in open warfare."

"You can be such a wet blanket!" Isaac huffed. "I just read that people will live in the ways of God. Not only that, but they will be personally guided in the way they should go. You're such a confusing person; why not agree that they will all be living in a happy paradise?"

Adam shakes his head as he answers. "I'd love for it to be a utopian paradise, if that was true. But people are people, with or without Satan. Our minds are continually bent towards sin. Read about what happens to those who don't follow God's ways. Some people have to be disciplined before they follow God."

"I'll look that up, along with the mind of man," said Isaac. "Ya, here it is. Genesis 6:5.

And God saw that the wickedness of man was great in the earth, and that every imagination of the thoughts of his heart was only evil continually.

As well as here,

Jeremiah 17:9
The heart is deceitful above all things, and desperately wicked: who can know it?

I suppose we are wicked. I will start to look for verses on those who don't follow God." Isaac types his next search into the lap top. "Here's some,

Zechariah 14:16-17
And it shall come to pass, that every one that is left of all the nations which came against Jerusalem shall even go up from year to year to worship the King, the LORD of hosts, and to keep the feast of tabernacles.
17 And it shall be, that whoso will not come up of all the families of the earth unto Jerusalem to worship the King, the LORD of hosts, even upon them shall be no rain."

"Yes, not everyone will willingly follow God. Notice that they aren't referred to as his children, but as his people, to become a child of God we have to be led by the Spirit, accept Jesus and have our sins forgiven," Adam tells Isaac.

"Yes I did notice that subtle difference. Jesus told us to call out to God, not only as father, but daddy, making it a much more intimate relationship. Here is a verse for your point," Isaac said before reading aloud.

Romans 8:14-15
For as many as are led by the Spirit of God, they are the sons of God.
15 For ye have not received the spirit of bondage again to fear; but ye have received the Spirit of adoption, whereby we cry, Abba, Father."

Adam continues laying out the plan as he understands it. "So here we have a world rebuilt and healed from the devastating legacy of mankind. Remember that if God had not stepped in, no flesh would have survived."

"Oh. I can find those easy." Isaac exclaimed excitedly.

"Mark 13:20
And except that the Lord had shortened those days, no flesh should be saved: but for the elect's sake, whom he hath chosen, he hath shortened the days.

And then again in,

Matthew 24:22.
And except those days should be shortened, there should no flesh be saved: but for the elect's sake those days shall be shortened.

I like those verses because the Christians are why the world gets saved. If it wasn't for us, God would let everyone die."

"Yes that is true," Adam agrees. "But don't forget that the word flesh is not only restricted to human beings. Animals are also referred to as flesh."

"I didn't think of that," Isaac admitted. "Christians are even more important in that context. The entire world is only saved because of us."

"Ya maybe, but I wouldn't go around bragging about it," Adam admonished. "Like I was saying, this group of people will not have Satan around to bother them. I believe the people who are born into this thousand year period will not be as spiritually strong as those of us who have to fight against Satan daily. My own speculation is that some of them will not believe that there is even such a being as Satan. Nothing in their world would have revealed him to them. Their life experience will be of generations of peace and prosperity. He potentially will be remembered only through ancient tales and stories.

I have no scriptural proof, but I believe that since these people will be taught and called by God to learn of his ways during their lives in the Millennium, free from the pull of sin, that this will be their time to choose to follow him and gain eternal life. This being the first time they have been alive, I think those who die not accepting Jesus during the millennium, will be included in the resurrection of the condemned as it ends with the second death. All those who willingly reject the deliverance of Jesus will be thrown into the lake of fire.

This resurrection of the condemned would provide closure for the family of God and a time of sober reflection for those brought back to physical life to face their punishment. They will have no excuses as there was no external force of sin that lead them to reject God. The decision to go their own way would have come from inside of them, reflecting who they truly are."

"What do you mean, I think, I believe, I have no scriptural proof?" Isaac asked indignantly. "You said that this was the provable plan of God? Not the imaginings of some old senile trucker. Why should anyone trust and believe in your speculations?"

"The only part I am speculating on is the process those alive during the millennium go through to become children of God," Adam strongly stated defensively. "Following the two prime directives, of everyone gets to choose Jesus and God wants all that will accept him as children, both of which we previously discussed and agreed on, then this is the most likely scenario to me. I could be wrong and I'm open to any ideas that you may have on how these millennial people come into the family of God, or meet their demise. Do you have any thoughts we should consider?"

"No no. This is your story time. I have no idea about what you might be imagining. I'm just shocked that you so openly admit the lack of scriptural proof for your speculations," Isaac's tone was mockingly snide.

"I am only speculating on one small aspect of the overall plan that God has laid out in his word. You read the verses talking about the millennium and the people who live during that time period. Were you not reading from the Bible?" Adam's voice was forceful and loud.

"Of course I was," Isaac wasn't expecting Adam's verbal retaliation. "But maybe your reference verses are all supposed to be understood as poetry and metaphor," Isaac said waving his hand in a dramatic gesture.

"Ya, the language used is a bit optimistic, but most of the verses describing the blessings of God, given to people rescued in the end times, are. It's certainly not as poetic as when trees have conversations with people who have died. Do you feel I have taken some verses out of context?" Adam questioned with concern. "If so, how and which ones?"

"Oh I couldn't critique them on the fly. To find all of your errors would take a lot of time and study. I am just doing my best to make sure your references are close to being accurate," Isaac explained, using his best scholarly tones.

"Well that's good. Just remember that those references are coming from the infallible word of God. It comes down to what you trust the most, Man's ideas, or the Bible?" Adam states bluntly.

"Oh for sure, I believe the Bible. I just don't know how accurately you put the scriptures together. But I am ready to look up more of them if you want to continue. That is if your rendition has any more scriptures to verify," Isaac returns to his demeaning tone.

"You will be finding several more before we get to the end," Adam says confidently. "At the closing of the millennium, the world will be left completely healed from its life ending wounds. This is when the bulk of humanity will have their time to come to God and accept Jesus as their saviour. Everyone since the Garden of Eden who never had the opportunity to hear or learn of Jesus and the forgiveness that comes only from him, can now have free access to that gift. Whether they died in infancy, or had their eyes blinded to God for whatever reason, they will now have a life time of one hundred years to decide if they want to follow God or not."

"Ha. You'll have to help me find those scriptures. What should I use for a search phrase, Aesop's fables?" Isaac jeered. "That's not from the Bible!"

"Have I been very wrong so far?" Adam asked. "We have already looked up verses showing that God has blinded the eyes of people. We have to be called by God to come to Jesus.

For this resurrection, look up something like, the rest did not live until after the thousands years were over."

"OK. I'll give it a try." Isaac tries skeptically a couple of times, then perks up with, "How about this?

Revelation 20:4-6
And I saw thrones, and they sat upon them, and judgment
was given unto them: and I saw the souls of them that
were beheaded for the witness of Jesus, and for the word
of God, and which had not worshipped the beast, neither
his image, neither had received his mark upon their
foreheads, or in their hands; and they lived and reigned
with Christ a thousand years.
5 But the rest of the dead lived not again until the
thousand years were finished. This is the first
resurrection.
6 Blessed and holy is he that hath part in the first
resurrection: on such the second death hath no power, but
they shall be priests of God and of Christ, and shall reign
with him a thousand years.

If the rest of the dead come back to life after the thousand
years is finished, why is this resurrection called the first
resurrection?"

"It's not. Those in the first resurrection are the ones who are
holy and blessed, the ones raised when Jesus returns. And that is
not the first resurrection if you believe Jesus led the way as the
first fruit. Jesus was the first to be resurrected to spirit-physical
life, as opposed to normal physical life, like many other
resurrections the Bible tells us about. So you can see the term, first
resurrection, depends on your starting point of reference," Adam
went on to explain further.

"Those raised at the end of the millennium would actually be
in the second mass resurrection of mankind. Counting from after
the resurrection of Jesus, those who are raised at his return are in
the first resurrection, they are holy and blessed. They rule with
Jesus during the millennium.

Then all of humanity that didn't have their opportunity to accept Jesus, are raised after the millennium is over, but before Satan is freed from his restraints. They have a lifetime of one hundred years free of Satan's influence, to decide if they want to follow Jesus or not. This would be the second major resurrection of mankind."

"Wow, this sure is nothing like what I have ever heard before. How do I find that in the Bible? Is it under, sinner's second chance, or, free pass to heaven?" Isaac shakes his head with a frown. "You sure are in left field. Heck, I don't even think you're in the ball park. Let me read Revelations twenty, verses four through six again.

And I saw thrones, and they sat upon them, and judgment was given unto them: and I saw the souls of them that were beheaded for the witness of Jesus, and for the word of God, and which had not worshipped the beast, neither his image, neither had received his mark upon their foreheads, or in their hands; and they lived and reigned with Christ a thousand years.
5 But the rest of the dead lived not again until the thousand years were finished. This is the first resurrection.
6 Blessed and holy is he that hath part in the first resurrection: on such the second death hath no power, but they shall be priests of God and of Christ, and shall reign with him a thousand years."

Adam jumps in, "Exactly, the sentence 'This is the first resurrection.' goes with verse six. The King James scholars added the punctuation as they saw best at the time, like they did with the thief on the cross. The punctuation is misleading there as well. Jesus told the thief he would be with him in paradise, but not on the same day. Jesus was in the grave for the next three days, proving he was our messiah."

"That's not how I've ever read it," Isaac says in a huff. "The thief was with Jesus in paradise that very day. Here let me read it.

Luke 23:39-43

39 And one of the malefactors which were hanged railed on him, saying, If thou be Christ, save thyself and us.
40 But the other answering rebuked him, saying, Dost not thou fear God, seeing thou art in the same condemnation?
41 And we indeed justly; for we receive the due reward of our deeds: but this man hath done nothing amiss.
42 And he said unto Jesus, Lord, remember me when thou comest into thy kingdom.
43 And Jesus said unto him, Verily I say unto thee, Today shalt thou be with me in paradise.

There is nothing wrong with the punctuation. Your just trying to twist the plain speaking word of God to suit yourself!" Isaac proclaims. "The word of God is truth. You just don't like how it doesn't fit in with all of your conspiracy theories."

"Oh. Didn't we already prove that Jesus was dead in the grave for three full days?" Adam quickly responded. "He told the women not to touch him on Sunday morning because he had not yet ascended to his father. He was in the grave for three days after talking to the thief on the cross, not in paradise that same day. You seem to have conflicting beliefs about some basic truths." Adam looks intently at Isaac, taking his eyes off the road for a brief moment. "Have you ever read those verses in the original Greek? Adam asked calmly. "You should give it a try before you come to any rash decisions."

"I'm not sure. I may have at school at some point, why would it matter? The words used would still be the same. I can understand what the words mean." Isaac replies sarcastically with unveiled anger.

"Humour me and give it a try." Adam directs. "Just do verse 43."

"OK, I don't know what good it will do but here goes." Isaac changes the translation on the lap top to a Greek translation. "I don't know if this is the original or not but here is a translation from the fifteen hundreds, the Stephanus New Testament." Isaac stumbles with the words of verse 43:

"και ειπεν αυτω ο ιησους αμην λεγω σοι σημερον μετ εμου εση εν τω παραδεισω.

I can't read this, it means nothing. It's all Greek to me," Isaac chuckles at his own joke.

"The words aren't the important part this time," Adam confirms. "It's the punctuation, or lack of it that matters."

"So, there is no punctuation in the Greek. What does that matter?" Isaac was sounding less confident.

"You'll see," Adam assures. "Read verse forty three again from the King James, but move the comma from after 'thee', and put it after 'today'. Now doe's that change the meaning?"

Isaac obliges,

"And Jesus said unto him, Verily I say unto thee today, shalt thou be with me in paradise'.

Ya it does change the tone somewhat." Isaac begrudgingly agrees. "I'd have to give it more thorough study before I could form a definite opinion on the subject."

"Needs further study, that seems to have become a reoccurring theme for you." Adam states confidently.

Referring back to the resurrection story Adam goes on, "Before you get too carried away with how inaccurately I am relaying the salvation plan of God, do a search for, child will die a hundred years old. See what you can come up with," Adam directs.

"OK. Here goes nothing," Isaac says, typing quickly. "I found one verse out of the entire Bible that refers to this, it's in Isaiah. I'll read some verses around it for context.

Isaiah 65:17-25
For, behold, I create new heavens and a new earth: and the former shall not be remembered, nor come into mind. 18 But be ye glad and rejoice for ever in that which I create: for, behold, I create Jerusalem a rejoicing, and her people a joy.
19 And I will rejoice in Jerusalem, and joy in my people: and the voice of weeping shall be no more heard in her, nor the voice of crying.
20 There shall be no more thence an infant of days, nor an old man that hath not filled his days: for the child shall die an hundred years old; but the sinner being an hundred years old shall be accursed.
21 And they shall build houses, and inhabit them; and they shall plant vineyards, and eat the fruit of them.
22 They shall not build, and another inhabit; they shall not plant, and another eat: for as the days of a tree are the days of my people, and mine elect shall long enjoy the work of their hands.
23 They shall not labour in vain, nor bring forth for trouble; for they are the seed of the blessed of the LORD, and their offspring with them.
24 And it shall come to pass, that before they call, I will answer; and while they are yet speaking, I will hear.

25 The wolf and the lamb shall feed together, and the lion shall eat straw like the bullock: and dust shall be the serpent's meat. They shall not hurt nor destroy in all my holy mountain, saith the LORD.

Well this is describing heaven. We will be greatly blessed when we are there with Jesus, living with God as his children," Isaac states boldly.

"I think you have it wrong, if I understand what people say about heaven," Adam disagrees. "There are no sinners in heaven is there? Yet there are sinners in this description of the future. Notice that the infant will die a hundred years old, but the sinner that is a hundred years old will be cursed.

These verses are describing how infants and all people that have died throughout the history of mankind will finally get to live an entire lifetime. After they are resurrected into physical bodies, these people, including babies will get to live a full and meaningful lifetime, to become the people they choose to grow into. They can learn about Jesus and make their own decision about following him. God will give everyone a fair opportunity to freely choose salvation. Their fate will be left for them to decide."

"Well that may be fine for innocent babies, but you said that everyone who didn't accept Jesus would be in this resurrection. That means that sinners get another chance at the salvation of Jesus. That would make all the sinners of the world, better off than the Christians who give up the pleasures of this life for Jesus. They will end up getting both the pleasures of this world and the next. Why should I bother being a Christian now if I am no better off than they are in the long run?" Isaac's face is red with anger as he bitterly responds to Adam's interpretations.

"I know this old truck is noisy, but you seem to have missed an important point about those who are resurrected in this second resurrection. Only the dead who have, not, had the opportunity to accept Jesus while they were alive, those who were blinded to the calling of God, now they will be resurrected to a physical body. They can live out a life, free of Satan and his pull towards sin. They will be resurrected back to who they were when they died. The sinful habits and attitudes they died with will still be inside of them. They will have a hundred years to overcome their sins and turn their attitudes into Godly ones."

"Ya, I know what you said! So why should I bother now if I can be saved later on?" Isaac is indignant.

"You talk as if they might be better off than Christians who have to struggle now with their sins. You short change the power of the Holy Spirit in your life to help you overcome sin and grow in the fruit of the Spirit. You don't seem to value the calling of God to come to Jesus now. No one will give up anything in this life that we won't receive a hundred fold in the Kingdom. We have been given a great opportunity to become rulers and priests in the Kingdom. Those from this resurrection will in no way be better off than the Christians who overcome the adversity of their own nature and the world," Adam sincerely explains.

"But the Bible clearly teaches that the sinner will die. They will not be part of the Kingdom of God," Isaac protests. "If what you say is true then those sinners will go unpunished, they will be forgiven and get to live with God anyway. Now that's not fair."

"You sound just like Jonah," Adam points out. "He didn't want to preach to the Ninavites because he knew that if they repented, God would forgive them. Jonah wanted them to die for their sins. But God so loved the world that he sent his only son to die, so that whoever believes in him will have everlasting life. None of us get what we deserve. We all get a chance to escape our sins and find life through Jesus. This is the only chance these people will have ever had, to learn of Jesus. This is not a second chance for them. This is their first and last chance to accept salvation."

Isaac sits in shock staring out the windshield. His eyes opened for the first time to his prejudices. "Do you really think I'm like Jonah?" he asks Adam shyly.

"Well it seems like you have a similar attitude," Adam said. "Why not look it up and see. I have been wrong before."

"OK, I will read it and see. Here it is, Jonah 4," Isaac reads the chapter.

"1 But it displeased Jonah exceedingly, and he was very angry.

2 And he prayed unto the LORD, and said, I pray thee, O LORD, was not this my saying, when I was yet in my country? Therefore I fled before unto Tarshish: for I knew that thou art a gracious God, and merciful, slow to anger, and of great kindness, and repentest thee of the evil.

3 Therefore now, O LORD, take, I beseech thee, my life from me; for it is better for me to die than to live.

4 Then said the LORD, Doest thou well to be angry?

5 So Jonah went out of the city, and sat on the east side of the city, and there made him a booth, and sat under it in the shadow, till he might see what would become of the city.

6 And the LORD God prepared a gourd, and made it to come up over Jonah, that it might be a shadow over his head, to deliver him from his grief. So Jonah was exceeding glad of the gourd.

7 But God prepared a worm when the morning rose the next day, and it smote the gourd that it withered.

8 And it came to pass, when the sun did arise, that God prepared a vehement east wind; and the sun beat upon the head of Jonah, that he fainted, and wished in himself to die, and said, It is better for me to die than to live.

9 And God said to Jonah, Doest thou well to be angry for the gourd? And he said, I do well to be angry, even unto death.

10 Then said the LORD, Thou hast had pity on the gourd, for the which thou hast not laboured, neither madest it grow; which came up in a night, and perished in a night:

11 And should not I spare Nineveh, that great city, wherein are more than sixscore thousand persons that cannot discern between their right hand and their left hand; and also much cattle?"

CHAPTER 14
SECOND LIFE

Isaac is quiet for a while as Adam drives. Then he breaks the silence with a question.

"So you are saying that everyone who ever lived will be given an opportunity to repent and learn about Jesus. Everyone, no matter what they have done, will be brought back to life in this resurrection?"

"Yes, but no. That is almost what I'm saying," Adam corrects in a gentle tone. "Yes everyone will have that choice to make. Everyone who hasn't been called to come to Jesus in this life, will be resurrected in the second resurrection. They will be resurrected to a physical life, so that if they reject Jesus after living for a hundred years, they will be choosing death rather than eternal life with Jesus. They will choose for themselves if they gain eternal life. If they reject Jesus, these resurrected people will die and remain that way for the rest of eternity. They will have had their chance and let it pass by. In time even the memory of them will be forgotten.

Their punishment will be everlasting as it takes an act of God to resurrect anyone back to life. God will respect the choice they willingly made and will let them have what they want; God will let them stay dead. They become the sinner that is cursed having lived a hundred years.

The people in this second resurrection should not be mixed up with those who willingly reject Jesus during this life. They have only the fear of the judgement to look forward to. They're resurrection of the condemned is still to come.

The plan of God gives everyone a full opportunity to come to Jesus for salvation. Some are called during this life to Jesus; the others will have to wait for the second resurrection to come back to a physical life, where they can finally learn about Jesus and his salvation. God wants as many children in his family as will willingly join."

"Oh. I think I am starting to get it," Isaac says tentatively. "Let me look up some of those references. Here is an easy one,

Hebrews 10:26-30
For if we sin wilfully after that we have received the knowledge of the truth, there remaineth no more sacrifice for sins,
27 But a certain fearful looking for of judgment and fiery indignation, which shall devour the adversaries.
28 He that despised Moses' law died without mercy under two or three witnesses:
29 Of how much sorer punishment, suppose ye, shall he be thought worthy, who hath trodden under foot the Son of God, and hath counted the blood of the covenant, wherewith he was sanctified, an unholy thing, and hath done despite unto the Spirit of grace?
30 For we know him that hath said, Vengeance belongeth unto me, I will recompense, saith the Lord. And again, The Lord shall judge his people.

Here is a story about Paul preaching to the Jews," Isaac said before continuing to read.

"Acts 13:44-48
44 And the next sabbath day came almost the whole city together to hear the word of God.
45 But when the Jews saw the multitudes, they were filled with envy, and spake against those things which were spoken by Paul, contradicting and blaspheming.

46 Then Paul and Barnabas waxed bold, and said, It was necessary that the word of God should first have been spoken to you: but seeing ye put it from you, and judge yourselves unworthy of everlasting life, lo, we turn to the Gentiles.

47 For so hath the Lord commanded us, saying, I have set thee to be a light of the Gentiles, that thou shouldest be for salvation unto the ends of the earth.

48 And when the Gentiles heard this, they were glad, and glorified the word of the Lord: and as many as were ordained to eternal life believed.

What key words should I use to find verses about a physical resurrection? I haven't learned much about that topic?"

"Try, valley of dead bones," Adam suggested.

"Good idea," Isaac said starting to type. "Yep here are some.

Ezekiel 37:1-14

The hand of the LORD was upon me, and carried me out in the spirit of the LORD, and set me down in the midst of the valley which was full of bones,

2 And caused me to pass by them round about: and, behold, there were very many in the open valley; and, lo, they were very dry.

3 And he said unto me, Son of man, can these bones live? And I answered, O Lord GOD, thou knowest.

4 Again he said unto me, Prophesy upon these bones, and say unto them, O ye dry bones, hear the word of the LORD.

5 Thus saith the Lord GOD unto these bones; Behold, I will cause breath to enter into you, and ye shall live:

6 And I will lay sinews upon you, and will bring up flesh upon you, and cover you with skin, and put breath in you, and ye shall live; and ye shall know that I am the LORD.

7 So I prophesied as I was commanded: and as I prophesied, there was a noise, and behold a shaking, and the bones came together, bone to his bone.

8 And when I beheld, lo, the sinews and the flesh came up upon them, and the skin covered them above: but there was no breath in them.

9 Then said he unto me, Prophesy unto the wind, prophesy, son of man, and say to the wind, Thus saith the Lord GOD; Come from the four winds, O breath, and breathe upon these slain, that they may live.

10 So I prophesied as he commanded me, and the breath came into them, and they lived, and stood up upon their feet, an exceeding great army.

11 Then he said unto me, Son of man, these bones are the whole house of Israel: behold, they say, Our bones are dried, and our hope is lost: we are cut off for our parts.

12 Therefore prophesy and say unto them, Thus saith the Lord GOD; Behold, O my people, I will open your graves, and cause you to come up out of your graves, and bring you into the land of Israel.

13 And ye shall know that I am the LORD, when I have opened your graves, O my people, and brought you up out of your graves,

14 And shall put my spirit in you, and ye shall live, and I shall place you in your own land: then shall ye know that I the LORD have spoken it, and performed it, saith the LORD.

These verses seem pretty specific to Israel. How do you prove it includes the rest of humanity?" Isaac challenges.

"We need to see who else is on the earth with them. Look up the prophesies for Gog and Magog," Adam directed.

"OK. I have heard a bit about them," Isaac said remembering a class from school. "Here is a reference in;

Revelation 20:7-9

And when the thousand years are expired, Satan shall be loosed out of his prison,

8 And shall go out to deceive the nations which are in the four quarters of the earth, Gog, and Magog, to gather them together to battle: the number of whom is as the sand of the sea.

9 And they went up on the breadth of the earth, and compassed the camp of the saints about, and the beloved city: and fire came down from God out of heaven, and devoured them.

This is to happen after Satan is released. So it is referring to the right time period," Isaac points out. "I suppose that if Gog and Magog are there then it wouldn't just be Israel who are resurrected back to life, others will be living with them."

"Exactly," Adam says nodding his head. "Like it told us in Revelations, the rest of the dead are not resurrected until after the thousand years are over, then the dead are brought back to life. At the end of the hundred years Satan is set loose, he deceives the nations and they fight against the saints of God. This will be the war to end all wars.

Finally all of humanity will have had an opportunity to choose God, or reject him. Those called in this life have to struggle against Satan and themselves so they can become Kings and Priests with Jesus in his Kingdom. Others will have to decide without the pulls of Satan during the Millennium, or have their chance to come to Jesus in the second resurrection. Not all will choose life with Jesus, but for those who do, eternal life awaits them, as children of God."

"So now God comes and lives with his people," Isaac says, anticipating Adam's next thought.

"Not quite yet," Adam says. "There are still some people that have to be dealt with for their poor choices."

"Who would those people be? I thought everyone would have had their chance by now," Isaac said in surprise. "All the people from the millennium and the second resurrection have had their turn at accepting Jesus and they have either been born into the spirit-physical realm like Jesus, or they chose not to accept him as saviour and are dead. Who's left?" Isaac was scratching his head.

"All the people who had their eyes opened and have been called by God in their first life, but ended up turning their backs on Jesus," Adam elaborates on the thought. "They have to receive the rewards of their choices. They have not tasted the second death yet. Those from the second resurrection have all died twice if they did not accept Jesus. One death after this life and once more dying a second and final time, after they reject salvation during their life in the second resurrection. People from this life, who know and accept Jesus, but do not follow him or the Spirit of God, as well as those born during the millennium but reject salvation, have to be dealt with and die their second death."

"What second death?" Isaac demands. "If someone accepts Jesus as their saviour, that is good for their entire life and nothing can take them from the safety of God's hand," Isaac said forcefully in the defense of his belief. "Once saved always saved!" he chanted.

"People who are Christians will not be hurt by the second death," Adam agreed. "We have already read that. Like I said earlier, a man convinced against his will, is still of the same mind still," Adam reminded, shaking his head. "We touched on these points earlier and I thought you understood, but it seems like we will have to more fully explore what it means to be, 'Saved', and how we need to be careful not to lose our salvation. Even Paul was concerned about being disqualified from the Kingdom and losing his eternal life."

"Even Paul! Oh you better explain this. Does this feed into your conspiracy theory as well? Conspiracy of some sort seems to be tied up with all of your resurrection talk," Isaac is back to his lofty, sarcastic, demeanor and tones."

CHAPTER 15
NOT ALL WHO CALL ME LORD

Brushing off the slights, Adam just smoothly shifts another gear keeping the Cummins engine running in its RPM sweet spot and says. "Well you are the one checking all my references from the Bible. We both agreed it is the only one true source for godly wisdom. If what I am saying is not supported correctly by the Bible, you haven't made much of a fuss so far."

Isaac is defensive in his response. "I told you it would take a lot of time and energy to find all of your errors. I can't be expected to find them all on the fly at the first hearing of such wild ideas."

Adam agrees. "That's fair, but you can believe the Bible. Have my wild ideas been far off the mark according to what the scriptures have to say?"

Isaac is quick to respond. "Well nothing painfully obvious so far. It's more the way you put scriptures together that is troubling. You don't follow any of the scripture flow that I am used to. You use verses I've never read, to contradict verses that I've studied and understand. Now those studied verses, don't seem to say, what I have been taught they say."

"It's like I have said before. If the Bible appears to be contradicting itself, we do not understand the scriptures properly," Adam assures him. "So, if I have not taken things out of context and the scriptures don't jive according to your teachings, where does the problem come from, my wacky ideas or yours?"

"Well maybe yours aren't completely wacky," Isaac begrudgingly admits. "But I know that I am saved through Jesus and I will never lose my salvation. I don't have to keep accepting Jesus, or worry that I might sin so badly that I can't be forgiven.

The salvation Jesus brings is bigger than any sin I could ever commit. I can rest assured in my salvation through Jesus."

"Amen. Again we agree," Adam chimed with a smile. "There is one way you may lose your salvation though, if you, abandon Jesus. No one can snatch us out of the hand of God, but we might willingly jump. The last resurrection is for those jumpers, those who believed in Jesus but did not follow him whole heartedly. Those who in this life, may appear to be doing his bidding but are only following their own passions, rather than following Jesus as they should be. Willfully sinning, knowingly not following the Holy Spirit. The third resurrection is for them."

"Some of that sounds familiar, the wicked going into eternal punishment I mean. I covered it in school. Let me look up some of the supportive scriptures for you," Isaac said with renewed zeal. "I think we have already read some of them. There may be some repeats, but it might help with the context. Here is an entire chapter, but I think it's relevant, if it's not too much for you to hear," Isaac said derisively."

"Sure. Go ahead and read it," Adam was pleased with the interest Isaac was displaying for the topic.

Isaac clears his throat and swigs down the last of his Dr. Pepper.

"Matthew 25," Isaac says in a flurry before wiping his mouth on his sleeve.

"Then shall the kingdom of heaven be likened unto ten virgins, which took their lamps, and went forth to meet the bridegroom.
2 And five of them were wise, and five were foolish.
3 They that were foolish took their lamps, and took no oil with them:
4 But the wise took oil in their vessels with their lamps.

5 While the bridegroom tarried, they all slumbered and slept.

6 And at midnight there was a cry made, Behold, the bridegroom cometh; go ye out to meet him.

7 Then all those virgins arose, and trimmed their lamps.

8 And the foolish said unto the wise, Give us of your oil; for our lamps are gone out.

9 But the wise answered, saying, Not so; lest there be not enough for us and you: but go ye rather to them that sell, and buy for yourselves.

10 And while they went to buy, the bridegroom came; and they that were ready went in with him to the marriage: and the door was shut.

11 Afterward came also the other virgins, saying, Lord, Lord, open to us.

12 But he answered and said, Verily I say unto you, I know you not.

13 Watch therefore, for ye know neither the day nor the hour wherein the Son of man cometh.

14 For the kingdom of heaven is as a man travelling into a far country, who called his own servants, and delivered unto them his goods.

15 And unto one he gave five talents, to another two, and to another one; to every man according to his several ability; and straightway took his journey.

16 Then he that had received the five talents went and traded with the same, and made them other five talents.

17 And likewise he that had received two, he also gained other two.

18 But he that had received one went and digged in the earth, and hid his lord's money.

19 After a long time the lord of those servants cometh, and reckoneth with them.

20 And so he that had received five talents came and brought other five talents, saying, Lord, thou deliveredst unto me five talents: behold, I have gained beside them five talents more.

21 His lord said unto him, Well done, thou good and faithful servant: thou hast been faithful over a few things, I will make thee ruler over many things: enter thou into the joy of thy lord.

22 He also that had received two talents came and said, Lord, thou deliveredst unto me two talents: behold, I have gained two other talents beside them.

23 His lord said unto him, Well done, good and faithful servant; thou hast been faithful over a few things, I will make thee ruler over many things: enter thou into the joy of thy lord.

24 Then he which had received the one talent came and said, Lord, I knew thee that thou art an hard man, reaping where thou hast not sown, and gathering where thou hast not strawed:

25 And I was afraid, and went and hid thy talent in the earth: lo, there thou hast that is thine.

26 His lord answered and said unto him, Thou wicked and slothful servant, thou knewest that I reap where I sowed not, and gather where I have not strawed:

27 Thou oughtest therefore to have put my money to the exchangers, and then at my coming I should have received mine own with usury.

28 Take therefore the talent from him, and give it unto him which hath ten talents.

29 For unto every one that hath shall be given, and he shall have abundance: but from him that hath not shall be taken away even that which he hath.

30 And cast ye the unprofitable servant into outer darkness: there shall be weeping and gnashing of teeth.

31 When the Son of man shall come in his glory, and all the holy angels with him, then shall he sit upon the throne of his glory:

32 And before him shall be gathered all nations: and he shall separate them one from another, as a shepherd divideth his sheep from the goats:

33 And he shall set the sheep on his right hand, but the goats on the left.

34 Then shall the King say unto them on his right hand, Come, ye blessed of my Father, inherit the kingdom prepared for you from the foundation of the world:

35 For I was an hungred, and ye gave me meat: I was thirsty, and ye gave me drink: I was a stranger, and ye took me in:

36 Naked, and ye clothed me: I was sick, and ye visited me: I was in prison, and ye came unto me.

37 Then shall the righteous answer him, saying, Lord, when saw we thee an hungred, and fed thee? or thirsty, and gave thee drink?

38 When saw we thee a stranger, and took thee in? or naked, and clothed thee?

39 Or when saw we thee sick, or in prison, and came unto thee?

40 And the King shall answer and say unto them, Verily I say unto you, Inasmuch as ye have done it unto one of the least of these my brethren, ye have done it unto me.

41 Then shall he say also unto them on the left hand, Depart from me, ye cursed, into everlasting fire, prepared for the devil and his angels:

42 For I was an hungred, and ye gave me no meat: I was thirsty, and ye gave me no drink:

43 I was a stranger, and ye took me not in: naked, and ye clothed me not: sick, and in prison, and ye visited me not.

44 Then shall they also answer him, saying, Lord, when saw we thee an hungred, or athirst, or a stranger, or naked, or sick, or in prison, and did not minister unto thee?

45 Then shall he answer them, saying, Verily I say unto you, Inasmuch as ye did it not to one of the least of these, ye did it not to me.

46 And these shall go away into everlasting punishment: but the righteous into life eternal.

Then we have more in;

Matthew 5:11-13

Blessed are ye, when men shall revile you, and persecute you, and shall say all manner of evil against you falsely, for my sake.

12 Rejoice, and be exceeding glad: for great is your reward in heaven: for so persecuted they the prophets which were before you.

13 Ye are the salt of the earth: but if the salt have lost his savour, wherewith shall it be salted? it is thenceforth good for nothing, but to be cast out, and to be trodden under foot of men.

I see what you mean, we can't be made salty, or Christian again if we abandon Jesus. Here are some more verses about those who were called and came to Jesus, but didn't take their salvation seriously.

Matthew 22:10-13 KJV.
10 So those servants went out into the highways, and gathered together all as many as they found, both bad and good: and the wedding was furnished with guests.
11 And when the king came in to see the guests, he saw there a man which had not on a wedding garment:
12 And he saith unto him, Friend, how camest thou in hither not having a wedding garment? And he was speechless.
13 Then said the king to the servants, Bind him hand and foot, and take him away, and cast him into outer darkness, there shall be weeping and gnashing of teeth.

Some Christians don't wear the Holy Spirit wedding cloths and are rejected," Isaac provides a running commentary for the scriptures as he reads them.

"Again, only the good ones are chosen. I have found plenty of examples. Here are a few more.

Matthew 13:47-50
Again, the kingdom of heaven is like unto a net, that was cast into the sea, and gathered of every kind:
48 Which, when it was full, they drew to shore, and sat down, and gathered the good into vessels, but cast the bad away.
49 So shall it be at the end of the world: the angels shall come forth, and sever the wicked from among the just,

50 And shall cast them into the furnace of fire: there shall be wailing and gnashing of teeth.

Matthew 24:45-51
45 Who then is a faithful and wise servant, whom his lord hath made ruler over his household, to give them meat in due season?
46 Blessed is that servant, whom his lord when he cometh shall find so doing.
47 Verily I say unto you, That he shall make him ruler over all his goods.
48 But and if that evil servant shall say in his heart, My lord delayeth his coming;
49 And shall begin to smite his fellowservants, and to eat and drink with the drunken;
50 The lord of that servant shall come in a day when he looketh not for him, and in an hour that he is not aware of,
51 And shall cut him asunder, and appoint him his portion with the hypocrites: there shall be weeping and gnashing of teeth.

The Bible warns us to be focused on following Jesus all the time and not drift off into carelessness thinking he will never come for us. We can't take a holiday from being Christian.

Luke 14:33-35 King James Version
33 So likewise, whosoever he be of you that forsaketh not all that he hath, he cannot be my disciple.
34 Salt is good: but if the salt have lost his savour, wherewith shall it be seasoned?

35 It is neither fit for the land, nor yet for the dunghill; but men cast it out. He that hath ears to hear, let him hear."

"There sure are a lot of verses supporting the topic, I get the picture," Adam said scratching his head. "Do we need to read them all?"

Isaac looks shocked at Adam's comment, when he replies, "It was you that said we couldn't be too sure of what the Bible had to say. I wouldn't want to be taking things for granted you know; besides I thought you liked reading the Bible." Isaac continues with his scripture search.

"I guise we can't be content with just being in the presence of Jesus, we have to be doers of his work.

James 1:22-25 KJV.
22 But be ye doers of the word, and not hearers only, deceiving your own selves.
23 For if any be a hearer of the word, and not a doer, he is like unto a man beholding his natural face in a glass:
24 For he beholdeth himself, and goeth his way, and straightway forgetteth what manner of man he was.
25 But whoso looketh into the perfect law of liberty, and continueth therein, he being not a forgetful hearer, but a doer of the work, this man shall be blessed in his deed."

Isaac sums up the last passage he read. "Hanging around with Jesus won't help us in the end. We have to be his servants, actively serving."

"You are contextualizing the pertinent thoughts of those scriptures very well," Adam agreed. "Is that all now, or have you found more?"

Isaac reads the next set of scriptures that he finds on the subject of, those who thought they were Christian only to be rejected in the end.

"Oh look, I've found some more golden nuggets of truth. Luke 13:22-28," Isaac announces.

"And he went through the cities and villages, teaching, and journeying toward Jerusalem.
23 Then said one unto him, Lord, are there few that be saved? And he said unto them,
24 Strive to enter in at the strait gate: for many, I say unto you, will seek to enter in, and shall not be able.
25 When once the master of the house is risen up, and hath shut to the door, and ye begin to stand without, and to knock at the door, saying, Lord, Lord, open unto us; and he shall answer and say unto you, I know you not whence ye are:
26 Then shall ye begin to say, We have eaten and drunk in thy presence, and thou hast taught in our streets.
27 But he shall say, I tell you, I know you not whence ye are; depart from me, all ye workers of iniquity.
28 There shall be weeping and gnashing of teeth, when ye shall see Abraham, and Isaac, and Jacob, and all the prophets, in the kingdom of God, and you yourselves thrust out.

This one is a bit different," Isaac says before he reads it.

"John 5:28-29
Marvel not at this: for the hour is coming, in the which all that are in the graves shall hear his voice,

29 And shall come forth; they that have done good, unto the resurrection of life; and they that have done evil, unto the resurrection of damnation.

So this must be when all the weeping and gnashing of teeth takes place. Is this resurrection of damnation what you call the third resurrection?"

"Yes," Adam loudly agrees so as to be clearly herd inside the old trucks raucous cab. "It's the last resurrection for mankind. Everyone has now had their opportunity to accept Jesus. This last resurrection is the end for those who rejected Jesus during their first life, either by decision or by neglectful indifference. They put the things of the world before him, even after counting the cost of discipleship. They will be pruned off and cast into the fire. Can I get back to explaining the plan now?"

"Wait, I can find a reference for that too," Isaac nods. "Here are some.

John 15:1-6

I am the true vine, and my Father is the husbandman.
2 Every branch in me that beareth not fruit he taketh away: and every branch that beareth fruit, he purgeth it, that it may bring forth more fruit.
3 Now ye are clean through the word which I have spoken unto you.
4 Abide in me, and I in you. As the branch cannot bear fruit of itself, except it abide in the vine; no more can ye, except ye abide in me.
5 I am the vine, ye are the branches: He that abideth in me, and I in him, the same bringeth forth much fruit: for without me ye can do nothing.

6 If a man abide not in me, he is cast forth as a branch, and is withered; and men gather them, and cast them into the fire, and they are burned.

Hebrews 6:4-8

For it is impossible for those who were once enlightened, and have tasted of the heavenly gift, and were made partakers of the Holy Ghost,

5 And have tasted the good word of God, and the powers of the world to come,

6 If they shall fall away, to renew them again unto repentance; seeing they crucify to themselves the Son of God afresh, and put him to an open shame.

7 For the earth which drinketh in the rain that cometh oft upon it, and bringeth forth herbs meet for them by whom it is dressed, receiveth blessing from God:

8 But that which beareth thorns and briers is rejected, and is nigh unto cursing; whose end is to be burned.

And there is still more. Here in;

2 Peter 2

But there were false prophets also among the people, even as there shall be false teachers among you, who privily shall bring in damnable heresies, even denying the Lord that bought them, and bring upon themselves swift destruction.

2 And many shall follow their pernicious ways; by reason of whom the way of truth shall be evil spoken of.

3 And through covetousness shall they with feigned words make merchandise of you: whose judgment now of a long time lingereth not, and their damnation slumbereth not.

4 For if God spared not the angels that sinned, but cast them down to hell, and delivered them into chains of darkness, to be reserved unto judgment;

5 And spared not the old world, but saved Noah the eighth person, a preacher of righteousness, bringing in the flood upon the world of the ungodly;

6 And turning the cities of Sodom and Gomorrha into ashes condemned them with an overthrow, making them an ensample unto those that after should live ungodly;

7 And delivered just Lot, vexed with the filthy conversation of the wicked:

8 (For that righteous man dwelling among them, in seeing and hearing, vexed his righteous soul from day to day with their unlawful deeds;)

9 The Lord knoweth how to deliver the godly out of temptations, and to reserve the unjust unto the day of judgment to be punished:

10 But chiefly them that walk after the flesh in the lust of uncleanness, and despise government. Presumptuous are they, selfwilled, they are not afraid to speak evil of dignities.

11 Whereas angels, which are greater in power and might, bring not railing accusation against them before the Lord.

12 But these, as natural brute beasts, made to be taken and destroyed, speak evil of the things that they understand not; and shall utterly perish in their own corruption;

13 And shall receive the reward of unrighteousness, as they that count it pleasure to riot in the day time. Spots they are and blemishes, sporting themselves with their own deceivings while they feast with you;

14 Having eyes full of adultery, and that cannot cease from sin; beguiling unstable souls: an heart they have exercised with covetous practices; cursed children:
15 Which have forsaken the right way, and are gone astray, following the way of Balaam the son of Bosor, who loved the wages of unrighteousness;
16 But was rebuked for his iniquity: the dumb ass speaking with man's voice forbad the madness of the prophet.
17 These are wells without water, clouds that are carried with a tempest; to whom the mist of darkness is reserved for ever.
18 For when they speak great swelling words of vanity, they allure through the lusts of the flesh, through much wantonness, those that were clean escaped from them who live in error.
19 While they promise them liberty, they themselves are the servants of corruption: for of whom a man is overcome, of the same is he brought in bondage.
20 For if after they have escaped the pollutions of the world through the knowledge of the Lord and Saviour Jesus Christ, they are again entangled therein, and overcome, the latter end is worse with them than the beginning.
21 For it had been better for them not to have known the way of righteousness, than, after they have known it, to turn from the holy commandment delivered unto them.
22 But it is happened unto them according to the true proverb, The dog is turned to his own vomit again; and the sow that was washed to her wallowing in the mire.

Wow that was a strong chapter; I have normally read it only in small sections. Reading it all at once gives me a much deeper impression of what God thinks about Christians that don't take their salvation seriously. Their end is to be worse than their beginning when they knew nothing of Jesus. Why do you think they will be worse off?

"Well probably because their fate will be sealed," Adam speculates. "They will have had eternal life all but theirs, only to trade it in favour of the sins of the world that will not last. They will only have the judgement of God to look forward to. So their end will be worse than their beginning. I'm glad that these scriptures are meaningful to you, but are all these scriptures new to you?"

"No, I have known these since I was little. That's why I can find them so fast." Isaac mused as he shrugged his shoulders. "I just figured that I better check out their context in case I had them wrong all along. I can't just take things for granted. Here are some more scriptures on the topic.

Jude 3-13

Beloved, when I gave all diligence to write unto you of the common salvation, it was needful for me to write unto you, and exhort you that ye should earnestly contend for the faith which was once delivered unto the saints.
4 For there are certain men crept in unawares, who were before of old ordained to this condemnation, ungodly men, turning the grace of our God into lasciviousness, and denying the only Lord God, and our Lord Jesus Christ.
5 I will therefore put you in remembrance, though ye once knew this, how that the Lord, having saved the people out of the land of Egypt, afterward destroyed them that believed not.

6 And the angels which kept not their first estate, but left their own habitation, he hath reserved in everlasting chains under darkness unto the judgment of the great day.

7 Even as Sodom and Gomorrha, and the cities about them in like manner, giving themselves over to fornication, and going after strange flesh, are set forth for an example, suffering the vengeance of eternal fire.

8 Likewise also these filthy dreamers defile the flesh, despise dominion, and speak evil of dignities.

9 Yet Michael the archangel, when contending with the devil he disputed about the body of Moses, durst not bring against him a railing accusation, but said, The Lord rebuke thee.

10 But these speak evil of those things which they know not: but what they know naturally, as brute beasts, in those things they corrupt themselves.

11 Woe unto them! for they have gone in the way of Cain, and ran greedily after the error of Balaam for reward, and perished in the gainsaying of Core.

12 These are spots in your feasts of charity, when they feast with you, feeding themselves without fear: clouds they are without water, carried about of winds; trees whose fruit withereth, without fruit, twice dead, plucked up by the roots;

13 Raging waves of the sea, foaming out their own shame; wandering stars, to whom is reserved the blackness of darkness for ever.

Teachers have a big responsibility to teach as God instructs, not going off with their own ideas. They will be twice dead if they do. You better be careful with all your conspiracy ideas. You may end up in a bad, bad, place," Isaac said staring at Adam.

"If what I was saying came from myself, I would be afraid of the second death. If I don't stay true to scripture, read in context, or if I was following my own agenda, I could miss out. I do my best to formulate my beliefs and understandings within the context of the scriptures. If you see where I have made an error please don't be shy about bringing it to my attention," Adam says, explaining his motives.

"Oh, I'm sure you do follow the scriptures, to the best of, your abilities," sneered Isaac. "Here is more scripture about those who are rejected by Jesus."

Staring at the lap top screen Isaac resumes reading.

"Revelation 3:15-16
I know thy works, that thou art neither cold nor hot: I would thou wert cold or hot.
16 So then because thou art lukewarm, and neither cold nor hot, I will spue thee out of my mouth.

Revelation 21:6-8
6 And he said unto me, It is done. I am Alpha and Omega, the beginning and the end. I will give unto him that is athirst of the fountain of the water of life freely.
7 He that overcometh shall inherit all things; and I will be his God, and he shall be my son.
8 But the fearful, and unbelieving, and the abominable, and murderers, and whoremongers, and sorcerers, and idolaters, and all liars, shall have their part in the lake which burneth with fire and brimstone: which is the second death.

Hey, you said that people who live and die during the second resurrection, not accepting Jesus, would stay dead, that would be their second death. This verse tells us the sinners and those who reject Jesus will be thrown into the lake of fire, which is the second death. Your understanding seems to be at odds with this verse. So who doesn't understand things properly after all?"

For a moment, Adam thinks about how to start his explanation. Taking in a deep breath he starts to talk.

"I believe this verse is talking about all who reject Jesus and are willfully sinning, even when they know better, during the first physical life they go through. Those who reject their calling during this life are resurrected back to physical life in the third resurrection, the resurrection of damnation. They will be judged and then cast into the lake of fire. Being mortal they will die in the flames, this will be the second and final time they will die. They had their opportunity to follow Jesus and rejected it. It will be their second death.

Those who reject Jesus from the second resurrection had their opportunity to follow Jesus without the influence of Satan. If they came back in this final resurrection of damnation, then it would be their third life and dying in the lake of fire would be their third death. Not the second death, as the scriptures refer to.

I haven't read anything in the Bible that tells us mankind will have more than two deaths and one opportunity at having their eyes opened and called to accept Jesus. I believe those who don't accept Jesus, after living a hundred years during the second resurrection, their death will be final, as that will have been their second death. But I could be wrong; do you have a better explanation?"

Surprised by Adams answer, Isaac side steps the question and goes on with his reading and synopses.

"No, I wouldn't want to speculate on the topic, I would need to do more research in order to give an informed opinion on the subject. These next verses are interesting though. They are the scriptures where Paul talks about the possibility of losing out on his own salvation after having shared the saving gospel with others. It sounds like we have to stay faithful to the end of our lives and not turn from our faith after we decide to follow Jesus.

1 Corinthians 9:16-27

For though I preach the gospel, I have nothing to glory of: for necessity is laid upon me; yea, woe is unto me, if I preach not the gospel!

17 For if I do this thing willingly, I have a reward: but if against my will, a dispensation of the gospel is committed unto me.

18 What is my reward then? Verily that, when I preach the gospel, I may make the gospel of Christ without charge, that I abuse not my power in the gospel.

19 For though I be free from all men, yet have I made myself servant unto all, that I might gain the more.

20 And unto the Jews I became as a Jew, that I might gain the Jews; to them that are under the law, as under the law, that I might gain them that are under the law;

21 To them that are without law, as without law, (being not without law to God, but under the law to Christ,) that I might gain them that are without law.

22 To the weak became I as weak, that I might gain the weak: I am made all things to all men, that I might by all means save some.

23 And this I do for the gospel's sake, that I might be partaker thereof with you.

24 Know ye not that they which run in a race run all, but one receiveth the prize? So run, that ye may obtain.

25 And every man that striveth for the mastery is temperate in all things. Now they do it to obtain a corruptible crown; but we an incorruptible.

26 I therefore so run, not as uncertainly; so fight I, not as one that beateth the air:

27 But I keep under my body, and bring it into subjection: lest that by any means, when I have preached to others, I myself should be a castaway."

"Yes. Jesus told us to count the cost of following him before we decide to commit," Adam explains. "We can't be double minded and try to serve two masters. We must give Jesus our all. Nothing can be allowed to side track us or be more important than following Jesus, for we willingly give up our lives to him, when we join with him through baptism.

You do know that I am aware of these verses that you're reading, right. I totally agree with them."

"Ya I thought so. But I told you I would be checking all of your references and I will, even if it kills you," Isaac flashes Adam a big fake smile. "Can't be too careful about our faith can we? Now those double minded verses sound familiar," Isaac nods knowingly. Remembering his parent's admonishment from when he was little. "Let me look them up. Here are a couple different ones that reflect your thoughts."

"Suit yourself," Adam said with a frown. "I was only trying to save your time and effort."

"Matthew 6:22-24," Isaac continued undaunted.

"The light of the body is the eye: if therefore thine eye be single, thy whole body shall be full of light.

23 But if thine eye be evil, thy whole body shall be full of darkness. If therefore the light that is in thee be darkness, how great is that darkness!

24 No man can serve two masters: for either he will hate the one, and love the other; or else he will hold to the one, and despise the other. Ye cannot serve God and mammon.

Luke 16:13-15

No servant can serve two masters: for either he will hate the one, and love the other; or else he will hold to the one, and despise the other. Ye cannot serve God and mammon.
14 And the Pharisees also, who were covetous, heard all these things: and they derided him.
15 And he said unto them, Ye are they which justify yourselves before men; but God knoweth your hearts: for that which is highly esteemed among men is abomination in the sight of God.

You're counting the cost scriptural references are quite long as they have several teaching points contained in them. I will read the long versions so we can be sure of the contextual accuracy."

"Sounds good to me," Adam agreed, rolling his eyes. "I don't want to be misrepresenting the scriptures, or refer to them out of their contextual meaning."

"OK I will start with Luke 14:25-34 King James Version," Said Isaac.

25 And there went great multitudes with him: and he turned, and said unto them,
26 If any man come to me, and hate not his father, and mother, and wife, and children, and brethren, and sisters, yea, and his own life also, he cannot be my disciple.
27 And whosoever doth not bear his cross, and come after me, cannot be my disciple.

28 For which of you, intending to build a tower, sitteth not down first, and counteth the cost, whether he have sufficient to finish it?

29 Lest haply, after he hath laid the foundation, and is not able to finish it, all that behold it begin to mock him,

30 Saying, This man began to build, and was not able to finish.

31 Or what king, going to make war against another king, sitteth not down first, and consulteth whether he be able with ten thousand to meet him that cometh against him with twenty thousand?

32 Or else, while the other is yet a great way off, he sendeth an ambassage, and desireth conditions of peace.

33 So likewise, whosoever he be of you that forsaketh not all that he hath, he cannot be my disciple.

34 Salt is good: but if the salt have lost his savour, wherewith shall it be seasoned?

These next verses tell us we are servants of the master we obey, do we serve sin and death, or do we have life and serve Jesus?

Romans 6

1 What shall we say then? Shall we continue in sin, that grace may abound?

2 God forbid. How shall we, that are dead to sin, live any longer therein?

3 Know ye not, that so many of us as were baptized into Jesus Christ were baptized into his death?

4 Therefore we are buried with him by baptism into death: that like as Christ was raised up from the dead by

the glory of the Father, even so we also should walk in newness of life.

5 For if we have been planted together in the likeness of his death, we shall be also in the likeness of his resurrection:

6 Knowing this, that our old man is crucified with him, that the body of sin might be destroyed, that henceforth we should not serve sin.

7 For he that is dead is freed from sin.

8 Now if we be dead with Christ, we believe that we shall also live with him:

9 Knowing that Christ being raised from the dead dieth no more; death hath no more dominion over him.

10 For in that he died, he died unto sin once: but in that he liveth, he liveth unto God.

11 Likewise reckon ye also yourselves to be dead indeed unto sin, but alive unto God through Jesus Christ our Lord.

12 Let not sin therefore reign in your mortal body, that ye should obey it in the lusts thereof.

13 Neither yield ye your members as instruments of unrighteousness unto sin: but yield yourselves unto God, as those that are alive from the dead, and your members as instruments of righteousness unto God.

14 For sin shall not have dominion over you: for ye are not under the law, but under grace.

15 What then? shall we sin, because we are not under the law, but under grace? God forbid.

16 Know ye not, that to whom ye yield yourselves servants to obey, his servants ye are to whom ye obey; whether of sin unto death, or of obedience unto righteousness?

17 But God be thanked, that ye were the servants of sin, but ye have obeyed from the heart that form of doctrine which was delivered you.

18 Being then made free from sin, ye became the servants of righteousness.

19 I speak after the manner of men because of the infirmity of your flesh: for as ye have yielded your members servants to uncleanness and to iniquity unto iniquity; even so now yield your members servants to righteousness unto holiness.

20 For when ye were the servants of sin, ye were free from righteousness.

21 What fruit had ye then in those things whereof ye are now ashamed? for the end of those things is death.

22 But now being made free from sin, and become servants to God, ye have your fruit unto holiness, and the end everlasting life.

23 For the wages of sin is death; but the gift of God is eternal life through Jesus Christ our Lord.

CHAPTER 16
FAMILY TIME

That was a lot of scripture," Isaac said. "I'm afraid I've lost track of where we are in your story. Could you catch me back up to where we left off?"

"Sure," Adam said, "glad to be getting back to the plan. Jesus has returned to the earth, the beast and false prophet are cast into the lake of fire. Satan is chained up and not allowed to influence the world or its inhabitants, as it is rebuilt during the millennium. Those who accept Jesus during the millennium are born into the family of God, those who don't, will have to wait in their graves for their final fate to arrive.

At the end of the millennium there is a second resurrection for everyone who lived and died without the opportunity to accept Jesus before the millennium got started. The vast majority of humanity will now have their eyes opened to salvation through Jesus. They will have a lifetime of one hundred years to choose salvation or death.

At the end of this hundred year period, Satan will again be loosed to deceive the nations who again make war against Jesus and the saints. They are defeated, in what will be the final war of all time. At the end of this war those who have died for the second time, not accepting Jesus, will most likely remain dead. Satan is cast into the lake of fire where he and the demons will be tormented for the rest of eternity.

Now the third resurrection takes place. The resurrection to damnation, because all who find themselves at this day of judgement, will have had their opportunity to accept Jesus, but never took advantage of that chance, they are cast into the lake of fire and die there.

They are not immortal like Satan, who is tormented in the flames forever. They are resurrected into physical mortal bodies and die in the flames and remain dead for the rest of eternity. Their punishment will be eternal as they will never be brought back to life again. They will become ashes under the feat of the saints. This will be their second death."

"Wait," Exclaimed Isaac. "That's new, becoming ashes under the feet of the saints. I'm not familiar with it; I need to look that up." Isaac starts a new search.

"Here it is,

Malachi 4:1-3

For, behold, the day cometh, that shall burn as an oven; and all the proud, yea, and all that do wickedly, shall be stubble: and the day that cometh shall burn them up, saith the LORD of hosts, that it shall leave them neither root nor branch.
2 But unto you that fear my name shall the Sun of righteousness arise with healing in his wings; and ye shall go forth, and grow up as calves of the stall.
3 And ye shall tread down the wicked; for they shall be ashes under the soles of your feet in the day that I shall do this, saith the LORD of hosts.

It seems to be talking about the end times, I suppose you are using it in the proper context," Isaac agrees skeptically.

"Can I go on now?" Adam asks with a big smile. "Are you satisfied?"

"No," Isaac said. "No I am not satisfied. How do you know that they are resurrected as mortal people? Why couldn't they be just as easily resurrected as immortal and then be thrown into the lake of fire and be tormented for the rest of eternity with Satan?

That would fit more closely to what the rest of Christendom believes. What makes you so sure your right?" Isaac demands.

"Well for one," Adam replies. "God will not violate his own prime directives. The first one clearly states that, we can only have eternal life if we accept Jesus. Remember we agreed on that? I believe to my very core that John 3:15-17 is the truth, the whole truth and nothing but the truth.

'That whosoever believeth in him should not perish, but have eternal life.

For God so loved the world, that he gave his only begotten Son, that whosoever believeth in him should not perish, but have everlasting life.

For God sent not his Son into the world to condemn the world; but that the world through him might be saved'.

This is the truth. We can only have eternal life if we believe in Jesus. Other scriptures we have covered, tell us that when we believe in Jesus, we will not be thrown into the lake of fire. Those who follow Jesus go on to become the children of God. These two points are undeniably true. Therefore, those who are thrown into the lake of fire have to be mortal, as they have not followed Jesus to receive their eternal life, which means they are mortal. Their mortality is self-evident by the fact they are thrown, into the lake of fire, where they are burned to ashes.

To argue they might somehow have an eternal life so they could suffer in the flames for all eternity, requires you to rewrite what is taught in John. As well, you would have to rethink your position on the belief that Jesus alone provides eternal life for those who believe on him. Is that what you believe? That Jesus, isn't, the only way to eternal life? Do you think there is some other way to gain immortality?"

"No! Of course not. I just hadn't thought of it quite like that before," Isaac stammered. "I thought you had a verse that said they would be mortal is all."

"I do. John 3:15-17," Adam said flatly. "It's either true or it's not. What do you think?"

"OK, OK, I'll go with those verses are understood within their proper context," Isaac responded soberly, happy to move the conversation along.

"One of the last things to happen is death and the grave are done away with, as there are now no more mortal people to go through them," Adam goes on with his Bible lesson. "Every human who has ever lived, is now an immortal spirit-physical being like Jesus, or they are dead for the rest of eternity, having suffered the second death. Then God brings down New Jerusalem and lives with his children here on the earth.

You can look that up. I have to stop up here at the brake check and do truck stuff." Running the Jake and down shifting Adam takes the right lane exit off of the highway leading to the brake check parking area. Pulling over to the far right by the shoulder of the pavement, he parks in front of the garbage cans chained to two big sign posts.

On the large, two post sign board, there's a road map of the upcoming decent along with the location of the runaway lanes. As well, it has distances and road grades for each section of the hill clearly marked out so the truck drivers would know what to expect as they proceed down the upcoming long steep hill.

"I'll be a bit," Adam said as he applied the truck spring brakes, leaving the parking brakes off on the trailer. "There's an outhouse toilet if you need to go. Last chance before we get to town."

"Ya. Maybe I had better do that," Isaac replied. "That pop was only rented and it would do me good to stretch my legs a bit."

They both got out of the cab. Adam went counter clockwise heading towards the back of the trailer, kicking tires and looking at various parts to make sure they were OK and good to go.

Isaac headed straight for the small concrete block building, not much larger than an old fashioned telephone booth. As he opened the door to walk in, he stopped and stepped back into the light breeze of the parking lot. Filling his lungs with as deep a breath as possible, he rushed into the building, the door slamming behind him.

A couple of minutes later he emerged just as fast, red faced and exhaling, awkwardly doing up the zipper of his pants. He walked briskly away from the outhouse for a few paces, then slowed noticeably, taking in deep breaths of the sweet mountain air.

Turning, he walked back towards the tattered looking old truck which was idling noisily where it had been parked. Not seeing Adam he headed towards the back of the trailer on the passenger side. Looking around bewilderedly for Adam at the rear of the trailer, he poked his head around the back corner of the reefer van to look down the driver's side. Adam was nowhere to be seen. Isaac was about to call out for Adam when he heard some scuffling sounds coming from under the trailer. Kneeling down he looked under the trailer to find Adam lying on his side with a long steel crowbar, prying against the trailer axles.

"What are you doing under there?" Isaac said with a mix of curiosity and disdain. "Is it broken or something?"

"No, not broken. Just checking the brakes like I'm supposed to," Adam explained. "Some guys just pretend to check their brakes by looking at them, but you never know for sure if your brakes are adjusted properly if you don't actually check them physically. Their all good, just as I had thought. This hill we are going to go down is over ten miles long and runs at a six to eight percent grade. So I wanted to check the trailer out, just to be safe."

Sliding on the lightly sanded pavement to get further back, Adam pries the slack adjusters, with his crow bar against the rear axle of the trailer. They have about half an inch of travel before he cannot move them any further.

Pleased with the test results Adam crawls out from under the reefer van, vigorously brushing the dirt off of his cloths with his hands. He walks over to some knee high green grass growing in the ditch, squeezing it tightly at the base he pulls it through his hands, freeing his fingers of most of their grimy dirt before he rubs the stubborn greasy bits off on his lower pant legs.

Kicking the rest of the tires on the passenger side of the trailer, he then heads towards the truck looking and checking for things amiss. Scanning under the truck he then kicks the rear duel tires and moves forward towards the front of the truck.

"Hey. Aren't you going to crawl under and check the truck brakes too?" Isaac asked shocked and slightly fearful. "You just said that you couldn't tell if they were OK by just looking at them, but that they need to be manually tested. I want to get home safe you know."

"I can't pull these slack adjusters because the spring brakes are on, that's what's keeping the truck from rolling down the hill right now. So I check the travel of the slacks with the markers that are on the push rods. They have about an inch of space from the face of the brake pot, which means the brakes are adjusted properly.

What I meant before about, just looking at them, was that some drivers just stop and pretend to check things out for show. You can get a fine if you don't check your brakes, but they aren't really checking anything, it's all pretend. With markers on the push rods you can check your brakes accurately by just looking at them when the spring brakes are applied, if you know what you're doing."

Adam explains his actions further, "I left the park brakes on the trailer off because I was planning to go under and check the brakes using the free stroke method. I wanted to do it here on the dry pavement; the next place I stop is likely to be muddy. You need to know your equipment and it has to be set up properly if you want to be efficient," Adam explains.

Not understanding a thing that Adam had just said, Isaac shrugged and said. "Oh ya, I can see that."

Using the hand rail and tank steps Isaac hoists himself back into the cab of the shabby old truck. Once comfortably settled back into the passenger seat, he starts searching for the last verses Adam referred to in his end time events scenario.

Adam continued with his checks around the truck until he finally got back into the cab behind the steering wheel.

"Well, everything seems to be fine," Adam said closing the door. "We can get on with our trip now. 'Just one more hour and I'll be, home and dry'." He was singing along with the Gerry Rafferty song that played in his head. "'Oww wa wa, oww ho ho, oww ho ho, I'll be home and dry'," he sang while releasing the truck brakes. Putting the truck into third gear he pointed it's nose for the highway. "Yup, we're just about there." He smiled at the thought of being with his wife for a couple of uninterrupted days.

Oblivious to Adam's singing and comments, Isaac is deep into his scripture search and just grunts in agreement. "Here is the first scripture for your last points," He said.

"1 Corinthians 15:24-26
24 Then cometh the end, when he shall have delivered up the kingdom to God, even the Father; when he shall have put down all rule and all authority and power.
25 For he must reign, till he hath put all enemies under his feet.
26 The last enemy that shall be destroyed is death.

Another one to support your point," Said Isaac, increasing his volume to match the truck noise.

"You're as tenacious as a dog with a bone," breaking in, Adam chuckles glancing at Isaac as he shakes his head.

"Thanks. I'll take that as a complement," Isaac smiled in return. Getting back to business he hollered out.

"Revelation 20:14.

And death and hell were cast into the lake of fire. This is the second death."

Isaac adds speculatively. "Then God will dwell with mankind."

"Or does mankind become the children of God and they dwell together as the one big family of God?" Adam interjects his question quickly.

"OK," Isaac responds. "That could be a better way of saying it, as mankind are the ones who are changed into new bodies, not God. Anyway, here is where the bible tells us about it.

Revelation 21.

1 And I saw a new heaven and a new earth: for the first heaven and the first earth were passed away; and there was no more sea.

2 I John saw the holy city, new Jerusalem, coming down from God out of heaven, prepared as a bride adorned for her husband.

3 And I heard a great voice out of heaven saying, Behold, the tabernacle of God is with men, and he will dwell with them, and they shall be his people, and God himself shall be with them, and be their God.

4 And God shall wipe away all tears from their eyes; and there shall be no more death, neither sorrow, nor crying, neither shall there be any more pain: for the former things are passed away.

5 And he that sat upon the throne said, Behold, I make all things new. And he said unto me, Write: for these words are true and faithful.

6 And he said unto me, It is done. I am Alpha and Omega, the beginning and the end. I will give unto him that is athirst of the fountain of the water of life freely.

7 He that overcometh shall inherit all things; and I will be his God, and he shall be my son.

8 But the fearful, and unbelieving, and the abominable, and murderers, and whoremongers, and sorcerers, and idolaters, and all liars, shall have their part in the lake which burneth with fire and brimstone: which is the second death.

9 And there came unto me one of the seven angels which had the seven vials full of the seven last plagues, and talked with me, saying, Come hither, I will shew thee the bride, the Lamb's wife.

10 And he carried me away in the spirit to a great and high mountain, and shewed me that great city, the holy Jerusalem, descending out of heaven from God,

11 Having the glory of God: and her light was like unto a stone most precious, even like a jasper stone, clear as crystal;

12 And had a wall great and high, and had twelve gates, and at the gates twelve angels, and names written thereon, which are the names of the twelve tribes of the children of Israel:

13 On the east three gates; on the north three gates; on the south three gates; and on the west three gates.

14 And the wall of the city had twelve foundations, and in them the names of the twelve apostles of the Lamb.

15 And he that talked with me had a golden reed to measure the city, and the gates thereof, and the wall thereof.

16 And the city lieth foursquare, and the length is as large as the breadth: and he measured the city with the reed, twelve thousand furlongs. The length and the breadth and the height of it are equal.

17 And he measured the wall thereof, an hundred and
forty and four cubits, according to the measure of a man,
that is, of the angel.

18 And the building of the wall of it was of jasper: and the
city was pure gold, like unto clear glass.

19 And the foundations of the wall of the city were
garnished with all manner of precious stones. The first
foundation was jasper; the second, sapphire; the third, a
chalcedony; the fourth, an emerald;

20 The fifth, sardonyx; the sixth, sardius; the seventh,
chrysolyte; the eighth, beryl; the ninth, a topaz; the tenth,
a chrysoprasus; the eleventh, a jacinth; the twelfth, an
amethyst.

21 And the twelve gates were twelve pearls: every several
gate was of one pearl: and the street of the city was pure
gold, as it were transparent glass.

22 And I saw no temple therein: for the Lord God
Almighty and the Lamb are the temple of it.

23 And the city had no need of the sun, neither of the
moon, to shine in it: for the glory of God did lighten it, and
the Lamb is the light thereof.

24 And the nations of them which are saved shall walk in
the light of it: and the kings of the earth do bring their
glory and honour into it.

25 And the gates of it shall not be shut at all by day: for
there shall be no night there.

26 And they shall bring the glory and honour of the
nations into it.

27 And there shall in no wise enter into it any thing that
defileth, neither whatsoever worketh abomination, or
maketh a lie: but they which are written in the Lamb's
book of life.

And a bit more in Revelation 22:1-5, KJV of course,

1 And he shewed me a pure river of water of life, clear as crystal, proceeding out of the throne of God and of the Lamb.

2 In the midst of the street of it, and on either side of the river, was there the tree of life, which bare twelve manner of fruits, and yielded her fruit every month: and the leaves of the tree were for the healing of the nations.

3 And there shall be no more curse: but the throne of God and of the Lamb shall be in it; and his servants shall serve him:

4 And they shall see his face; and his name shall be in their foreheads.

5 And there shall be no night there; and they need no candle, neither light of the sun; for the Lord God giveth them light: and they shall reign for ever and ever.

Those scriptures cover your points so far. Culminating with God coming to live with man here on the earth," Isaac said.

"And that's it," Said Adam with finality. "That is how the plan of God plays out, bringing salvation to all of humanity that accept it. Humanities destiny, if we choose to accept it, is to become the spirit born children of God. At least that is how I see it explained from the Bible.

Understanding the Bible this way gives everyone that has ever lived, no matter where, or when, an opportunity to come to Jesus for salvation. It also punishes the wicked, who willingly reject Jesus, for the rest of eternity. They will never partake in eternal life, that is reserved exclusively for the followers of Jesus.

Finally, when everyone has made their choice, when death and the grave are destroyed forever, then God the Father will come and live with mankind as a family. We will all be spirit-physical beings, the same way Jesus is. We will truly be children of the most high."

CHAPTER 17
WHY THAT WAY

"Well that would be nice, if it were true," Isaac blurted out without thinking.

"If it were true?" Adam exclaimed in astonishment. "Weren't you the one reading the proof verses out of the Bible? How can you say, if it were true?"

"Well I just meant that I couldn't believe it all without studying it diligently," Isaac replied defensively. "It will take a lot of time to work through the twists and turns of your story."

"And why do you think it would be nice? Is it because you think it's unfair to confine people, that have no knowledge of Jesus, to the torments of Hell for all eternity. The belief that God punishes mankind without giving them a chance at repentance doesn't portray him as very loving," Adam says, continuing to push his point.

Isaac stammers back with a rehearsed response. "God is sovereign and his ways are a mystery to us. I'm sure he will treat everyone fairly and let them choose Jesus if they want to. Just after they die perhaps, before they go into Hell."

"Perhaps! Perhaps! And you were just giving me the gears for not having any scriptural backing, where's your proof for that thought? You seem to be short of contextual scriptural proof for a lot of your doctrines. Tell me, did you take a lot of time proving what you believe now? Did you search the scriptures before you accepted the belief that mankind has an immortal soul? I think it rests in whether you want to believe all of what the Bible teaches or not," Adam contended heatedly.

"My parents taught me about those fundamentals when I was a child," Isaac protested. "I could hardly be expected to do an in depth Bible study of them before I could read!"

"Well you're not a child any more are you!" Adam retorts.

"Oh, so I should change my beliefs in one day because of what you have told me?" Isaac challenges.

"No. I'm not suggesting you do that, you should be sure and prove all things diligently. But you make it sound like it was some major, lifelong undertaking and that my points were in some way inaccurate to what the Bible teaches," Adam was uncharacteristically sensitive to Isaac's opinions. "You haven't been taking notes and you're not likely going to remember half of what we talked about by tomorrow."

"Oh, I'm sure that I'll be able to find the important scriptures," Isaac said self-assuredly. "But tell me, why would have God devised such an elaborate scheme? Why doesn't God just have everyone choose their fate now, in their first life?"

"Those who lived, before Jesus paid the penalty for sin, couldn't accept his sacrifice before it was made," Adam pointed out. "It was not available to humanity until after the deed was done," Adam prefaced what he was about to say.

"I don't have scripture to back up these ideas, but I think God wanted to let humanity try their own ideas first. That way there would be no doubt by anyone that we need Jesus to save us, as we are helpless on our own. There would be plenty of examples of people who had tried and failed at living a sin free life. Letting everyone try would undeniably prove that humanity is lost, utterly incapable of living without sin. They would have to admit that Jesus is their only hope for salvation.

I'm reminded of my daughter when she was little; she was determined to do things for herself no matter what. She would push my help aside and stubbornly say, 'me do'. I think humanity would have the same attitude that she did when it comes to living a sin free life. People would believe they could do it on their own. So

God let them try, he knew they would fail, but until that belief was tested, it could not be proven wrong. Until we know we need saving, we don't need a saviour."

"OK I can buy that. People can be hard headed," Isaac says in a calmer tone. "But that doesn't explain about giving the Old Testament law to the Israelites. God told them to obey him and they would be saved. What was that for? The Bible tells us that the law can't save anyone; we must all go through Jesus to get to God. Having the law didn't get those Old Testament people any closer to salvation, they needed faith," Isaac quickly looks up some scriptures to prove his point. "Here," He said. "I'll read you some scriptures.

Romans 10:16-17
But they have not all obeyed the gospel. For Esaias saith, Lord, who hath believed our report?
17 So then faith cometh by hearing, and hearing by the word of God.

Here's another, found in.

Galatians 3:1-5
O foolish Galatians, who hath bewitched you, that ye should not obey the truth, before whose eyes Jesus Christ hath been evidently set forth, crucified among you?
2 This only would I learn of you, Received ye the Spirit by the works of the law, or by the hearing of faith?
3 Are ye so foolish? having begun in the Spirit, are ye now made perfect by the flesh?
4 Have ye suffered so many things in vain? if it be yet in vain.

5 He therefore that ministereth to you the Spirit, and worketh miracles among you, doeth he it by the works of the law, or by the hearing of faith?

More still in.

Acts 13:38-39
38 Be it known unto you therefore, men and brethren, that through this man is preached unto you the forgiveness of sins:
39 And by him all that believe are justified from all things, from which ye could not be justified by the law of Moses.

And Ephesians.

1:13-14
In whom ye also trusted, after that ye heard the word of truth, the gospel of your salvation: in whom also after that ye believed, ye were sealed with that holy Spirit of promise,
14 Which is the earnest of our inheritance until the redemption of the purchased possession, unto the praise of his glory.

Finally, we are carnal and completely incapable of keeping the law of God perfectly.

Romans 8:7
Because the carnal mind is enmity against God: for it is not subject to the law of God, neither indeed can be.

So why did God even bother with giving us his laws when he knew we couldn't keep them anyways?"

"Do you enjoy reading out loud?" Adam asks, but the question went unnoticed by Isaac, it was lost in the noise of the truck. Then with a cheeky tone and a smirk he looked Isaac in the eye and yelled earnestly. "I could keep the laws perfectly if given a chance. Why do I need Jesus?"

"What?" asked Isaac with surprise. "You know the nature of man. There is no way you could keep the law of God perfectly without ever making one single mistake at some time."

"Oh yes I can, I just have to know what the rules are and be allowed to try!" Adam insisted noisily.

"What are you on? You're not making any sense at all. It's not possible," Isaac was shaking his head in bewilderment. "No one has ever lived a sin free life except Jesus, the history of mankind has taught us that."

"Exactly, no one ever has, and with the exception of Jesus, no one ever will," Agreed Adam. "But mankind didn't know they couldn't keep the laws of God, until they had time to try and fail at it. Without the chance to try some people would come back to life in a resurrection claiming, like I just did, that they would have been able to live sinlessly, if only God had allowed them to try by spelling out the rules they needed to keep. So he did.

God gave his rules to a chosen nation, a nation that he blessed when they obeyed him and let them fall when they didn't follow his rules and went their own way. We still have the laws of God with us today, if people want to try and keep them perfectly.

Humanity will never be able to accuse God of forcing them to follow him. God has always let mankind make their own decisions on how to live their lives. God lets us try our own ways so we will finally come to the realization that we are incapable of living without sin. Otherwise some would reject the salvation of Jesus. They would believe they could follow the laws of God perfectly, or that they could live a life of their own making that would be acceptable to God, without the help of Jesus. People would reject their saviour because they wouldn't recognize their need, for a saviour.

No, no. God won't allow that to happen. He gives mankind plenty of rope to hang themselves with. On the day of reckoning, there will be no excuses or loopholes for people to say they never got a chance to try. Our failings will be clear for all to see. Every possibility for personal perfection will have been tried and tested at some point in mankind's collective history."

"Huh, I hadn't given that much thought. You make a good point," Isaac said thoughtfully. "I suppose it's like that for everyone, you have to recognize your shortcomings, before you can fix them.

But you make it sound like God isn't concerned that people don't follow him or accept Jesus. So why should I follow Jesus now? Why don't I just wait till later for my salvation when it's easier? Why should I struggle against everything now?"

"I have never said that," Adam states. "God calls whoever he wants to come to Jesus in this life. He gives those he calls the opportunity to become leaders in his coming Kingdom. We need to grow the fruit of his Spirit in our lives now, so we can be kings and priests with Jesus. Christians will be helping to harvest the future children of God during the resurrections.

Spreading the good news about Jesus now is important, that is how people can be called by God in this life. If they are called, now is their time to follow Jesus, there will be no later, or second chance. As far as why follow now, I don't know about you, but where else would I go? It's like what Peter said; Jesus has the words of life."

"Oh let me look that up," Isaac jumped in, fingers flying on the key board. "Here it is,

John 6:68

Then Simon Peter answered him, Lord, to whom shall we
go? thou hast the words of eternal life."

"Exactly, I have no choice but to follow Jesus if I want eternal
life," said Adam. "I know too much to turn back now. Besides,
what makes you think it will be easier for those in the second
resurrection?

They will still have their own personalities and addictions to
struggle with. They aren't resurrected washed clean of their
problems. They will have a lifetime of sin to overcome and forget.
The personalities they developed during this life will still be who
they are in the next.

Ask anyone overcoming an addiction how easy it is to do.
Satan may not be there constantly tempting them, but it is
overcoming Satan's temptations through the Holy Spirit working in
us, that makes Christians spiritually strong today. Some of those
resurrected, whose lives are mired in depraved sin, may never be
able or want to escape their old habits once they are resurrected.

It's called neural plasticity. Our minds work through electronic
connections in our brains. The more we reuse the same thought
connections the more engrained the pathways get. Before long
those paths becomes a paved highway, making it easier for the
thoughts to flow through. Building new pathways and making our
thoughts flow through new connections is a difficult process as the
electrical connections want to take the quickest, easiest way. It
takes a lot of effort to retrain our brains, but it can be done.

Besides, that resurrection isn't a way to escape the call of God.
It is there to provide a chance for people who never received their
call to finally come to Jesus. Chances are, if you are trying to avoid
being a servant of Jesus in this life, then you probably are being
called to Jesus. If you want life, then you better follow that calling.
Otherwise you may be counting yourself unworthy of eternal life
like some of the Pharisees did."

"Ya, and some of those last verses we covered had a lot of people fighting against God in the final war at the end of the second resurrection. I get the impression that a lot of people don't use their opportunity to accept Jesus even in their second life," Isaac says, thinking back on some of the verses he had read.

"That doesn't surprise me," Adam was having to almost yell now, to be heard above the screaming Jake brake. Since they had left the brake check, the steep decline of the road forced Adam to alternate between using his brakes and engine brake to safely keep the speed of the truck in check.

He would use a light brake application, around fifteen psi to gradually slow the speed of the truck. Then he would release the brakes and let the engine brake keep the trucks speed from increasing too quickly. This pattern would alternate about every thirty seconds; brakes applied for ten seconds, then off for twenty, giving the foundation brakes time to cool. The whole time the Jacobs Engine brake barked out its song, from loud, to an intense roar that made the tin cab of the old truck echo angrily.

Adam was trying to make himself heard now at the loudest part of the pattern. "That doesn't surprise me," He yelled again louder to make sure he had been heard. "One third of the angles rejected God when they rebelled. They knew God, they had lived with him in heaven, yet they still rejected him."

Lowering his volume as he applied the rigs brakes, hushing the Jake's bark, Adam continued. "Why should people be all that different than the Angles? I think the percentage of people who reject God's offer of eternal life will be just as large as that of the Angles. I wouldn't be surprised if at least one third of mankind rejects God."

"Let me recap your thoughts to see if I got this right," hollered Isaac, as the loud side of the braking cycle began. "God created people because he wanted a family. Humanity can eventually become his children if they choose to be. Why not just create us as spirit beings, like he did with the Angels?" Isaac asked.

"I believe God created us physical so we could die if we didn't accept Jesus and his ways of love," Adam speculated. "The angels cannot die. The angels who rejected God are doomed to be tormented in the lake of fire for the rest of eternity. By making us mortal God has spared sinful humans an eternity of pain and sorrow. Those who reject Jesus will die, some in the lake of fire to be cremated, but all who don't accept Jesus will never again see life of any kind.

God wants a family who will live in love and harmony. By withholding immortality from humanity, until after we decide to follow God's ways of love, keeps us from a potential eternity of suffering. God takes no pleasure in punishing; he is much more interested in loving others and showing that love extravagantly to them."

"Let's see. We were created mortal, so we could die and become completely nonexistent, if we fail to become children of God," Isaac restates Adam's thoughts. "To aid people in their choosing process, God let everyone follow their own wicked ways, just so mankind would realize they need Jesus and the forgiveness he alone offers.

Then, to make sure people wouldn't think they could keep the laws of God by their own power, he gives his laws to a nation so they could try and keep them, proving through that nation, that humans are incapable of living without sin, even when they know what sin is. In the end, everyone will have to admit the only way to escape their sin is to let Jesus take them away through his atoning sacrifice."

"That's good so far," Adam agreed encouragingly, "then what?"

"Then," Isaac continued. "After Jesus came, was crucified and resurrected, defeating sin for everyone, God now draws the people he chooses out of this world to Jesus, so they can become his followers. Those followers learn to put sin out of their lives by following the Holy Spirit and putting Jesus first in their lives.

Having the Holy Spirit doesn't give Christians eternal life right away though. Having the Holy Spirit now, is more like a down payment to the spirit-physical life we will be resurrected into, at the return of Jesus. We are only heirs now, having to wait for our inheritance of perfection, when we are resurrected as children of God. This physical life we live now, as Christians, could be likened to the gestation period of our new life to come as children of God. Our future potential is to be Kings and Priests, teaching the way of God first for the thousand years of rebuilding, as humanity decides if they will follow Jesus. We will be their leaders under Jesus.

The rest of humanity who haven't been called by God, have to wait in their graves for their resurrection that comes at a later time. Their second lifetime of a hundred years is when they will have their eyes opened to Jesus; they will need to decide for themselves if they accept Jesus or not, during their newly resurrected physical lifetime.

All those who were called by God in this life, but reject Jesus, will also be eventually resurrected to a physical life, but they will be thrown into the lake of fire after their day of judgement. They had their opportunity to follow Jesus in this life, but rejected it. Being mortal they will die in the lake of fire, never to have life again. Even the memory of them will die and they will be forgotten for the rest of eternity. Their punishment will be eternal as they will never live again. They will not be in eternal punishing, as they won't have eternal life. Only the true followers of Jesus will gain eternal life, either at his return, or by following him in their resurrected life. Eventually everyone will have the opportunity to make their own decision to follow Jesus or not."

"Wow. You paid better attention than I gave you credit for," Adam admitted with embarrassment. "Your outline for humanity was pretty accurate to the way the Bible verses we read explained it."

"Thanks. You see I was paying attention," Isaac said, recognizing Adam's regret. "Your plan does give everyone a time to come to God. I can see how it would help those who had no knowledge about Jesus, or the forgiveness he brought."

CHAPTER 18
CHANCE MEETING

"One thing that comes to my mind though," Isaac says thoughtfully. "You seem to be focused on death and dying all the time. I would rather focus on showing the love of God to people. I want to tell them about the love of Jesus and his gospel, not be fixated on death and where we all end up. The gospel is about love," Isaac stressed.

"Yes, the gospel is a message about the love of God," Adam agreed. "But that message is rooted in the death of Jesus. Forgiveness and redemption would not be possible if it were not for the death of Jesus. Even the often quoted John 3:15-17 stresses the sacrifice and love of Jesus; but it also tells us how we can escape death and obtain eternal life.

Life and how to keep it, is one interest all humanity shares. Since death figures so prominently with life, death is unavoidably part and parcel with life. If you have one you don't have the other. It is through death, that the love of God is displayed to the world. It is through death, that his love found its way to us."

"Well how does this great conspiracy you keep talking about affect the love of God?" Isaac asked exasperatedly. "How does my belief in having an immortal soul affect the death of Jesus?"

"Your misunderstanding doesn't affect the death of Jesus at all," Adam continued to explain. "But your misunderstanding of humanities true nature does affect how you interact with those who you say you want to show God's love to. If you are unaware of their potential now, as well of their future potential, you may expect them to make unrealistic choices based on your misconception of how humanity gains eternal life and what will happen to them if they don't."

"Give me an example of what you mean. I don't see how being wrong about the mortality of our soul could hinder us in showing the love of Jesus to people," Isaac said emphatically.

"In school did you get any instruction on doing outreach to people who didn't know Jesus? Adam asked curiously.

"Oh yes, we did that a lot," Isaac replied. "We called it outreach training, or discipleship class. The instructor would run us through all sorts of different scenarios. We did lots of role playing in those classes. It was good to imagine some of the different excuses people would come up with for not accepting Jesus.

As Christians, it is vital we bring the love of Jesus to those who are lost. They need him so badly and it's up to Christians to reach them, but there are so many out there that don't seem to recognize their need for Jesus or the salvation he brings. They are in danger of being in hell's fires for the rest of eternity. 'Behold the fields are white, ready for harvest'," Isaac's voice crackled with emotion as he talked about the lost souls of humanity.

"Let's do some role playing," Adam suggests. "It may be easier to address any doctrinal inconsistencies, while we are actually practicing. I will be the unconverted newcomer and you can be you."

"OK," Isaac replied. Feeling confident in his abilities, Isaac seemed motivated to put into practice his outreach talents through role play. "But I want to be an aid worker in a refugee camp. I will be one of the nurses, no wait, I will be a trauma evacuation technician, flying in a medevac chopper. That way I can cover a wider area and interact with a broader diaspora of people."

"Ya, that job may let you see a wider range of people," Adam agreed. "And it does sound exciting, it is sure to impress people back home, but it may not give you much time to build a relationship with the people you are there to serve. It would be hard to have a meaningful relationship with someone who is so close to death that they need to be evacuated to be saved. It seems to me that it would produce a very one sided conversation, as the sick person would likely be preoccupied with staying alive.

Besides, being so hopped up on drugs, or in such pain, they would hardly be thinking straight, even if coherent. I would think it best to be in a role where you can interact with people when they are relaxed and have time to think and ponder the life altering topics you are discussing."

"Oh, I didn't think of it in that way. I wanted to be in a role that addressed people's most urgent needs," Isaac replied thoughtfully. "Helping them through a trauma, or an emergency, seemed like the best place to be. So what should I do there to help, pass out food and water?"

"Well I'm not sure either, I've never been in a refugee camp," Admitted Adam. "And I don't think there are many people who get medevacked out of those camps anyway. I think for the most part if they get sick or hurt, they are just left there to die."

"I suppose your right. Those camps sound like unpleasant places to end up," Isaac thoughtfully agreed. "Hey, how about if I was an ESL teacher, that would be helpful to the people there who are trying to immigrate to an English speaking country and it would give me the time to build a rapport with the students and their families."

"Good idea, an ESL teacher it is. I will be one of your students trying to improve my English," Adam said, starting to imagine the kind of refugee he would be playing. "I'll be Ting, a refugee from North Korea, he escaped northwards into China, but has ended up in the Mae La refugee camp in Thailand, along the border with Myanmar."

"How do you know about that stuff?" Isaac was surprised by Adam's quick response.

"I told you earlier," Adam said with a smile. "You can't judge a book by the cover. The good radio stations have a lot of interesting and informative programs and with this job; I have a lot of time to listen to them."

"OK," Isaac agreed warily. "I'll be the missionary ESL teacher and you can be Ting, the refugee from North Korea."

"Ooh tank you, Mr. Isak sur. Tat wus a verwy good lesson. You come my hows for food. Clas over for today. Yu come, we tok abot stuff," Adam hollered in his best broken English.

They had been going down the long steep hill for a while now and were still a long ways from the bottom, the engine brake oscillating from loud to obnoxious keeping the rig at a manageable speed. It would be difficult to stop the truck on the hill as it would take quite some distance, at least an eighth of a mile to safely. Adam was watching the road ahead as far as he could; constantly planning ways to avoid any obstacle that they should encounter as stopping in time may not be a viable option.

"I hav questons fo u abowt yo God. I wont to go Canada an need to no abowt yo Kristan holiday an beleefs. Plees come, eet food, an tok."

"It would be my pleasure to come and talk with you," Isaac replied sincerely. "I have some yummy food treats that came in a care package from home, let me go get them and we can share them as we talk."

"Tat good, I like yumy kare food," Adam continued in his broken English spiel.

"Maybe we could do without the broken English and bad accent," Isaac complained. "I get the picture of who Ting is and it's hard enough to hear in here without having to guess at what you're saying as well," Isaac hollered at Adam.

"No problem. I don't think that I could keep up with the acting anyway," Adam said, relieved to be free from the vocal acting part of Ting's character.

"How about I talk in my normal English, but you hear it in the broken English of Ting? It will sort of be like hearing in tongues rather than speaking in them."

"That would be better for me," Agreed Isaac. "I'll imagine I am hearing Ting the whole time.

So how do I get to your house Ting? I don't know where you live," Isaac said looking at Adam intently.

"It is hard to describe as there are no signs for the streets and allies. Me and a couple other men have a small house above a shop-front in a back ally. It would be easier if you came with me the first time, so you don't get lost," Ting replied in Adam's much better English.

"OK. We will have to stop by my house first for the treats, and then go on to your place," Isaac replied, keeping in character and staying with the plot.

"Here we are. This is what I call home, for now," Adam makes a sweeping gesture with his right hand across the windshield of the truck.

"I could have gone to South Korea, but I want to get to Canada. I was told that I might have a better chance of immigrating as a refugee to Canada from this camp, rather than from South Korea. My applications are being processed now, but it takes time and the policies are always evolving and changing.

Please sit down and I will put on some tea to go with your appetizers. Supper may not be fancy but it will be filling."

"Here are the treats from my care package," Isaac said, pretending to hand something to Adam.

"We can eat them before the meal. So, you have gotten me curious, what questions do you have about Christianity," Isaac boldly asks. "How can I help you?"

"I have many questions about your Christian culture," Ting explained. "I have heard random bits about Canada since I was a small boy. My Dad was a respected professor and nuclear scientist in North Korea. Ever since North Korea acquired Canadian nuclear technology, he was a fan of Canada and liked to tell my family Canadian facts and stories."

"Wait a minute," Isaac interjected bluntly. "Canada never sent nuclear technology to North Korea. Canadians, my uncle included, fought against North Korea during the Korean War. There is no way Canada helped North Korea gain nuclear weapons!"

"Things aren't always that straight forward," Ting said, as Adam wagged his finger at Isaac. "North Korea didn't get the nuclear technology directly from Canada. But if Canada hadn't sold its Cando reactors to India, who used them to produce nuclear weapons, then Pakistan wouldn't have stolen that nuclear weapons technology from India. Who in turn, wouldn't have sold weapons grade nuclear material and know how, derived from Canadian technology, to North Korea. After all this espionage took place, my father always had a warm place in his heart for Canada. He saw Canada as helping to liberate the outcasts of the world, intentionally or not."

Adam leans back in his driver's seat as Ting reminisces. "Oh yes, my father saw things differently than most others in our secular, non-religious North Korean society. He was a true man of science and evolution. Until the day my twin brother was hit by a car and killed in front of our house. We were only three years old when he died. My mother was so overcome with grief that she jumped off a bridge to her death, leaving Dad to raise me and my older brother by himself.

Dad was never satisfied with the teachings of evolution when it came to the death of humans. He felt it made our lives so meaningless, if we just died and that was it. Our energy going to fertilizing some flower or weed with no other purpose or future good.

He started studying the origins of the universe and learned science taught that before there was the big bang there was nothing at all. Then something happened that made the big bang boom. He could never learn what that something was. He wanted to know, what started everything before there was anything?

After several years of looking for answers, dad started to go a bit crazy with grief over my mom and brother dying. Along with the stress of his job at the university and raising two rambunctious boys, he started to say things he normally would have not said out loud to others."

"I can see how he might have been pushed to his breaking point," Isaac said sympathetically. "What kind of things did he start to say?" Isaac's curiosity was getting the better of him.

"Oh, he would mock his fellow scientists by saying that, everything came from nothing, or he would misquote Marx by saying, if religion is the opium for the masses, then evolution is heroin for the learned."

Ting is silent for a short while as he remembers his past.

"But what really got us all in trouble was when he kept saying that Kim Il-sung, North Korea's first supreme leader should have learned more from his Presbyterian minister grandfather. That was when our family was relocated to a re-education camp in the northern mountains. We were starving there, forced to memorize and chant state policy and rules. We suffered through mindless work and brutal beatings if we didn't adhere to the smallest rule."

Adam now fully immersed into Ting's character, pulls his t-shirt up over his right side ribs and back, exposing a nasty series of scars he had received from crashing his dirt bike when he was in his late teens. "See, the guards would beat us with sticks if we got out of line. They enjoyed their jobs," Ting complained.

"Sounds like your family fell out of favour with the government. What happened next? How did you end up here?" Isaac was intrigued by Ting's life story, seemingly unaware that it was Adam doing the talking.

"You have to remember that Dad's sanity unraveled slowly," Ting reminded. "We were in the camp for a year before we started to plan our escape. By then my older brother was the true leader of our family. I was barely fifteen when we got our chance to escape. It is all a blur to me now, running in the snow and cold, heading north, north to more cold, but to the warmth of freedom. I have been running ever since.

It took me three years to get through China to Myanmar. Working at any job I could to get transport and food. Living wherever I could, to keep from getting caught and sent back to North Korea. Almost another year of struggle to get here and now, I am out of winters frozen grip of oppression and I can relax a bit in my spring time of release. Here in this refugee camp, I am the closest to my summertime of freedom in Canada than I have ever been."

"Well I hate to break the news to you but summer in Canada is short, but we make up for it with freedom. It's not utopia, but it's pretty good," Isaac boasts. "Do you live here with your dad and brother? I haven't seen them at classes. How is their English?"

Adam bows his head with a sad dis-meaner. "My father and brother died escaping. They both sacrificed themselves to save me. If it hadn't been for their acts of selflessness, I would have died a long time ago," Ting's voice was quivering with emotion and Isaac could tell he was on the verge of tears.

Tenderly Isaac said. "We don't have to talk about it now; we can give it a rest if you want to."

Adam shakes his head and sits up straighter in his driver's seat as he gently applies the brakes to slow the trucks decent. "No. I want to tell you. It will bring honour to them if I do," Ting says with optimism in his cracking voice. Adam takes in a long deep breath. "My brother was the first one to go. We were almost to the Chinese border. A couple of days more and he might have made it all the way here with me.

We had to cross a frozen river. It wasn't very wide, ten meters or so. I was supposed to follow in dad's footsteps on solid ice and then my brother followed behind me in my footsteps. Dad stepped over a fallen tree, frozen in the ice, it was too high for me to get over, and so I went around it. I broke through a patch of thin ice and into the bone chilling water. I couldn't hold onto the edge of the ice with the fast current pulling at me legs. Dad was too far away to get to me and I was going under.

My older brother jumped in behind me, pushing me upwards to dad's reaching hands and forced himself deeper into the cold dark water. Dad barely got to me in time to grab my sleeve before my brother and I both disappeared under the ice. What Dad did to warm me up, I can't say. I only know that when I woke up, I was warm and dry, but my brother was gone.

Dad didn't, or couldn't talk again after that day. I think that the losses he suffered in his life had finally overwhelmed him. We walked for two more days, stealing any food we could find. Then we came to the border with China. North Korea had armed guards at the crossings and they were checking for permits. We hid in the bushes and saw two defectors, hiding under the deck of a truck, get shot and killed for their efforts. I didn't know how we would get across safely. Dad just watched the guards as they checked everyone.

It was almost dark before Dad got up from our hiding spot and motioned for me to follow him. We walked out onto the road and joined up with a group of families. There was about fifteen or twenty of us as we headed towards the border check point.

Some of the guards had left for the barracks and now there were only three manning the crossing. We waited in line at the crossing towards the end of the group, but not the last. Dad was pushing me into the guy in front of me as he was showing his papers to the guard. Then just as the papers were being handed back to him, dad yells for me to 'GO'. Giving me a huge push, shoving me into the guy and the guard. All three of us fell to the ground, papers flying everywhere in the dwindling light.

Then dad starts to run around like a crazy man and yelling his head off, all of the guards start to chase him down the road back into North Korea. As they disappeared into the darkness, I heard shots from a machine gun. The rest of the group and I quickly fled over the border crossing and got into China. The Chinese guards were so busy trying to see what was going on, they completely ignored us. If it hadn't been for my brother and dad, I never would have gotten out of there. My freedom came at their expense," Ting was beginning to choke up talking about his dad and brother. Adam wiped his eyes with the back of his hand.

"I am truly sorry for your loss Ting. You have suffered a lot in your life already; I hope that I can help bring you some piece of mind. When you're ready, I will try to give you all the answers you need," Isaac sits thoughtfully quiet, waiting for Ting to be ready to continue.

CHAPTER 19
SHOW THEM LOVE

This time as the Jake reaches its maddening crescendo, Adam up shifts rather than braking. The truck quickly picks up speed again, as the Jake brake reaches its frantic pitch. Several more cycles of these up shift patterns and the semi has started to vibrate with freeway speed as the wind whistled through the window seal cracks.

Isaac started to look less contemplative and more worried as he stares wide eyed through the windshield as the highway drops below them, down the hill for as far as he could see. He glances at Adam who is unconcernedly making his last up shift into top gear. The Jake brake was beginning its slow advance into the realm of overwhelmingly loud.

"She certainly can run," Adam yells over the noise with a growing smile. "Wind resistance can hold her back now. When we get to the bottom we'll almost be able to coast into Kelowna."

With growing alarm, Isaac asks, "Should we be going this fast down such a steep hill?"

"Maybe not, depends who you ask. All sorts of things, could, happen, but not much is likely to. I think it's called risk management. We'll know for sure when, or if, we get to the bottom," Adam's weak attempt at reassurance was a complete failure. Isaac nervously watched in the side mirror as the air turbulence from the speeding semi, buffeted the young saplings growing in the ditch.

"I would like to start out on a happy note. With a subject that is not so sad," Ting explained. "Who is Santa Claus and how does he fit into the birth of Jesus at Christmas?" Tang light-heartedly asks Isaac his first question.

Glad for the distraction from his present mode of transportation, Isaac thought how best to answer Ting's question.

"He doesn't really have anything to do with the birth of Jesus," Isaac began. "The real life Santa Claus is believed to have been a monk named St. Nicholas from Patara, in modern-day Turkey. He was born sometime around 280 A.D. He was known for his kindness and generosity. He is believed to have given presents out to the children at Christmas. That is why it is St. Nicholas who distributes toys to children around the world at Christmas.

We know that it isn't the original St. Nicholas giving out the presents, but those who do give presents out to others could be said to be doing it in the spirit, or tradition of St. Nicholas."

"Oh. I didn't know that," Said Ting with surprise. "There is such a fuss about Santa that I thought he was there when Jesus was born."

"No, he came into the picture later on. In fact a lot of the traditions surrounding Christian holidays don't come from the bible at all. Many come from the pagan world that the early Christians encountered when they were spreading out from Jerusalem during the first century," Isaac explained.

"The early Christians would try to make the concepts of Jesus and God relevant to the new converts by using symbols they were already accustomed to. The apostle Paul did this in Corinth by introducing the people there to God the creator by telling them he was the god they already had a shrine to, as the unknown god. Paul used something they could relate to, to introduce them to Jesus. Early Christians often found, having a cultural reference point to start with helped them introduce Jesus to those who had no concept of the true God.

Familiar symbols like the yule log, a decorated tree, coloured eggs and even the symbol of the cross, all can be traced back to pre-Christian times. These were the symbols the early Christians used as conversation starting points that the new converts would recognize. Christians gave new interpretations to these familiar symbols to introduce the pagan world to Jesus.

And I hate to be the one to break the news to you, but not everyone in Canada are Christian. North America may be thought of as, Christian, but most people who live there are not living their lives in an effort to follow the example of Jesus. Christian holidays have been commercialized in an effort to sell more merchandise. Christian ideals are being replaced with marketing," Isaac frowns as he explains to Ting.

"Oh, I think I understand," Replied Ting. "So Christian traditions were made up by Christians themselves? I thought those traditions represented truth about God, but they are really just made up stories. I've always wondered how Jesus could have been born of a virgin. What you are telling me now explains a lot," Adam nods his head and has a look of awakened understanding on his face.

"No, no," Isaac quickly says trying to correct the misunderstanding. "Not everything is made up, only some of the traditions. For example, December the 25 may not be the actual day Jesus was born on, we don't know the real day. So we picked a day that was already celebrated as the return of the sun, using that day to introduce the coming of God's son to the world.

All of the truths about the birth of Jesus come from the Bible. In fact the Bible is the only source of all Godly truth. Jesus was born to a virgin as the Bible tells us. Traditions were made by man, but truth comes from God and can be verified through studying the Bible."

Isaac thinks of another example, "Take the wise men for instance. The Bible doesn't tell us how many there were, but it's a Christian tradition that there were three because the Bible tells us they brought three different kinds of gifts, gold, frankincense and myrrh, one for each wise man. There could have been ten wise men with these gifts, Christians just made it a tradition there was only three.

In a similar way, Christians have the tradition that the wise men came to see Jesus in the manger. The Bible tells us that they came to a house, and refers to Jesus as a child, not a baby. More evidence that Jesus was older, is that Herod had all boys from two years old and younger killed.

These Bible facts are left out of Christian, traditional Christmas celebrations. To get all the facts you need to study the Bible. Christmas is a joyous holiday where Christians celebrate the coming of Jesus to the world. Without his coming mankind would still be doomed and mired in their sins. The celebrations give us a fun way to proclaim Jesus to those around us."

"Oh, you Christians make it hard to know what is true and what is tradition. Why not just stick to the facts?" Ting asks in frustration.

"Yes, Christian denominations do vary in what they believe, but they all want to follow Jesus. They just understand the Bible teachings a bit different from each other. Some seem to hold tighter to their traditions than they do to the Bible though," Isaac agreed. "I can see how it might be difficult to sort out."

"That is why I wanted to talk to you, I would like to get a real Bible answer," Said Ting. Adam lightly pressed on the brake in an effort to control the speed of the semi, still rapidly descending the hill.

"I want to know where my family is. My mom, dad and brothers, where are they now? When and where do I get to be with them? I miss them," A tear slowly runs down Adam's cheek as Ting croaks out his words.

"Some Christians who helped me in China told me that I had to believe and accept Jesus in order to have eternal life with him and God. They said there was no other way, except to be saved through Jesus. Is that true?"

"Yes. That is absolutely true," Confirmed Isaac "There is only one way to have our sins forgiven and dwell with God forever and that is if we let Jesus wash our sins away by the blood of his sacrifice. Only those who believe in Jesus can have eternal life. Salvation comes through the death, burial and resurrection of Jesus. We know this to be true, Jesus is our example to follow. He was dead but is now alive with God in heaven, if you want to have eternal life with your heavenly Father, then you must accept Jesus as you saviour. No one can make it on their own."

"Yes I do want that eternal life," Ting replied enthusiastically. "But I am not asking for myself, I am asking about my family. Where are they? They went through so many hardships and died, so that I could live free and have a better life. Where are they? I am not as concerned about myself, as I am concerned for them. What does your God and Jesus have for them?" Ting asks bluntly, as Adam looked directly into Isaac's eyes.

"Well, I don't know that I can give you much good news for them. The Bible clearly tells us that the only path to salvation is through Jesus. Only those who follow and accept him will gain eternal life. Unfortunately, those who don't have their sins cleansed by Jesus will be in the fires of Hell, where they will be tortured for the rest of eternity," Isaac pauses for a moment of thought.

"Your twin brother could be spared from Hell though, as he may have been too young to be responsible for his sins. God is merciful and won't punish those who aren't emotionally responsible for their sins. Infants and young children would fall into that category, so it is a possibility that your twin brother is already waiting in Heaven for you. Don't you want to get to be with him there when you die?" Isaac's voice sounds excited with the possibility of Ting's Heavenly future.

"Yes, of course I would like to be with my twin brother, but also with the rest of my family," Ting protests. "You say that your God is merciful to those who are not emotionally responsible for their sins because of their age. What about those who never herd the message about Jesus and sin forgiveness? Why isn't your God merciful towards them? No one in my family knew about Jesus, salvation, or eternal life.

They tried to be the best people they could be. Their selfless acts during my life prove that to me. They might not have been chronological infants when they died, but concerning the knowledge of Jesus, they were newborns."

"I'm sure they were good people and did their best, but that isn't what brings salvation. Salvation is found only in Jesus," Isaac reiterated forcefully.

"No matter how good we are, our righteousness is like filthy rags compared to God's standard of good. Jesus lived a life free of sin so that he could pay the death penalty for all of humanity. His one perfect sacrifice redeems all those who accept it. We must willingly take Jesus to be our saviour and follow him, otherwise we are lost."

"But my family would have accepted Jesus if only they had heard about him and his salvation," Ting reasoned. "They never got a chance to hear about him in North Korea. How were they to learn about him there?

It's easy for you to say they have no chance, your family have all heard about Jesus. They probably grew up knowing about him. We knew nothing about him; it's not fair to send my family to Hell to be punished for the rest of eternity without the opportunity to repent."

"I am sorry Ting," Isaac said sympathetically. "I can see how much you love your family, but I can't change what the Bible teaches me. There is no salvation without Jesus."

Ting goes silent as Adam keeps the truck barreling down the hill. Stepping slightly on the throttle Adam turns off the Jake brake. The truck cab goes quiet with the exception of the wind whistling around the windows. This calming reprieve takes Isaac by surprise. Looking forward out of the windshield he sees that they are finally at the bottom of the hill. Before he has time to comment on their progress they are bouncing over the Trepanier Creek bridge.

"See going fast wasn't a problem after all," Adam said with a smile. "We aren't going over the speed limit by much. I like to let the truck run out the last bit of the hills. You worry too much about things you don't know anything about. We would still be up there on that hill for another half hour if you were in charge."

Steering side to side for a better viewing angle, Adam checks out the trailer the best he can through the big side mirrors. As far as he could tell, all looked well.

Briefly looking at Isaac, Adam asks. "So how is showing the love of Jesus to Ting going? Is it the positive life affirming gospel you were describing, or does it include the subject of death?"

"Showing the love of Jesus to others is more than just telling them about Jesus. It also includes meeting the physical needs they have. Ting will see the love of Jesus through my act of teaching him English. Love is useful and informative," Isaac insists.

"Yes, it can be both of those," Adam agreed. "But Ting is in need of some emotional healing. So far you have only seemed to make him feel bad for his family and mad with your unfair God. Is that the good news of Jesus you were talking about? If it is, Ting isn't feeling the love."

"That's because he wants his family to be safe in heaven," retorted Isaac. "They can't be in heaven if they don't accept Jesus. Jesus is the only way for salvation and they must personally accept him. You know that."

"Yes I agree with you, we can only be saved from our sins through Jesus," Adam said nodding his head. "But you give no possibility for those who had never heard about Jesus. Your lack of understanding of human mortality and the plan of God is limiting the potential for Ting's family. You are only bringing good news for him and bad news for his family."

Isaac sits silently pondering Adam's words as the semi rapidly climbs the last hill of the connector before they merge onto highway 97 heading into West bank.

"Hey," Ting breaks into the void of conversation. "How can my family be alive in the agonizing torments of Hell for the rest of eternity?

Adam turns his head and looks at Isaac.

"You said the only way to have eternal life is to accept Jesus. No ifs ands or buts. Since they didn't get the chance to accept Jesus they can't be alive. They must be dead. And they won't live in Hell forever, as that would mean they have eternal life. Is this more of your made up Christian tradition stuff like Christmas? I want to know what the bible truly teaches. I have no patience for fables," Ting was struggling to keep his emotions in check and be polite, as he forcefully talked to his honoured guest.

Isaac was taken aback by the stinging charges. "Yes, we do need Jesus, to receive eternal life," Isaac stammers. "And the wicked will be punished forever in Hell."

"How?" asks Ting. "My English needs improving, not my reasoning. If I need Jesus to gain eternal life, I can't have eternal life without him. So those who reject Jesus, end up in Hell, without eternal life. It only stands to reason.

Without eternal life you can't be tormented forever. Your teaching doesn't add up, are you sure that your doctrine didn't come from those pagans the early Christians were trying to convert? Like the Christmas tree?" Ting added sarcastically.

Ting continues angrily. "How can I trust Christian tradition when their most celebrated times and holidays were made up by themselves? I would be no better off than some of the religious people I met on my way here. Hindus and Buddhists who worship statues and gods of their own making, their beliefs seem to all be based on stories and ancient legends. To me, you sound just like them, sure that what you are teaching is right, but have no proof, except some hollow fables of man."

"Now I take exception to that," Isaac protested. "Yes some of the Christian traditions were made up by Christians themselves, but the basic truths come from the word of God, found in the Bible. I can find the scriptures for you if you would like."

"Oh, I am sure you have some Bible verse that you believe proves your point, but would all Christians agree with you?" Ting questioned.

"There seems to be no end to the variety of Christian denominations and their beliefs, how do I know which one is right? They all say they follow the Bible, yet they all can't agree on what is true, even though I have been told, the Bible will not contradict itself. All I want to know for sure is, where is my family and when do I get to be with them.

If what you have told me is true and my family has nothing to look forward to, other than to be tormented in hell for the rest of eternity, simply because they never had the chance to hear about Jesus, then I don't want to become a Christian. I would never forsake my loved ones to be in hell by themselves. I would rather join them there in torment. We could at least be together in suffering. I don't want to be with a God in paradise, who would condemn uninformed people to eternal torment without giving them a chance to learn. It feels so wrong!" Ting's voice was defiant, as Adam's face started to twist in rage.

"The ways of God are mysterious to us mortals," Chirped Isaac.

Ting interrupted, cutting Isaac's words short before he could continue with more platitudes.

"Yes, you see, you just said it yourself. Us mortals," Ting said in a flurry, clearly agitated. "We don't have an eternal life. The evolutionists are right. When we die, we are dead; we become dust, just like what is said at Christian funerals. 'Ashes to ashes, dust to dust'. Man is mortal. So my family is not in hell now, they are just dead. Dead, like Jesus was dead after being crucified.

I was told by the Chinese Christians I met, all Christians believe Jesus came back to life after being dead and buried for three days in the grave. Apparently, that was the only sign he gave to prove he was the Messiah. Then God would bring him back to life after three days. If Jesus truly died to save me, why isn't my family just dead and waiting for God to bring them back to life, same as he did for Jesus? Why do you say that my family is alive now, being tormented in Hell.

You are saying, they have immortality without believing in Jesus, yet you also say, we must accept Jesus to have eternal life and gain immortality. Your words are not consistent with your stated beliefs. How can I trust you? You just aren't credible," Adam monumentally lets go of the steering wheel throwing his hands in the air, while Ting makes a huffing, scoffing sound with his breath.

"I don't mean to upset you," Isaac reassured. "I want to show you how much Jesus loves you. I am here to help you because I want to demonstrate the love of Jesus to you and let you hear the good news of how you can have your sins forgiven and gain eternal life with God," Isaac talked earnestly, trying to make a fresh start in the conversation. Ting was having none of it, as the safety of his family was his biggest concern.

"You need to consider your eternal salvation. By rejecting Jesus, you will be no help to your family. You will only be hurting yourself. We all must make our own choices as they are presented to us. You can't help your family choose now, they are in God's hands," Isaac continued.

"Yes we must make the best choice we can with the options we are given," Ting agreed. "But how can I accept and worship a God who condemns people to a horrible fate without giving them the opportunity to accept his free gift of salvation? I find that so unfair, I don't want to worship a God like that, let alone have to spend eternity with him. I don't think I could last that long without getting mad at him for imprisoning my family, as well as all the others that share in their fate.

I could never love this God of yours as you describe him. I had been led to believe the Christian God was our heavenly father, a father who loves his children and wants the best for them, not one who destroys the uneducated rather than teaching them."

Isaac is silent while his mind raced through the rehearsed scenarios he had practiced in school. Adam was busy negotiating the increased traffic through Westbank. They had to stop for a couple red lights and Adam was complaining about the other road users having no idea about the limitations trucks have when it comes to stopping quickly.

"They should teach beginner drivers about how hard it is for trucks to stop," Adam complained loudly after a car pulled tight in front of him and then stopped for the changing traffic light. "This guy is lucky we have no load. If we did, he would have become a bumper ornament. When a car is involved in a crash with a truck, the truck driver is only hurt ten percent of the time. Probably trips getting out of the truck to help the car driver! If people remembered that statistic, they might give trucks a bit more room to stop, it would be in their best interest."

Isaac remains oblivious to what is going on around him as he tries to think of answers for Ting.

"Ting," Isaac called over to Adam. "This is your time to accept Jesus. God wants you to be his son. If you don't accept Jesus, you will lose your soul in the fires of Hell. God doesn't want that to happen, he loves you so much that he sent his only begotten son to die for you, paying for your sins, so that you should not die, but have everlasting life.

You can be redeemed of your sins through Jesus and live forever in heaven with God. Your penalty has been paid in full through the love of Jesus. He doesn't want you to die. He wants you to live with him forever."

"That sounds very nice," said Ting. "Most people would want to live forever in paradise. But I don't think you have thought through your terminology, or your doctrine."

"What do you mean by that?" Isaac asked with a mixture of shock and annoyance in his tone of voice. "I have been telling you the Bible truth through our entire conversation."

"Well could you please give me your definition of life and death?" Ting asked with exasperation. "It seems to me you use them to mean the same thing. If I accept Jesus, I have eternal life in heaven, but if I reject Jesus, I have eternal life in hell. Yet I can only gain, eternal life, if I accept Jesus, so by not accepting Jesus, I should die.

What is death and what is life? You seem to be making them both the same thing. The only difference is, one is pleasant and one is nasty. You just told me that God doesn't want me to die, but wants me to live. Then you tell me I must choose, that I can be in bliss forever in heaven, or be tormented in hell for the rest of eternity. What is it, because it can't be both? I'm either dead, or alive."

"You focus too much on death," Scolded Isaac. "Jesus wants to give you, life eternal. All you have to do is accept him and you can have true life."

"Of course I'm focused on death. My family are all dead. Where are they, what's happening to them, that's what I want to know about?" Ting exclaimed. "That's what I have been asking you about. Their outcome is what I want to know, not mine. Don't you first world people think of others, or is your only concern for yourself?" Ting's voice was loud and accusational. Adam was talking so forcefully that he was beginning to spray small amounts of saliva onto the windshield.

"Well of course you die," Isaac said slowly and purposefully as if he was talking to someone who didn't have all of their mental faculties. "We all die physically, but your soul lives on. That's why you need to choose Jesus now while you can. Once you die it will be too late to save your soul from the fires of hell, 'For it is appointed unto men once to die, then comes the judgement'."

"Am I not a man, made the same as Jesus?" Ting asked inquisitively. "I was told he was fully man and fully God. Jesus was supposed to have died for my sins providing me access to salvation and eternal life. Wasn't he dead for three days and then came back to life? Wasn't that the proof of his messiah-ship?"

"Yes he did die physically. But the Bible tells us that he preached to the spirits in bondage when he was in the grave. Here I'll read it to you," Isaac explained. Then he read out loud from the lap top.

"1 Peter 3:18-20 KJV
18 For Christ also hath once suffered for sins, the just for the unjust, that he might bring us to God, being put to death in the flesh, but quickened by the Spirit:
19 By which also he went and preached unto the spirits in prison;
20 Which sometime were disobedient, when once the longsuffering of God waited in the days of Noah, while the ark was a preparing, wherein few, that is, eight souls were saved by water.

There, do you see? That confirms it. Jesus preached to the imprisoned spirits after he died and was in the grave," Isaac said confidently. "His body died like ours will, but his soul lived on to preach to others. Our souls are immortal, when we die they go on to be with Jesus in heaven, or they go to be punished in hell. That's what the bible tells us."

Adam runs his fingers through his hair and shakes his head as Ting replies to Isaac. "You just said we could only have eternal life if we accepted Jesus. Now you say we have a soul that has eternal life, without the sacrifice of Jesus. What you should be saying, is that Jesus is only needed to get to heaven and avoid hell.

Your also saying that Jesus didn't really die to forgive my sins; he was just extremely physically handicapped. Dead people have none of the aspects of life. You can't be dead, if you are alive and conscience outside of your body. That would only make you physically challenged.

If what you say now is true, then what you told me were the basic truths of Christianity are false. Like I said earlier it appears as though you don't know your terminology and you haven't thought through your doctrine. Alive is alive, dead is the opposite. You can't be both at the same time. Your beliefs make the Bible very contradictory."

"No, no, no," Isaac retorted in a huff. "You only die physically. Your essence, you soul, your spirit if you will, lives on. Your body and you soul are separate entities but go together to make up who you are. The body dies but the spirit lives on."

"Then I don't need Jesus to receive the gift of eternal life. In fact it's not much of a gift from God if I already possess it, I have had it since birth," Ting reasoned. "The eastern religions are right; they believe I only need to become a better person in this life to have a good afterlife. My karma will determine my destiny, good or bad. At least they offer hope to everyone, dead or alive and not just to those who have heard about Jesus and have accepted him."

CHAPTER 20
NEW IDEAS

"No," Isaac groaned in emotional agony. "Jesus is the answer. We can never be good enough by our own efforts. Our hearts are destined to sin, that's why Jesus came to this earth. He lived a sinless life and then shed his blood to wash away our sins.

You know yourself that you could never live a sinless week, let alone a lifetime, or an eternity. The whole of mankind has yet to produce a sinless person, save Jesus. Our only hope is to trust in Jesus and let him cover our sins through the cleansing of his blood."

Isaac is trembling with passion as he speaks of the sacrifice Jesus willingly made for all. "The other religions of the world are hollow; there is only one name by which we can be saved.

Maybe I am wrong about your family not being able to have an opportunity to accept Jesus. A guy I met recently was telling me about an, after death scenario, that I had never heard before. He seemed to have, some, scriptural backing for his ideas, but I haven't had a chance to look into it all yet. As far as after death beliefs go, it's really out there in left field. I don't know of any popular denomination that would agree with his understanding. His belief would seem to provide some hope for the salvation of your family though. He did use a lot of scriptures for support, but he put them together very differently than I have ever been taught.

I thought he was an old, odd ball crank, a real eccentric type. I mostly just listened to his ramblings to make the time pass quicker and to give him someone to talk to. I felt sorry for the lonely old guy."

"Oh. That sounds interesting," Said Ting, as Adam scowled at Isaac's comments. "If his doctrines were accurately supported from the Bible, then why wouldn't I want to believe them, especially if those beliefs can show a way for my family to receive salvation? That would give me a firm hope for them and a hope that we will be together again, as the family we always wanted to be."

"Well like I said, I haven't had the chance to look into it yet. To be perfectly honest I thought the belief was rather flaky, as it was so far away from what I had always been taught. But I have to admit, it would give your family the opportunity to accept Jesus.

That's not to say they would be saved, only that they would have the chance to get to know Jesus. They would still have to willingly accept him as their Savior. There are no guaranties what they will decide when the time comes," Isaac tries to temper Ting's expectations.

"Ya, but at least they get a chance at salvation. That's more than they had with your beliefs. Tell me about the strange ideas this, odd ball guy, told you. I am curious to hear how my family might learn of Jesus now that they are dead," Ting's voice was excited with the hopeful prospect of a future reunion.

Adam hits the brakes hard as the traffic in front of him comes to an unexpected and seemingly unnecessary stop. Quickly checking his left hand mirror Adam bats at the signal light lever. The lights barely have time to flash before he is changing lanes to the left veering around the cars stopped in the curb lane.

After blowing past fifteen cars or so the reason for their stagnant motion became apparent. A car was waiting for a pedestrian to clear the crosswalk before it could proceed with a right hand turn. The pedestrian seemed to be in no hurry to get out of the way as he sauntered slowly towards the sidewalk. Adam said nothing as he shook his head. Once they were clear of the jam he reluctantly signaled his intentions and changed back into the right lane.

"Once we get onto the three lane road we will be able to stay in the center lane. That will help keep us out of any potential vehicular conflicts. I don't need any of those headaches today,"

Adam said thoughtfully. "Today I just want to get home without any complications."

Isaac is so focused on his conversation with Ting, that he doesn't even notice Adam's comments or the abrupt course change of the truck. "Well like I said, I haven't had time to look into his ideas to find where he has undoubtedly gone wrong. Cause let's face it, it's been over two thousand years since Jesus walked on the earth, and these ideas of his are not supported by any of the major Christian religions of the world. If his ideas were to be true, then everyone else would have been getting it wrong for a long time. When I think of all the Godly people who have gone before me, it is ludicrous to think that Christendom should be in need of his understandings."

"Yes that may be true. But if his ideas are supported by the Bible then they shouldn't be minimalized either," Ting countered. "What makes his beliefs so different than everyone else's?"

"First off, his whole concept seems to be based on the notion that God created humans fully mortal. He believes that we have no soul that will live on after we die. When we are dead, that's it, we are dead."

"So more like an evolutionist," Ting pondered out loud.

"Kind of I guess. But he still believes in creation," Isaac explained. "He insists that God created us mortal at the Garden of Eden. He calls the idea of the, immortal soul, a lie foisted onto Adam and Eve in the beginning by Satan, to keep us blinded to the plans God has for mankind's salvation.

He calls the notion of humans having an immortal soul, or spirit, a worldwide satanic conspiracy. He insists that's why all cultures have the notion of an afterlife. Satan planted the notion that we wouldn't die at the beginning of mankind's start and it has infected everyone ever since," Isaac turns to Adam with a look of terror on his face and trembled with mock fear. "It's all so very scary, the mother of all conspiracy theories."

Traffic was congested and Adam ignored the insult as he continued to drive past the seemingly endless strip malls heading into Kelowna.

"Are his beliefs justified? Is that what the Bible tells us?" Ting asks sincerely. "If they are, that would explain why God tells us the only way to have eternal life is by accepting Jesus, it would also support the teaching that Jesus died to save me from my sins and death. Not just becoming, extremely physically handicapped." Ting pondered his thoughts and then added.

"It also lines up with the definitions for life and death. Life lets you receive stimulation from the world around us, as well as make signals out to the world. It also enables us to have internal function or thoughts. Death is the opposite of life. There is no internal function, no sending out or receiving stimulation. Death is a complete stop of all functions that we associate with life, no matter how faint or seldom. Someone isn't mostly dead, they are barely alive. You can't be dead, if you are alive in some other state of existence."

"I wouldn't say the Bible explicitly tells us that we have an immortal soul, any more than it tells us that we don't have one," Isaac says. "It's more in the way you understand what the scriptures are saying."

"That doesn't sound very convincing," Ting broke in. "You were quite clear about the fate of my family ten minutes ago. Now you say it's more in the way the scriptures are understood. I don't know who to believe. I think I need to find out more about this new insight. Maybe it offers more hope than all of the teachings from, Christendom's Godly people that have gone before you.

The Bible proof is ether there or it isn't. Maybe your idea of the eternal soul is like your idea of Christmas, a nice story, but not completely backed up by the Bible. Some facts may have been altered or amended to fit with tradition," The tone of Ting's voice was heavy with accusation and disappointment. Adam took quick fleeting glances at Isaac as he maneuvered the big rig in the congested traffic.

"Like I said," Isaac reiterated. "His ideas are new to me. They did appear to have some merit, but I am not going to abandon what I have been taught all my life and believe to be true, without serious study. He may have had some compelling scriptures to support his beliefs, but I am in no position to endorse them. You would be best to look into those beliefs yourself.

There was a host of ideas that are new to me. Being completely mortal was just the start. For example I have always been taught and believe that a person goes to heaven or hell immediately at their death. He has those who accept Jesus, asleep, waiting in the grave until the return of Jesus at his second coming. He says this is when they receive their new spirit bodies and eternal life.

Then they start to rule with Jesus as the kingdom of God takes over the world. The old guy teaches that it is a literal physical kingdom that will rule over all nations of the world. The saints are to be the kings and priests, leading what's left of mankind, as they rebuild the world over a thousand year period. Not only that, but he believes Satan will be bound in chains, during this thousand years of rejuvenation, unable to influence the world into sin."

"Wow!" said Ting. "That is different from anything I have ever heard. Are you sure he's a Christian?"

"Oh yes, I believe he is. He definitely believes everyone needs to accept Jesus for salvation. That is the basic essential for all Christians. No one can be saved by any other name, we must all go through Jesus," Isaac nods his agreement with Adam's belief for salvation.

"Well how does that help my family? They are dead and haven't accepted Jesus. They will still be left out of this Godly Kingdom," Ting complains in bewilderment.

"Yes they do miss out on this resurrection. This resurrection, at the second coming of Jesus, is only for those who have accepted

Jesus as their Savior now during this life. He believes all other people, including your family, will stay dead until God brings them back to life. He thinks they will be in the safe keeping of their graves for a long time yet," Isaac tries hard to remember Adam's beliefs and get them in the proper sequence.

"Your dead family won't be introduced to Jesus until they are resurrected after this thousand year period is over. He thinks there will be a hundred year period, at the close of the thousand years of rejuvenation. That's when everyone who didn't get the opportunity to learn about Jesus, during this life, will be brought back to physical life in another resurrection.

They supposedly will have a hundred year, mortal life span, to learn of Jesus and decide if they want to accept him and Gods ways of love. This would give your family time to work out their emotional problems and experience life free from the influence of Satan to make them sin. They could follow Jesus free from outside interference. This will be their time to exercise their free moral agency; the only thing keeping them from salvation would be their own choices."

"Wow," Ting said with delight. "These notions seem to be more fair than yours. At least people who have never had the chance to hear about Jesus during this life, will get the opportunity to hear about salvation and accept it if they want to. They don't go directly to hell because they didn't know about the salvation Jesus offers. To me this plan makes God seem much more loving. What happens to those who refuse to follow Jesus and reject God during this second life? What happens to them?"

"Well I believe he said that those who reject God, and decide not to choose life will get what they want," Isaac remembered confidently.

"What do you mean? They will get what they want?" Ting questioned.

"Well since they are resurrected, for those hundred years, back into the same mortality they died with, God will let them refuse the eternal life brought by Jesus and they will die, never to be resurrected back to life again. Their punishment for rejecting Jesus will be everlasting, even the memory of them will be forgotten.

This hundred year life time, will be their time to gain salvation and eternal life, if they refuse it, God will respect their choice and let them die," Isaac is trying hard to get the time sequencing and facts of the resurrections correct. He pauses at times to replay Adam's rantings in his mind.

"How do they die?" Ting asks intrigued.

"I believe the old guy said that Satan is released from his pit at the end of the hundred years for a short time," Isaac continues, reciting the events Adam had described to him the best he could.

"Satan goes out and deceives those who don't choose Jesus. He incites them to make war against the saints of God who are living peacefully in undefended cities. This will be the final war mankind will ever fight against God. Needless to say, God wins, everyone who is not on the side of God and Jesus, die in this final battle. You know, he actually has some obscure Bible scriptures that support all this?" Isaac has a slight hint of admiration in his voice.

Ting blurts out in amazement. "You are right; this is not like anything I have heard from a Christian before. When you said he was way out, in the left field position, you weren't joking. But his thoughts do give me comfort that my family and all those in their position are not doomed without hope. According to the scriptures he reads, they all will have their chance to freely choose Jesus and receive salvation.

But what about Hell and the wicked being thrown into the lake of fire? Where does that come in with his scenario? You haven't mentioned it yet. Surely he believes in punishment for the wicked."

"Oh yes, he believes in the fires of Hell all right," Isaac confirms with a laugh. "But he believes that the people who are thrown into the flames are from still yet another resurrection. They too will be resurrected as mortals and shown how they chose not to follow Jesus. A heavenly judge will pass sentence on them. They will be thrown into the lake of fire and die there, never to exist again. There will never be another opportunity for them to have life.

He says that it is Satan and the demons, the immortal spirit beings; they will be alive to be tormented in the flames forever. The humans that are sent to the flames will die in the fire because they are mortal."

"That's logical," Ting agrees, raising his left eye brow. "But who are they. What time did they come from? If everyone gets to freely choose Jesus in their second life, who are the ones getting thrown into the fires of hell? Is this their second life?

"Well I only talked with him the one time. I can't remember everything he said perfectly," Isaac complained defensively. "But I think he said that those who have been called by God, coming to Jesus in this life, but reject Jesus by their actions and decisions have no further opportunity to change their ways.

They will have used up their chance for eternal life in the kingdom of God. He was quite clear; everyone will get a chance to repent, but only one. Their choice will come either now in this life, if they are called by God to be leaders in the coming kingdom, or they will have an opportunity when they are resurrected back to mortal life before the last battle during the hundred year period."

"Which is better? To be called to Jesus now, or get to learn of him without Satan and his influence around?" Ting Questions almost to himself.

"Beats me," Isaac retorts. "Without Satan it should be easier. But then again, without gravity to work against, we wouldn't build any muscle. Maybe it will be like that for those who learn about Jesus later, they won't have much spiritual muscle to ward off Satan when he is finally released from his chains.

And those who are called now and fight Satan during this life get to rule with Jesus as kings and priests from the beginning of God's kingdom. They may have a better position, or receive better rewards for their efforts. It's all speculation as God doesn't tell us much about what his kingdom, or heaven will be like, only that it will be great. Either way, we will still have eternal life in the kingdom as a son of God, which is pretty awesome no matter what you do there."

"I wonder why God would set it up like this, not calling everyone to himself now, like you teach?" Ting asks Isaac, as Adam watched the flow of traffic ahead of him slow to a crawl heading down bridge hill entering Kelowna.

"I don't know," Isaac said resolutely. "That old crazy guy I was talking to said it was so that great people wouldn't start to think they were anything special. To keep the mighty humble, God calls the week and broken now. That way the focus stays on Jesus as the only way to salvation. Otherwise people might get the idea they could have salvation through their own power and righteousness. If he was right and only the foolish are called, he was living proof of his own belief, if you get my drift?" Isaac adds with a chuckle.

"So if I understand these ideas properly, God isn't that concerned with having humanity saved during this life now. He isn't in some kind of a race with the Devil to save the souls of mankind before each one dies. God has the power to bring them back to life again anyway, where they can learn about him in a world of peace, free of Satan's temptations," Ting was starting to congeal his thoughts, connecting them together.

"If most people throughout history, like my family, die without having heard the salvation message brought by Jesus. That's alright, as they will have their time for salvation later. The trials and struggles they have with sin during this life will only highlight their utter lack of ability to live a sinless life when they are resurrected. None of them will think they could live perfectly on their own. Their need for Jesus will be clear to them and to those around them."

Ting speculates further. "I suppose then, the reason why Christians are to spread the gospel about Jesus, in this life, is so God can draw those who he wants now. The weak and broken people, who know they couldn't make it on their own and are open to him, they are to become the leaders in the coming kingdom of God. They wrestle during this life against sin, building spiritual muscle, denying their own will through the help of the Holy Spirit, following the examples of Jesus. That way God will have strong leaders ready to take charge with Jesus when it is time for his kingdom to start ruling the nations."

CHAPTER 21
PERSECUTION

"Sounds like the plans of God are a bit more detailed than I had been led to believe," Ting said disappointedly. "And you said there are Bible scriptures that support these thoughts? How can it be these ideas are not more widely talked about? After all, like you said, there has been over two thousand years of Christian teaching. Why are these ideas so far out of the main stream of Christianity?" Ting questioned in amazement.

"I don't know," replied Isaac. "If I was to guess though, I would have to say it's because the Bible as we know it, was not put together until later in the first century by scholars from the Catholic Church. Common believers had no access to a Bible or its teachings.

The Churches clergy were the sole purveyors for the word of God. The Church had its traditions and beliefs firmly in place and actively put down any dissension. These traditions and doctrines weren't challenged successfully until the reformation.

Look at the life story of Galileo. He was a renowned scientist until he was punished by the Roman Church for the heresy of teaching that the earth revolved around the sun. After being found 'vehemently suspect of heresy' by an inquisition, he spent the rest of his life under house arrest. These events took place in the early sixteen hundreds. The global Christian society hasn't had freedom of religious thought for very long.

After the reformation things weren't any better with the Protestant denominations. It was also a death sentence if you preached against their orthodoxy. None of the leading churches seemed to tolerate freedom of thought if you were going to express it loudly to others.

That is why the Pilgrims fled Europe to come to the new world of America, they wanted religious freedom. Personal and religious freedom, was still a strong desire decade later, demonstrated by the American bill of rights. Freedom to live life without being told how to think was denied to most of the world up till then. Had liberty and freedom been available, there would have been no need to demand, or fight for it.

Most Christian denominations seem to have stifled diversity, rather than embrace it," Isaac ponders his rant against exclusive orthodoxy. He couldn't explain what brought it on, his mind was just flooded with facts he had studied in church history class. Though he had never given them much thought before, as the class was mandatory and not one he had been keen on taking.

It had never occurred to him that it was the established churches that were squelching Bible based ideas, in favour of church doctrine and tradition. His mind was awash with stories of faithful people being martyred for their beliefs, refusing to recant some of the same Bible truths that he also believed in. Beliefs Isaac had held to be true, for as long as he could remember.

He felt a kinship to those martyrs that went before him, their faith in Bible beliefs such as, baptism is for those who choose Jesus, that faith alone could lead to salvation, or that the Bible alone, not church doctrine, governed the source and requirements of faith. Along with those martyrs he too didn't recognize the authority of the Pope or the Catholic Church as the sole purveyors of the Christian faith.

It finally dawned on him who was doing the persecuting; it was not some Satan worshippers, out to tear down Christianity. Those who were stoking the fires of intolerance were from the Christian establishment. The very ones who were supposed to be spreading the life giving message of Jesus to the world.

In an instant he recognizes his own hypocrisy and intolerance towards other Bible based beliefs. "Would I have been there with an arm full of wood myself?" he quietly asks out loud.

"What," said Ting? "I couldn't hear you in this noisy old truck. You'll have to yell at me."

"Oh, I wasn't saying anything," Isaac muttered. "It just came to me that I was wrong about there being two thousand years of unfettered Christian biblical scrutiny. Major Christian denominations have not truly encouraged open debate of their Bible teachings. Instead, for the most part, they did their best to stifle any beliefs other than their own. Most denominations want conformity to their ideas rather than thoughtful Bible based discussion.

So when I said that there has been two thousand years of Bible study since Jesus died for us, I was wrong. It seems to me now that there has been mostly two thousand years of conformity, interspersed by bursts of enlightenment. Perhaps I should look at these new ideas more seriously, as they do appear to have at least some biblical support. My traditional thoughts on several beliefs were successfully challenged by this crazy old guy, so maybe his ideas on immortality do have some merit."

"How does that help me?" Ting said in a huff. "What am I supposed to believe? Do I believe that my family is dead waiting for their chance to accept Jesus, or are they in the flames of Hell! You need to tell me!"

"No. I don't need to tell you," Isaac snapped back. "You need to find out for yourself. I am not responsible for your salvation, you are. 'Work out your own salvation with fear and trembling'," Isaac quotes roughly from Philippians 2:12. "You need to do some work for yourself and not outsource your faith to others. I can tell you about Jesus and your need for salvation, which is at the core of Christianity, it is essential.

These issues of where, when and how we get to our final destination with Jesus is not an essential belief, they are peripheral. You will get a different opinion depending which Christian denomination you ask. You should do some study into what the Bible has to say and then decide for yourself.

Your beliefs may change as you discover new things the Bible has to tell you. Doctrines don't need to be stagnant. If you uncover new truth and you prove it to be true, then believe it. Christians are allowed to make new discoveries of wisdom, that's why our Christian walk is a growing one, we are to grow in wisdom and faith. We can't grow if we are constrained by our erroneous beliefs of the past."

"You mean to say I can be a Christian and not believe my family is burning in Hell?" Ting questions Isaac bluntly. "I only have to believe in Jesus to be saved. Are you telling me that as a Christian I have freedom in the peripheral areas of doctrine to choose for myself what I believe? I would much rather believe my family will get the chance to accept Jesus at some future time. But I don't want to be wrong, I want to be correct. I believe accepting Jesus is a personal decision. But at least with this new way, my family will get to have an opportunity for salvation. It is much preferable to what, you, told me would happen to them.

There is much more to this Christian stuff than I had thought. I suppose I do need to put the time and energy in to see what the Bible teaches for myself, rather than just believe what others tell me it teaches. Now that I can get on the internet here at the camp, research resources should be easily accessed."

"Your right, you have just given me a thought," Isaac exclaimed with eyes wide. "In order to do good in depth Bible study, the resources needed were not readily available to the general population until the internet was developed. For instance, if I wanted to get different translations of the bible, or get explanations for ideas, it would've had to come from books that were not always available. Now with the world wide web, those resources are only a mouse click away.

One could argue that the time for Christian understanding and debate on a worldwide scale has only just gotten underway. After all, the Bible was not even translated into the common language of the people until the fourteen hundreds. Before that, to even read it would have been impossible, except for the elite scholars. I wonder what new discoveries in biblical understanding will come from this world wide accessibility."

"I don't know," said Ting. "But I will be doing my own study from now on. I will prove my beliefs from the Bible and make sure they do not contradict other Bible teachings. I need to be careful not to blindly believe what others tell me, but prove what they say from all relevant Bible scripture.

To be a knowledgeable Christian I need to prayerfully decide what is right from careful study of the Bible scriptures. From my conversation with you today it is clear to me that a scripture's meaning can be twisted from what the original intent was. I want to know for myself what is true. You are right, I need to do the work of study for myself and not leave my beliefs of faith for others to figure out."

"That would be the safest thing to do for your own satisfaction," Isaac agreed. "If you don't study you will never know for sure. It reminds me of a Bible story about the believers who lived in Berea. Here let me read some verses to you. I brought my lap top with me to lunch and the camp has Wi-Fi everywhere, thanks to the donations from one of those Hi-Tec billionaires," Isaac does a search on the lap top and starts to read to Ting. "Here it is in

Acts 17:10-11 KJV.
10 And the brethren immediately sent away Paul and Silas by night unto Berea: who coming thither went into the synagogue of the Jews.
11 These were more noble than those in Thessalonica, in that they received the word with all readiness of mind, and searched the scriptures daily, whether those things were so.

They didn't blindly believe the stories from Paul and Silas. They proved themselves noble by putting in the hard work of studying scripture to prove that what they were told was the truth. They have left us a great biblical example to follow," Isaac said confidently.

"There are many verses that warn us about those who would lead us away from the truth of Jesus. Here let me read you some," Isaac does a search on the net. He starts to read before Ting thinks to reply.

"We are warned to be careful about who we choose to believe," Isaac states. "We need to recognize false teaching when we hear it. 1 John 4:1-6 instructs us in what to look for in recognizing the spirit of truth.

Beloved, believe not every spirit, but try the spirits whether they are of God: because many false prophets are gone out into the world.
2 Hereby know ye the Spirit of God: Every spirit that confesseth that Jesus Christ is come in the flesh is of God:
3 And every spirit that confesseth not that Jesus Christ is come in the flesh is not of God: and this is that spirit of antichrist, whereof ye have heard that it should come; and even now already is it in the world.
4 Ye are of God, little children, and have overcome them: because greater is he that is in you, than he that is in the world.
5 They are of the world: therefore speak they of the world, and the world heareth them.
6 We are of God: he that knoweth God heareth us; he that is not of God heareth not us. Hereby know we the spirit of truth, and the spirit of error."

Hardly stopping for a breath Isaac continues to read to Ting from the verses he found on the lap top.

"Here is more Bible direction for us," Isaac said clearing his throat. "Those who deny Jesus as Savior are singled out as false prophets.

2 Peter 2:1-3
But there were false prophets also among the people, even as there shall be false teachers among you, who privily shall bring in damnable heresies, even denying the Lord that bought them, and bring upon themselves swift destruction.
2 And many shall follow their pernicious ways; by reason of whom the way of truth shall be evil spoken of.
3 And through covetousness shall they with feigned words make merchandise of you: whose judgment now of a long time lingereth not, and their damnation slumbereth not.

These people only want to make a living from the people of God. They don't care about the people, only about themselves and their own well-being.

Romans 16:17-19
Now I beseech you, brethren, mark them which cause divisions and offences contrary to the doctrine which ye have learned; and avoid them.
18 For they that are such serve not our Lord Jesus Christ, but their own belly; and by good words and fair speeches deceive the hearts of the simple.
19 For your obedience is come abroad unto all men. I am glad therefore on your behalf: but yet I would have you wise unto that which is good, and simple concerning evil."

Ting tries to say something but can't get a word in edgewise.

"Jesus himself warned us about these predators trying to devour his people." Isaac goes on excitedly.

"Matthew 7:15
Beware of false prophets, which come to you in sheep's clothing, but inwardly they are ravening wolves.

Mark 7:6-9
He answered and said unto them, Well hath Esaias prophesied of you hypocrites, as it is written, This people honoureth me with their lips, but their heart is far from me.
7 Howbeit in vain do they worship me, teaching for doctrines the commandments of men.
8 For laying aside the commandment of God, ye hold the tradition of men, as the washing of pots and cups: and many other such like things ye do.
9 And he said unto them, Full well ye reject the commandment of God, that ye may keep your own tradition.

This behaviour is nothing new to religious denominations. That last passage was about the Jews in the days of Jesus. Things haven't changed much since then. Humans are still willing to lead others astray, all for the sake of power, prestige and position. This next section tells us more about those who claim to be followers of Jesus but aren't.

Jude 3-21
Beloved, when I gave all diligence to write unto you of the common salvation, it was needful for me to write unto

you, and exhort you that ye should earnestly contend for the faith which was once delivered unto the saints.

4 For there are certain men crept in unawares, who were before of old ordained to this condemnation, ungodly men, turning the grace of our God into lasciviousness, and denying the only Lord God, and our Lord Jesus Christ.

5 I will therefore put you in remembrance, though ye once knew this, how that the Lord, having saved the people out of the land of Egypt, afterward destroyed them that believed not.

6 And the angels which kept not their first estate, but left their own habitation, he hath reserved in everlasting chains under darkness unto the judgment of the great day.

7 Even as Sodom and Gomorrha, and the cities about them in like manner, giving themselves over to fornication, and going after strange flesh, are set forth for an example, suffering the vengeance of eternal fire.

8 Likewise also these filthy dreamers defile the flesh, despise dominion, and speak evil of dignities.

9 Yet Michael the archangel, when contending with the devil he disputed about the body of Moses, durst not bring against him a railing accusation, but said, The Lord rebuke thee.

10 But these speak evil of those things which they know not: but what they know naturally, as brute beasts, in those things they corrupt themselves.

11 Woe unto them! for they have gone in the way of Cain, and ran greedily after the error of Balaam for reward, and perished in the gainsaying of Core.

12 These are spots in your feasts of charity, when they feast with you, feeding themselves without fear: clouds

they are without water, carried about of winds; trees whose fruit withereth, without fruit, twice dead, plucked up by the roots;

13 Raging waves of the sea, foaming out their own shame; wandering stars, to whom is reserved the blackness of darkness for ever.

14 And Enoch also, the seventh from Adam, prophesied of these, saying, Behold, the Lord cometh with ten thousands of his saints,

15 To execute judgment upon all, and to convince all that are ungodly among them of all their ungodly deeds which they have ungodly committed, and of all their hard speeches which ungodly sinners have spoken against him.

16 These are murmurers, complainers, walking after their own lusts; and their mouth speaketh great swelling words, having men's persons in admiration because of advantage.

17 But, beloved, remember ye the words which were spoken before of the apostles of our Lord Jesus Christ;

18 How that they told you there should be mockers in the last time, who should walk after their own ungodly lusts.

19 These be they who separate themselves, sensual, having not the Spirit.

20 But ye, beloved, building up yourselves on your most holy faith, praying in the Holy Ghost,

21 Keep yourselves in the love of God, looking for the mercy of our Lord Jesus Christ unto eternal life."

"Wow. You really like reading out loud, don't you," Ting said in amazement, finally getting the opportunity to speak. "The Bible has a lot to say about people who don't walk their talk," Ting said. "No wonder it's so hard to know who to trust."

"That's the point," Isaac observed, staying focused on the topic. "We should only trust Jesus and what God has recorded for us in the Bible. I have made some mistakes before by not reading all that the Bible has to tell me and I don't want that to happen again. The most important thing is to stay in and display the love of God. These next verses will help explain it," Isaac continues reading to Ting enthusiastically.

"2 Peter 1:5-10
And beside this, giving all diligence, add to your faith virtue; and to virtue knowledge;
6 And to knowledge temperance; and to temperance patience; and to patience godliness;
7 And to godliness brotherly kindness; and to brotherly kindness charity.
8 For if these things be in you, and abound, they make you that ye shall neither be barren nor unfruitful in the knowledge of our Lord Jesus Christ.
9 But he that lacketh these things is blind, and cannot see afar off, and hath forgotten that he was purged from his old sins.
10 Wherefore the rather, brethren, give diligence to make your calling and election sure: for if ye do these things, ye shall never fall:

See. God has our backs. He tells us that even when people try to harm us it will ultimately turn out for our good. Here I'll find that verse for you," Isaac does yet one more search to find an elusive verse.
"Here it is.

Romans 8:28

And we know that all things work together for good to them that love God, to them who are the called according to his purpose.

That's one of my favourite verses. I find it comforting to know God will work things out for those who love him."

Graciously accepting all of the oral scripture reading, Adam lets Ting Respond. "Yes. It gives me confidence that if I prayerfully study the word of God, the Holy Spirit will lead me into the knowledge God wants to reveal to me," Ting said confidently. "I want to study into those different ideas you told me about. I feel better about becoming a Christian knowing God has a plan of salvation for everyone. Not just those who were lucky enough to learn about Jesus during this life.

I can't wait to do some in-depth Bible study on those topics. I only hope I will be able to remember the plan as you laid it out, it may be hard to find others who promote those ideas on the web. I will do my best to study since we have such good internet service here in the camp," Adam lets out a chuckle.

"Thank you for pointing out this other possibility for those who have died not knowing Jesus. I realize it is not what you personally endorse or believe, but like you said it is a peripheral belief. It has helped me in my understanding of God's love for us. It's good to have choices and freedom of thought, to follow the Spirit as I am led into the Bible's light."

"It was my pleasure to be of service to you. I hope I helped and didn't confuse you too much," Isaac smiled shyly.

"I am so glad you came to my house today and talked with me. It was very insightful. I have much to learn, and many truths to prove," Ting's voice was filled with gratitude as Adam repeatedly made a bowing gesture with his head.

Then checking his mirrors repeatedly, he pulls the truck and trailer into the curb lane. He continues a few hundred yards then signals to the right as he prepares to make a right hand turn onto Spall road, at the Burger Barron.

The corner is tight and he narrowly misses the curbing for the sidewalk as he squiggles the truck and trailer across several lanes of traffic. His hands swiftly shifting the big steering wheel in alternating circles as he gets the trailer tracking in the correct lane avoiding the congestion. He lets the engine idle as the truck approaches the first intersection. A red traffic light is keeping him from faster progress.

"Here's the mall," Adam points to his left as he waits for the light to change to green. "There is not much room to maneuver in there," he states, gesturing at the crowded mall parking lot. "I will park on the road just across Springfield, in front of the church. You'll have to walk back across to the mall to meet your ride.

There's plenty of room there for me to park on the wide road shoulder. I do it often when I'm in town. I run across to the mall and pick up stuff, or meet my wife there for shopping sometimes. It can be hard to park these trucks in a shopping district."

"I can see that. It looks difficult to get around," Isaac replies with growing esteem for Adam's abilities. "There is a lot more to driving a big rig than I had thought."

"Most things are like that, you don't recognize the difficulty until you're in the middle of the problem," Adam jokes with a slight chuckle. Handing Isaac his cell phone he says. "Here's my phone you can call your ride if you want to. I was going to give it to you sooner but you were so absorbed in conversation with Ting, that I didn't want to disturb your train of thought."

"Thanks anyway. But I think I will look around the mall for a bit, then call. I need to just stretch and think for a while," Isaac had a calm humble tone in his voice.

"No problem," Adam smiled, pulling the truck over onto the gravel between the sidewalk and the paved bike lane. "Here we are safe and sound. I can't wait to get home for a couple of days off,"

Adam dynamites the brakes, securely fixing the truck in its parking spot.

"Well thanks for the ride home. It has been an interesting trip with you, I'm sure I will not forget it anytime soon. You've given me lots to think about," Isaac said extending his right hand to Adam.

Grasping Isaac in the firm grip of his own right hand, Adam smiled as he shakes his hand vigorously. "Hope I have given you some food for thought, good luck with the rest of your year here at home. I hope you get to continue with your studies."

"Thanks," Isaac smiles back warmly. "I am pretty sure that I will, although they may be more self-directed, rather than the formal variety."

"That's alright, as long as you are growing in wisdom and knowledge," Adam nods.

Reaching for the door handle Isaac pulls it back and swings the door open, then in one fluid motion vaults himself out of the truck sliding his hand down the grab rail the way he had seem Adam do it. Lightly touching down on his feet, he nods and smiles back up at Adam. "I guise I did learn a few things from you," Isaac hollered back up to Adam with a laugh. "Thanks for the ride and say goodbye to Ting for me when you get the chance."

Dragging his suitcase out of the vibrating, rattily truck he closes the door behind himself and turns towards the mall. Shuffling towards the crosswalk, Isaac is reminded of his prayer from earlier that morning. Talking silently to God he offers up praise. "Thank you father for getting me safely back home and for opening my eyes to glimpse some of your mysteries. You sure do work in mysterious ways. I can see that I will have a lot of studying to do in the near future. Please guide me."

"Well that made for a quick trip, passed the time nicely," Adam said to the empty cab. Releasing the brakes and then putting the truck into gear he said out loud, still talking to himself. "I think that was a divine appointment after all. Now it's time to get all of us lost lambs home. Oh, and Ting, Isaac says goodbye."

The End

About The Author

Clayton and his wife live in the Okanagan Valley of southern British Colombia, Canada. They have two adult children and enjoy getting out to explore the outdoors, camping and quading. Clayton started his working career as an owner-operator in the trucking industry. After an industrial accident he retrained as a heavy duty mechanic and driving instructor. He enjoys working with his hands. Being a tradesman provides a good living for his family, but his passion is to study the Bible as the Bereans did, proving what is true from the scriptures.

Clayton is a published freelance author within the Christian genre. He writes articles and Bible studies for the www.biblists.com web site, and has audio books and articles appearing on various podcast websites.

Connect With Clayton B Carlson

Find Clayton on Facebook: https://www.facebook.com/biblists/
Visit his website: www.biblists.com

Books By Clayton B Carlson

Biblist Apologetics
"In The Beginning" Chronologically Speaking Bible Supports
Richard Dawkins
My Baby Died. Where is My Baby?
Searching For Immortality
The Eden Conspiracy
Thy Kingdom Come, The Next Big Thing.

www.ingramcontent.com/pod-product-compliance
Lightning Source LLC
Chambersburg PA
CBHW071257170626
46809CB00001B/247